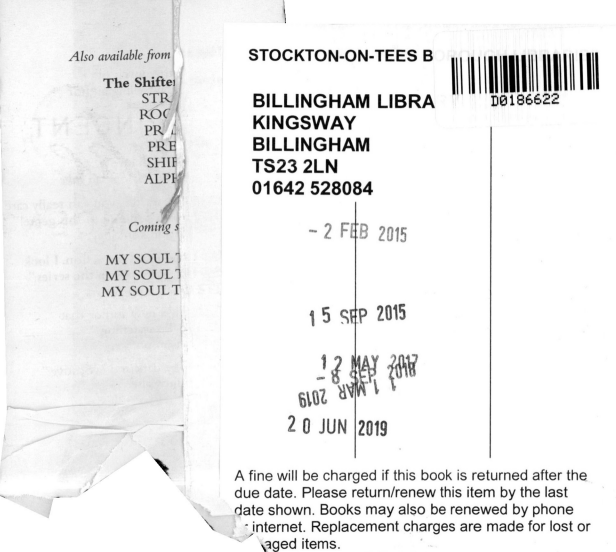

Also available from

The Shifter
STR
ROC
PR
PRE
SHIF
ALPH

Coming s

MY SOUL T
MY SOUL T
MY SOUL T

my SOUL to Take

RACHEL VINCENT

All the characters in this book have no existence outside the imagination of the author, and have no relation whatsoever to anyone bearing the same name or names. They are not even distantly inspired by any individual known or unknown to the author, and all the incidents are pure invention.

Published in Great Britain 2011
MIRA Books, Eton House, 18-24 Paradise Road,
Richmond, Surrey, TW9 1SR

© Rachel Vincent 2009

ISBN 978 0 7783 0355 8

47-0111

Printed and bound by
CPI Group (UK) Ltd, Croydon, CR0 4YY

For Number 1,
who knows that fajitas will fix any plot hole

ACKNOWLEDGEMENTS

First of all, thanks to Rayna and Alex, for letting me pick your teenage brains, and again to Alex, for being the first reader in my target audience.

Thanks to Rinda Elliott, for showing me what I couldn't see. Thanks to my agent, Miriam Kriss, for believing I could do this, before there was any evidence to support that claim. Thanks to Elizabeth Mazer and everyone else behind the scenes at MIRA for making it happen.

Thanks to my editor, Mary-Theresa Hussey, for all the questions—for answering mine along the way and knowing just which ones to ask in the margins. *And finally, thanks to Melissa, for being there.*

1

"COME ON!" EMMA whispered from my right, her words floating from her mouth in a thin white cloud. She glared at the battered steel panel in front of us, as if her own impatience would make the door open. "She forgot, Kaylee. I should have known she would." More white puffs drifted from Emma's perfectly painted mouth as she bounced to stay warm, her curves barely contained in the low-cut shimmery red blouse she'd "borrowed" from one of her sisters.

Yes, I was a little envious; I had few curves and no sister from whom to borrow hot clothes. But I did have the time, and one glance at my cell phone told me it was still four minutes to nine. "She'll be here." I smoothed the front of my own shirt and slid my phone into my pocket as Emma knocked for the third time. "We're early. Just give her a minute."

My own puff of breath had yet to fade when metal creaked and the door swung slowly toward us, leaking rhythmic flashes of smoky light and a low thumping beat into the cold, dark alley. Traci Marshall—Emma's youngest older sister—stood with one palm flat against the door, holding it open. She wore a snug, low-cut black tee, readily displaying the family resemblance, as if the long blond hair wasn't enough.

"'Bout time!" Emma snapped, stepping forward to brush past her sister. But Traci slapped her free hand against the door frame, blocking our entrance.

She returned my smile briefly, then frowned at her sister. "Nice to see you too. Tell me the rules."

Emma rolled wide-set brown eyes and rubbed her bare, goose-pimpled arms—we'd left our jackets in my car. "No alcohol, no chemicals. No fun of any sort." She mumbled that last part, and I stifled a smile.

"What else?" Traci demanded, obviously struggling to maintain a rare scowl.

"Come together, stay together, leave together," I supplied, reciting the same lines we'd repeated each time she snuck us in—only twice before. The rules were lame, but I knew from experience that we wouldn't get in without them.

"And…"

Emma stamped her feet for warmth, chunky heels clacking on the concrete. "If we get caught, we don't know you."

As if anyone would believe that. The Marshall girls were all cast from the same mold: a tall, voluptuous mold that put my own modest curves to shame.

Traci nodded, apparently satisfied, and let her hand fall from the door frame. Emma stepped forward and her sister frowned, pulling her into the light from the hall fixture overhead. "Is that Cara's new shirt?"

Emma scowled and tugged her arm free. "She'll never know it's gone."

Traci laughed and motioned with one arm toward the front of the club, from which light and sound flooded the back rooms and offices. Now that we were all inside, she had to shout to be heard over the music. "Enjoy the rest of your life while it lasts, 'cause she's gonna *bury* you in that shirt."

Unperturbed, Emma danced her way down the hall and into the main room, hands in the air, hips swaying with the pulse of the song. I followed her, keyed up by the energy of the Saturday-night crowd from the moment I saw the first cluster of bodies in motion.

We worked our way into the throng and were swallowed by it, assimilated by the beat, the heat and the casual partners pulling us close. We danced through several songs, together, alone and in random pairs, until I was breathing hard and damp with sweat. I signaled Emma that I was going for a drink, and she nodded, already moving again as I worked my way toward the edge of the crowd.

Behind the bar, Traci worked alongside another bartender, a large, dark man in a snug black tee, both oddly lit by a strip of blue neon overhead. I claimed the first abandoned bar stool, and the man in black propped both broad palms on the bar in front of me.

"I got this one," Traci said, one hand on his arm. He nodded and moved on to the next customer. "What'll it be?" Traci smoothed back a stray strand of pale, blue-tinted hair.

I grinned, leaning with both elbows on the bar. "Jack and Coke?"

She laughed. "I'll give you the Coke." She shot soda into a glass of ice and slid it toward me. I pushed a five across the bar and swiveled on my stool to watch the dance floor, scanning the multitude for Emma. She was sandwiched between two guys in matching UT Dallas fraternity tees and neon, legal-to-drink bracelets, all three grinding in unison.

Emma drew attention like wool draws static.

Still smiling, I drained my soda and set my glass on the bar.

"Kaylee Cavanaugh."

I jumped at the sound of my own name and whirled toward the stool to my left. My gaze settled on the most hypnotic set of hazel eyes I'd ever seen, and for several seconds I could only stare, lost in the most amazing swirls of deep brown and vivid green, which seemed to churn in time with my own heartbeat—though surely they were just reflecting the lights flashing overhead. My focus only returned when I had to blink, and the momentary loss of contact brought me back to myself.

That's when I realized who I was staring at.

Nash Hudson. Holy crap. I almost looked down to see if ice had anchored my feet to the floor, since hell had surely frozen over. Somehow I'd stepped off the dance floor and into some weird warp zone where irises swam with color and Nash Hudson smiled at me, and me alone.

I picked up my glass, hoping for one last drop to rewet my suddenly dry throat—and wondered fleetingly if Traci *had* spiked my Coke—but discovered it every bit as empty as I'd expected.

"Need a refill?" Nash asked, and that time I made my mouth open. After all, if I was dreaming—or in the Twilight Zone—I had nothing to lose by speaking. Right?

"I'm good. Thanks." I ventured a hesitant smile, and my heart nearly exploded when I saw my grin reflected on his upturned, perfectly formed lips.

"How'd you get in here?" He arched one brow, more in amusement than in real curiosity. "Crawl through the window?"

"Back door," I whispered, feeling my face flush. Of course he knew I was a junior—too young even for an eighteen-and-over club, like Taboo.

"What?" He grinned and leaned closer to hear me above the music. His breath brushed my neck, and my pulse pounded so hard I felt light-headed. He smelled sooo good.

"Back door," I repeated into his ear. "Emma's sister works here."

"Emma's here?"

I pointed her out on the dance floor—now swaying with three guys at once—and assumed that would be the last I saw of Nash Hudson. But to my near-fatal shock, he dismissed Em at a glance and turned back to me with a mischievous gleam in those amazing eyes.

"Aren't you gonna dance?"

My hand was suddenly sweaty around my empty glass. Did that mean he wanted to dance with me? Or that he wanted the bar stool for his girlfriend?

No, wait. He'd dumped his latest girlfriend the week before, and the sharks were already circling the fresh meat. *Though they're not circling him now…* I saw no one from Nash's usual crowd, either clustered around him or on the dance floor.

"Yeah, I'm gonna dance," I said, and again, his eyes were swirling green melting into brown and back, flashing blue occasionally in the neon glow. I could have stared at his eyes for hours. But he probably would have thought that was weird.

"Let's go!" He took my hand and stood as I slid off the bar stool, and I followed him onto the dance floor. A fresh smile bloomed on my face, and my chest seemed to tighten around my heart in anticipation. I'd known him for a while—Emma had gone out with a few of his friends—but had never been the sole object of his attention. Had never even considered the possibility.

If Eastlake High School were the universe, I would be one of the moons circling Planet Emma, constantly hidden by her shadow, and glad to be there. Nash Hudson would be one of the stars: too bright to look at, too hot to touch and at the center of his own solar system.

But on the dance floor, I forgot all that. His light was shining directly on me, and it was *sooo warm*.

We wound up only feet from Emma, but with Nash's hands on me, his body pressed into mine, I barely noticed. That first song ended, and we were moving to the next one before I even fully realized the beat had changed.

Several minutes later, I glimpsed Emma over Nash's shoulder. She stood at the bar with one of the guys she'd been grinding with, and as I watched, Traci set a drink in front of each of them. When her sister turned around, Emma grabbed her partner's drink—something dark with a wedge of lime on the rim—and drained it in three gulps. Frat boy smiled, then pulled her back into the crowd.

I made a mental note not to let Emma drive my car— ever—then let my eyes wander back to Nash, where they wanted to be in the first place. But on the way, my gaze was snagged by an unfamiliar sheet of strawberry-blond hair, crowning the head of the only girl in the building to rival Emma in beauty. This girl, too, had her choice of dance partners, and though she couldn't have been more than eighteen, she'd obviously had much more to drink than Emma.

But despite how pretty and obviously charismatic she was, watching her dance twisted something deep inside my gut and made my chest tighten, as if I couldn't quite get enough air. Something was wrong with her. I wasn't sure how I knew, but I was absolutely certain that something was *not right* with that girl.

"You okay?" Nash shouted, laying one hand on my shoulder, and suddenly I realized I'd gone still, while everyone around me was still writhing to the beat.

"Yeah!" I shook off my discomfort and was relieved to find that looking into Nash's eyes chased away that feeling of *wrongness,* leaving in its place a new calm, eerie in its depth and reach. We danced for several more songs, growing more comfortable with each other with every moment that passed. By the time we stopped for a drink, sweat was gathering on the back of my neck and my arms were damp.

I lifted the bulk of my hair to cool myself and waved to Emma with my free hand as I turned to follow Nash off the dance floor—and nearly collided with that same strawberry blonde. Not that she noticed. But the minute my eyes found her, that feeling was back in spades—that strong discomfort, like a bad taste in my mouth, only all over my body. And this time it was accompanied by an odd sadness. A general melancholy that felt specifically connected to this one person. Whom I'd never met.

"Kaylee?" Nash yelled over the music. He stood at the bar, holding two tall glasses of soda, slick with condensation. I closed the space between us and took the glass he offered, a little frightened to notice that this time, even staring straight into his eyes couldn't completely relax me. Couldn't quite loosen my throat, which threatened to close against the cold drink I so desperately craved.

"What's wrong?" We stood inches apart, thanks to the throng pressing ever closer to the bar, but he still had to lean into me to be heard.

"I don't know. Something about that girl, that redhead over there—" I nodded toward the dancer in question "—bothers me." *Well, crap.* I hadn't meant to admit that. It sounded so pathetic aloud.

But Nash only glanced at the girl, then back at me. "Seems okay to me. Assuming she has a ride home..."

"Yeah, I guess." But then the current song ended, and the girl stumbled—looking somehow graceful, even when obviously intoxicated—off the dance floor and toward the bar. Headed right for us.

My heart beat harder with every step she took. My hand curled around my glass until my knuckles went white. And that familiar sense of melancholy swelled into an overwhelming feeling of grief. Of dark foreboding.

I gasped, startled by a sudden, gruesome certainty.

Not again. Not with Nash Hudson there to watch me completely freak out. My breakdown would be all over the school on Monday, and I could kiss goodbye what little social standing I'd gained.

Nash set his glass down and peered into my face. "Kaylee? You okay?" But I could only shake my head, incapable of answering. I was *far* from okay, but couldn't articulate the problem in any way resembling coherence. And suddenly the potentially devastating rumors looked like minor blips on my disaster meter compared to the panic growing inside me.

Each breath came faster than the last, and a scream built deep within my chest. I clamped my mouth shut to hold it back, grinding my teeth painfully. The strawberry blonde stepped up to the bar on my left, and only a single stool and its occupant stood between us. The male bartender took her order and she turned sideways to wait for her drink. Her eyes met mine. She smiled briefly, then stared out onto the dance floor.

Horror washed over me in a devastating wave of intuition. My throat closed. I choked on a scream of terror. My glass slipped from my hand and shattered on the floor. The redheaded dancer squealed and jumped back as ice-cold soda splattered her, me, Nash, and the man on the stool to my left. But I barely noticed the frigid liquid, or the people staring at me.

I saw only the girl, and the dark, translucent shadow that had enveloped her.

"Kaylee?" Nash tilted my face up so that our eyes met. His were full of concern, the colors swirling almost out of control now in the flashing lights. Watching them made me dizzy.

I wanted to tell him…something. Anything. But if I opened my mouth, the scream would rip free, and then anyone who wasn't already looking at me would turn to stare. They'd think I'd lost my mind.

Maybe they'd be right.

"What's wrong?" Nash demanded, stepping closer to me now, heedless of the glass and the wet floor. "Do you have seizures?" But I could only shake my head at him, refusing passage to the wail trying to claw its way out of me, denying the existence of a narrow bed in a sterile white room, awaiting my return.

And suddenly Emma was there. Emma, with her perfect body, beautiful face and heart the size of an elephant's. "She'll be fine." Emma pulled me away from the bar as the male bartender came forward with a mop and bucket. "She just needs some air." She waved off Traci's worried look and frantic hand gestures, then tugged me through the crowd by one arm.

I clamped my free palm over my mouth and shook my head furiously when Nash tried to take that hand in his. I should have been worried about what he would think. That he would want nothing else to do with me now that I'd publicly embarrassed him. But I couldn't concentrate long enough to worry about anything but the redhead at the bar. The one who'd watched us leave through a shadow-shroud only I could see.

Emma led me past the bathrooms and into the back hall, Nash close on my heels. "What's wrong with her?" he asked.

"Nothing." Emma paused to turn and smile at us both, and gratitude broke through my dark terror for just an instant. "It's a panic attack. She just needs some fresh air and time to calm down."

But that's where she was wrong. It wasn't time I needed, so much as space. Distance, between me and the source of the panic. Unfortunately, there wasn't enough room in the whole club to get me far enough away from the girl at the bar. Even with me standing by the back door, the panic was as strong as ever. The unspoken shriek burned my throat, and if I unclenched my jaws—if I lost control—my scream would shatter eardrums all over Taboo. It would put the thumping dance beat to shame, and possibly blow out the speakers—if not the windows.

All because of some redhead I didn't even know.

Just thinking about her sent a fresh wave of devastation through me, and my knees collapsed. My fall caught Emma off guard, and I would have pulled her down if Nash hadn't caught me.

He lifted me completely off the ground, cradling me like a child, and followed Emma out the back door with me secure in his arms. The club had been dim, but the alley was *dark,* and it went quiet once the door thumped shut behind us, Emma's bank card keeping the latch from sliding home. The frigid near-silence should have calmed me, but the racket in my head had reached its zenith. The scream I refused to release slammed around in my brain, reverberating, echoing, punctuating the grief still thick in my heart.

Nash set me down in the alley, but by then my thoughts had lost all semblance of logic or comprehension. I felt something smooth and dry beneath me, and only later would I realize Emma had found a collapsed box for him to set me on.

My jeans had ridden up on my legs when Nash carried me, and the cardboard was cold and gritty with grime against my calves.

"Kaylee?" Emma knelt in front of me, her face inches from mine, but I couldn't make sense of a word she said after my name. I heard only my own thoughts. Just *one* thought, actually. A paranoid delusion, according to my former therapist, which presented itself with the absolute authority of long-held fact.

Then Emma's face disappeared and I was staring at her knees. Nash said something I couldn't make out. Something about a drink…

Music swelled back to life, then Emma was gone. She'd left me alone with the hottest guy I'd ever danced with— the last person in the world I wanted to witness my total break with reality.

Nash dropped onto his knees and looked into my eyes, the greens and browns in his still churning frantically somehow, though there were no lights overhead now.

I was imagining it. I had to be. I'd seen them dance with the light earlier, and now my traumatized mind had seized upon Nash's eyes as a focal point of my delusion. Just like the strawberry blonde. Right?

But there was no time to think through my theory. I was losing control. Successive waves of grief threatened to flatten me, crushing me into the wall with an invisible pressure, as if Nash weren't even there. I couldn't suck in a deep breath, yet a high-pitched keening leaked from my throat now, even with my lips sealed shut. My vision began to go even darker than the alley—though I wouldn't have thought that possible—like the whole world had been overlaid with an odd gray filter.

Nash frowned, still watching me, then twisted to sit beside me, his back against the wall too. On the edges of my graying vision, something scuttled past soundlessly. A rat, or some other scavenger attracted by the club's garbage bin? *No.* Whatever I'd glimpsed was too big to be a rodent—unless we'd stepped into Buttercup's fire swamp—and too indistinct for my shattered focus to settle on.

Nash took my free hand in his, and I forgot whatever I'd seen. He pushed my hair back from my right ear. I couldn't understand most of what he whispered to me, but I gradually came to realize that his actual words weren't important. What mattered was his proximity. His breath on my neck. His warmth melting into mine. His scent surrounding me. His voice swirling in my head, insulating me from the scream still ricocheting against my skull.

He was calming me with nothing more than his presence, his patience and whispered words of what sounded like a child's rhyme, based on what little I caught.

And it was working. My anxiety gradually faded, and dim, gritty color leaked back into the world. My fingers relaxed around his hand. My lungs expanded fully, and I sucked in a sharp, frigid breath, suddenly freezing as sweat from the club dried on my skin.

The panic was still there, in the shadowed corners of my mind, in the dark spots on the edge of my vision. But I could handle it now. Thanks to Nash.

"You okay?" he asked when I turned my head to face him, the bricks cold and rough against my cheek.

I nodded. And that's when a new horror descended: utter, consuming, inescapable mortification, most awful in its longevity. The panic attack was all but over, but humiliation would last a lifetime.

I'd completely lost it in front of Nash Hudson. My life was over; even my friendship with Emma wouldn't be enough to repair the damage from such a nasty wound.

Nash stretched his legs out. "Wanna talk about it?"

No. I wanted to go hide in a hole, or stick my head in a bag, or change my name and move to Peru.

But then suddenly, I *did* want to talk about it. With Nash's voice still echoing softly in my head, his words whispering faintly over my skin, I wanted to tell him what had happened. It made no sense. After knowing me for eight years and helping me through at least half a dozen previous panic attacks, Emma still had no idea what caused them. I couldn't tell her. It would scare her. Or worse, finally convince her I really was crazy.

So why did I want to tell Nash? I had no answer for that, but the urge was undeniable.

"...the strawberry blonde." There, I'd said it out loud, and committed myself to some sort of explanation.

Nash's brow furrowed in confusion. "You know her?"

"No." Fortunately. Merely sharing oxygen with her had nearly driven me out of my mind. "But something's wrong with her, Nash. She's...dark."

Kaylee, shut up! If he wasn't already convinced I was certifiable, he would be soon....

"What?" His frown deepened, but rather than bewildered or skeptical, he looked surprised. Then came vague comprehension. Comprehension, and...dread. He might not know exactly what I meant, but he didn't look completely clueless either. "What do you mean, 'dark'?"

I closed my eyes, hesitating at the last second. What if I'd misread him? What if he did think I was crazy?

Worse yet, what if he was right?

But in the end, I opened my eyes and met his gaze frankly, because I had to tell him something, and surely I couldn't damage his opinion of me much more than I already had. Right?

"Okay, this is going to sound weird," I began, "but something's wrong with that girl at the bar. When I looked at her, she was…shadowed." I hesitated, scrounging up the courage to finish what I'd started. "She's going to die, Nash. That girl is going to die very, very soon."

2

"WHAT?" NASH's eyebrows rose, but he didn't roll his eyes, or laugh, or pat my head and call for the men in white coats. In fact, he looked like he almost believed me. "How do you know she's gonna die?"

I rubbed both temples, trying to wipe away a familiar frustration rearing inside me. He might not be laughing on the outside, but surely he was cracking up on the inside. How could he not be? *What the hell was I thinking?*

"I don't know how I know. I don't even know that I'm right. But when I look at her, she's…darker than everyone around her. Like she's standing in the shadow of something I can't see. And I know she's going to die."

Nash frowned in concern, and I closed my eyes, barely noticing the sudden swell of music from the club. I knew that look. It was the one mothers give their kids when they fall off the slide and sit up talking about purple ponies and dancing squirrels.

"I know it sounds—" *crazy* "—weird, but…"

He took both of my hands, twisting to face me more fully on the flattened box beneath us, and again the colors in his irises seemed to pulse with my heartbeat. His mouth opened, and I held my breath, awaiting my verdict. Had I lost him with talk of creepy black shadows, or did my mistakes start all the way back with the spilled drink?

"Sounds pretty weird to me."

We both glanced up to find Emma watching us, a chilled bottle of water in one hand, dripping condensation on the grimy concrete, and I almost groaned in frustration. Whatever Nash had been about to say was gone now; I could see that in the cautious smile he shot at me, before redirecting toward Emma.

She twisted open the lid and handed me the bottle. "But then, you wouldn't be Kaylee if you didn't weird-out on me every now and then." She shrugged amiably and hauled me to my feet as Nash stood to join us. "So you had a panic attack because you think some girl in the club is going to die?"

I nodded hesitantly, waiting for her to laugh or roll her eyes, if she thought I was joking. Or to look nervous, if she knew I wasn't. Instead, her brows arched, and she cocked her head to one side. "Well, shouldn't you go tell her? Or something?"

"I…" I blinked in confusion and frowned at the brick

wall over her shoulder. Somehow, that option had never occurred to me. "I don't know." I glanced at Nash, but found no answer in his now-normal eyes. "She'd probably just think I was crazy. Or she'd get all freaked out." And really, who could blame her? "Doesn't matter, anyway, because it's not true. Right? It can't be."

Nash shrugged but looked like he wanted to say something. But then Emma spoke up, never hesitant to voice her opinion. "Of course not. You had another panic attack, and your mind latched onto the first person you saw. Could've been me, or Nash, or Traci. It doesn't mean anything."

I nodded, but as badly as I wanted to believe her theory, it just didn't feel right. Yet I couldn't make myself warn the redhead. No matter what I thought I knew, the prospect of telling a perfect stranger that she was going to die felt just plain crazy, and I'd had enough of crazy for the moment.

For the rest of my life, in fact.

"All better?" Emma asked, when she read my decision on my face. "Wanna go back in?"

I was feeling better, but that dark panic still lingered on the edge of my mind, and it would only get worse if I saw the girl again. I had no doubt of that. And I would not give Nash an encore of the night's performance, if at all possible.

"I'm just gonna head home." My uncle had taken my aunt out for her fortieth birthday, and Sophie was on an overnight trip with the dance team. For once I'd have the house to myself. I smiled at Emma in apology. "But if you want to stay, you could probably catch a ride with Traci."

"Nah, I'll go with you." Emma took the water bottle from my hand and gulped from it. "She told us to leave together, remember?"

"She also told us not to drink."

Emma rolled her big brown eyes. "If she really meant that, she wouldn't have snuck us into a *bar*."

That was Emma-logic, all right. The longer you thought about it, the less sense it made.

Emma glanced from me to Nash. Then she smiled and headed down the alley toward the car lot across the street, to give us some privacy. I dug my keys from my pocket and stared at them, trying to avoid Nash's gaze until I knew what I was going to say.

He'd seen me at my worst, and rather than flipping out or making fun, he'd helped me regain control. We'd connected in a way I wouldn't have thought possible an hour earlier, especially with someone like Nash, whose one-track mind was a thing of legends. Still, I couldn't fight the certainty that this evening's dream would end in tomorrow's nightmare. That daylight would bring him to his senses, and he'd wonder what he was doing with me in the first place.

I opened my mouth, but no sound came out. My keys

jangled, the ring dangling from my index finger, and he frowned when his gaze settled on them.

"You okay to drive?" He grinned, and my pulse jumped in response. "I could take you home and walk from there. You live in the Parkview complex, right? That's just a couple of minutes from me."

He knew where I lived? I must have looked suspicious, because he rushed to explain. "I gave your sister a ride once. Last month."

My jaw tightened, and I felt my expression darken. "She's my cousin." Nash had given Sophie a ride? *Please don't let that be a euphemism…*

He frowned and shook his head in answer to my unspoken question. "Scott Carter asked me to give her a lift."

Oh. Good. I nodded, and he shrugged. "So you want me to take you guys home?" He held his hand out for my keys.

"That's okay, I'm good to drive." And I wasn't in the habit of letting people I barely knew behind the wheel of my car. Especially really hot guys who—rumor had it—had gotten two speeding tickets in his ex's Firebird.

Nash flashed a deep set of stubbly dimples and shrugged. "Then can I have a lift? I rode with Carter, and he won't be ready to go for hours."

My pulse jumped into my throat. Was he leaving early just so he could ride with me? Or had I ruined his evening with my freak-tastic hysterics?

"Um…yeah." My car was a mess, but it was too late

to worry about that. "But you'll have to flip Emma for shotgun."

Fortunately, that turned out to be unnecessary. Em took the back, shooting me a meaningful glance and pointing at Nash as she slid across the seat, swiping a corn-chip bag onto the floor. I dropped her off first, a full hour and a half before her curfew, which had to be some kind of record.

As I pulled out of Emma's driveway, Nash twisted in the passenger seat to face me, his expression somber, and my heart beat so hard it almost hurt. It was time for the easy letdown. He was too cool to say it in front of Emma, and even with her gone, he'd probably be really nice about it. But the bottom line was the same; he wasn't interested in me. At least, not after my public meltdown.

"So you've had these panic attacks before?"

What? My hands clenched the wheel in surprise as I took a left at the end of the street.

"A couple of times." *Half a dozen, at least.* I couldn't purge suspicion from my voice. My "issues" should have driven him screaming into the night, and instead he wanted details? Why?

"Do your parents know?"

I shifted in my seat, as if a new position might make me more comfortable with the question. But it would take much more than that. "My mom died when I was little, and my dad couldn't handle me on his own. He moved to Ireland, and I've been with my aunt and uncle ever since."

Nash blinked and nodded for me to go on. He gave me none of the awkward sympathy or compulsive, I'm-not-sure-what-to-say throat-clearing I usually got when people found out I'd been half-orphaned, then wholly abandoned. I liked him for that, even if I didn't like where his questions were heading.

"So your aunt and uncle know?"

Yeah. *They think I'm one egg shy of a dozen.* But the truth hurt too much to say out loud.

I turned to see him watching me closely, and my suspicion flared again, settling to burn deep in my gut. Why did he care what my family knew about my not-so-private misery? Unless he was planning to laugh with his friends later about what a freak I was.

But his interest didn't seem malicious. Especially considering what he'd done for me at Taboo. So maybe his curiosity was feigned, and he was after something else to tell his friends about. Something girls rarely denied him, if the rumors were true.

If he didn't get it, would he tell the entire school my darkest, most painful secret?

No. My stomach pitched at the thought, and I hit the brake too hard as we came to a stop sign.

My foot still wedged against the brake, I glanced in the rearview mirror at the empty street behind me, then shifted into Park and turned to face Nash, steeling my nerve for the question to come. "What do you want from me?" I spat it out before I could change my mind.

Nash's eyes widened in surprise, and he sat back hard against the passenger's side door, as if I'd shoved him. "I just… Nothing."

"You want nothing?" I wanted to see the deep greens and browns of his irises, but the beam from the nearest streetlight didn't reach my car, so only the dim light from my dashboard shone on him, and it wasn't enough to illuminate his face. To let me truly read his expression. "I can count the number of times we've really spoken before tonight on one hand." I held that hand up for emphasis. "Then you come out of nowhere and play white knight to my distressed damsel, and I'm supposed to believe you want nothing in return? Nothing to tell your friends about on Monday?"

He tried to laugh, but the sound was stilted, and he shifted uncomfortably in his seat. "I wouldn't—"

"Save it. Rumor has it you've conquered more territory than Genghis Khan."

A single dark brow rose in the shadows, challenging me. "You believe everything you hear?"

My eyebrow shot up to mirror his. "You denyin' it?"

Instead of answering, he laughed for real and propped one elbow on the door handle. "Are you always this mean to guys who sing to you in dark alleys?"

My next retort died on my lips, so surprised was I by the reminder. He had sung to me, and somehow talked me down from a brutal panic attack. He'd saved me from public humiliation. But there had to be a reason, and I wasn't that great of a conquest.

"I don't trust you," I said finally, my hands limp and worthless on my lap.

"Right now I don't trust you either." He grinned in the dark, flashing pale teeth and a single shadowed dimple, and his open-armed gesture took in the stopped car. "Are you kicking me out, or do I get door-to-door service?"

That's the only *service you get.* But I shifted into Drive and faced the road again, then turned right into his subdivision, which was definitely more than a couple of minutes from my neighborhood. Would he really have walked if I'd let him drive me home?

Would he have taken me straight home?

"Take this left, then the next right. It's the one on the corner."

His directions led me to a small frame house in an older section of the development. I pulled into the driveway behind a dusty, dented sedan. The driver's side door stood open, spilling light from the interior to illuminate a lopsided square of dry grass to the left of the pavement.

"You left your car door open," I said, shifting into Park, glad for something to focus on other than Nash, though that's where my gaze really wanted to be.

Nash sighed. "It's my mom's. She's gone through three batteries in six months."

I stifled a smile as her car light flickered. "Make that four."

He groaned, but when I glanced at him, I found him watching me rather than the car. "So…do I get a chance to earn your trust?"

My pulse jumped. Was he serious?

I should've said no. I should have thanked him for helping me at Taboo, then left with him staring after me from his front yard. But I wasn't strong enough to resist those dimples. Even knowing how many other girls had probably failed that same task.

I blame my weakness on the recent panic attack.

"How?" I asked finally, then flushed when he grinned. He'd known I'd give in.

"Come over tomorrow night?"

To his house? *No way.* I was weak-willed, not stupid. Not that I could make it anyway… "I work till nine on Sundays."

"At the Ciné?"

He knows where I work. Surprise warmed me from the inside out, and I frowned in question.

"I've seen you there."

"Oh." Of course he'd seen me there. Probably on a date. "Yeah, I'll be in the ticket booth from two on."

"Lunch, then?"

Lunch. How much could I possibly be tempted into in a public restaurant? "Fine. But I still don't trust you."

He grinned and opened his door, and the overhead light flared to life. His pupils shrank to pinpoints in the sudden glare, and as my heart raced, he leaned forward like he would kiss me. Instead, his cheek brushed mine and his warm breath skimmed my ear as he whispered, "That's half the fun."

My breath hitched in my throat, but before I could speak, the car bobbed beneath his shifting weight and suddenly the passenger seat was empty. He closed the car door, then jogged up the driveway to slam his mother's.

I backed away from his house in a daze, and when I parked in front of my own, I couldn't remember a moment of the drive home.

"Good morning, Kaylee." Aunt Val stood at the kitchen counter, bathed in late-morning sunlight, holding a steaming mug of coffee nearly as big as her head. She wore a satin robe the exact shade of blue as her eyes, and her sleek brown waves were still tousled from sleep. But they were tousled the way hair always looks in the movies, when the star wakes up in full makeup, wearing miraculously unwrinkled pajamas.

I couldn't pull my own fingers through my hair first thing in the morning.

My aunt's robe and the size of her coffee cup were the only signs that she and my uncle had had a late night. Or rather, an early morning. I'd heard them come in around 2:00 a.m., stumbling down the hall, giggling like idiots.

Then I'd stuck my earbuds in my ears so I wouldn't have to listen as he proved just how attractive he still found her, even after seventeen years of marriage. Uncle Brendon was the younger of the pair, and my aunt resented each of the four years she had on him.

The problem wasn't that she looked her age—thanks to Botox and an obsessive workout routine, she looked thirty-five at the most—but that he looked so young for his. She jokingly called him Peter Pan, but as her big 4-0 had approached, she'd ceased finding her own joke funny.

"Cereal or waffles?" Aunt Val set her coffee on the marble countertop and pulled a box of blueberry Eggos from the freezer, holding them up for my selection. My aunt didn't do big breakfasts. She said she couldn't afford to eat that many calories in one meal, and she wasn't going to cook what she couldn't eat. But we were welcome to help ourselves to all the fat and cholesterol we wanted.

Normally Uncle Brendon served up plenty of both on Saturday mornings, but I could still hear him snoring from his bedroom, halfway across the house. She'd obviously worn him out pretty good.

I crossed the dining room into the kitchen, my fuzzy socks silent on the cold tile. "Just toast. I'm going out for lunch in a couple of hours."

Aunt Val stuck the waffles back in the freezer and handed me a loaf of low-calorie whole wheat bread—the only kind she would buy. "With Emma?"

I shook my head and dropped two slices into the toaster, then tugged my pajama pants up and tightened the drawstring.

She arched her brows at me over her mug. "You have a date? Anyone I know?" Meaning, "Any of Sophie's exes?"

"I doubt it." Aunt Val was constantly disappointed that, unlike her daughter—the world's most socially ambitious sophomore—I had no interest in student council, or the dance team, or the winter carnival–planning committee. In part, because Sophie would have made my life miserable if I'd intruded on "her" territory. But mostly because I had to work to pay for my car insurance, and I'd rather spend my rare free hours with Emma than helping the dance team coordinate their glitter gel with their sequined costumes.

While Nash would no doubt have met with Aunt Val's hearty approval, I did not need her hovering over me when I got home, eyes glittering in anticipation of a social climb I had no interest in. I was happy hanging with Emma and whichever crowd she claimed at the moment.

"His name's Nash."

Aunt Val took a butter knife from the silverware drawer. "What year is he?"

I groaned inwardly. "Senior." *Here we go…*

Her smile was a little too enthusiastic. "Well, that's wonderful!"

Of course, what she really meant was "Rise from the shadows, social leper, and walk in the bright light of acceptance!" Or some crap like that. Because my aunt and overprivileged cousin only recognize two states of being:

glitter and grunge. And if you weren't glitter, well, that only left one other option…

I slathered strawberry jelly on my toast and took a seat at the bar. Aunt Val poured a second cup of coffee and aimed the TV remote across the dining room and into the den, where the fifty-inch flat-screen flashed to life, signaling the end of the requisite breakfast "conversation."

"…coming to you live from Taboo, in the West End, where last night, the body of nineteen-year-old Heidi Anderson was found on the restroom floor."

Nooo…

My stomach churned around a half slice of toast, and I twisted slowly on my bar stool, dread sending a spike of adrenaline through my veins. On screen, a too-poised reporter stood on the brick walkway in front of the club I'd snuck into twelve hours earlier, and as I watched, her image was replaced by a still shot of Heidi Anderson sitting in a lawn chair in a UT Arlington T-shirt, straight teeth gleaming, reddish-blond hair blown back by the relentless prairie wind.

It was her.

I couldn't breathe.

"Kaylee? What's wrong?"

I blinked and sucked in a quick breath, then looked up at my aunt to find her staring at my plate, where I'd dropped my toast jelly-side down. It was a miracle I hadn't lost the half I'd already eaten.

"Nothing. Can you turn that up?" I pushed my plate

away and Aunt Val turned up the volume, shooting me a puzzled frown.

"No cause of death has yet been identified," the reporter said on-screen. "But according to the employee who found Ms. Anderson's body, there was no obvious sign of violence."

The picture changed again, and now Traci Marshall stared into the camera, pale with shock and hoarse, as if she'd been crying. "She was just lying there, like she was sleeping. I thought she'd passed out until I realized she wasn't breathing."

Traci disappeared and the reporter was back, but I couldn't hear her over Aunt Val. "Isn't that Emma's sister?"

"Yeah. She's a bartender at Taboo."

Aunt Val stared at the television, her expression grim. "That whole thing is so tragic…"

I nodded. *You have no idea.* But I did.

I also had chill bumps. *It really happened.*

With my previous panic attacks, my aunt and uncle had had no reason to heed my hysterical babble about looming shadows and impending death. And with no way to shush me once the screaming began, they'd taken me home—coincidently away from the source of the panic— to calm me down. Except for that last time, when they'd driven me straight to the hospital, checked me into the mental-health ward and begun looking at me with eyes full of pity. Concern. Unspoken relief that I was the one losing my mind, rather than their own, blessedly normal daughter.

But now I had proof I wasn't crazy. Right? I'd seen Heidi Anderson shrouded in shadow and known she would die. I'd told Emma and Nash. And now my premonition had come true.

I stood so fast my bar stool skidded against the tiles. I had to *tell* somebody. I needed to see confirmation in someone's eyes, assurance that I wasn't imagining the news story, because really, if I could imagine death, how much harder could it be for my poor, sick mind to make up the news story? But I couldn't tell my aunt what had happened without admitting I'd snuck into a club, and once I'd said that part, she wouldn't listen to the rest. She'd just take away my keys and call my father.

No, telling Aunt Val was out of the question. But Emma would believe me.

While my aunt stared, I dropped my plate into the sink and ran to my room, ignoring her when she called after me. I kicked the door shut, collapsed on my bed then snatched my phone from my nightstand where I'd left it charging the night before.

I called Emma's cell, and almost groaned out loud when her mother answered. But Emma had gotten home more than an hour early for once. What could she possibly be grounded for *this* time?

"Hi, Ms. Marshall." I flopped onto my back and stared

at the textured, eggshell ceiling. "Can I talk to Em? It's kind of important."

Her mom sighed. "Not today, Kaylee. Emma came home smelling like rum last night. She's grounded until further notice. I certainly hope you weren't out drinking with her."

Oh, crap. I closed my eyes, trying to come up with an answer that wouldn't make Em sound like a delinquent by comparison. I drew a total blank. "Um, no, ma'am. I was driving."

"Well, at least *one* of you has a little sense. Do me a favor and try sharing some of that with Emma next time. Assuming I ever let her out of the house again."

"Sure, Ms. Marshall." I hung up, suddenly glad I hadn't spent the night at the Marshalls', as had been my original plan. With Emma grounded and Traci probably still in shock, breakfast could *not* have been a pleasant meal.

After a minute's hesitation, and much anticipatory panic, I decided to call Nash, because in spite of his reputation and my suspicion about his motives, he hadn't laughed at me when I told him the truth about the panic attack.

And with Emma grounded, he was the only one left who knew.

I picked up my phone again—then I realized I didn't have his number.

Careful to avoid my aunt and uncle, who was now awake and frying bacon, based on the scent permeating the entire house, I snuck into the living room, snagged the phone book from an end table drawer and took it back to my room. There were four Hudsons with the right prefix, but only one on his street. Nash answered on the third ring.

My heart pounded so hard I was sure he could hear it over the phone, and for several seconds, silence was all I could manage.

"Hello?" he repeated, sounding almost as annoyed as sleepy now.

"Hey, it's Kaylee," I finally blurted, fervently hoping he remembered me—that I hadn't imagined dancing with him the night before. Because frankly, after the night's premonition and the morning's newscast, even *I* was starting to wonder if Sophie was right about me.

Nash cleared his throat, and when he spoke, his voice was husky with sleep. "Hey. You're not calling to cancel, are you?"

I couldn't resist a smile, in spite of the reason for the call. "No. I… Have you seen the news this morning?"

He chuckled hoarsely. "I haven't even seen the *floor* yet this morning." Nash yawned, and springs creaked over the line. He was still in bed.

I stamped down the scandalous images that knowledge brought to mind and forced myself to focus on the issue at hand. "Turn on your TV."

"I'm not really into current events…." More springs squealed as he rolled over, and something whispered against his phone.

My eyes closed and I leaned against my headboard, sucking in a deep breath. "She's dead, Nash."

"What?" He sounded marginally more awake this time. "Who's dead?"

I leaned forward, and my own bed creaked. "The girl from the club. Emma's sister found her dead in the bathroom at Taboo last night."

"Are you sure it's her?" He was definitely awake now, and I pictured him sitting straight up in bed. Hopefully shirtless.

"See for yourself." I aimed my remote at the nineteen-inch set on my dresser and scrolled through the local channels until I found one still running the story. "Channel nine."

Something clicked over the phone, and canned laughter rang out from his room. A moment later, the sounds from his television synched with mine. "Oh, shit," Nash whispered. Then his voice went deeper. Serious. "Kaylee, has this happened to you before? I mean, have you ever been right before?"

I hesitated, unsure how much to tell him. My eyes closed again, but the backs of my eyelids offered me no advice. So I sighed and told him the truth. After all, he already knew the weirdest part. "I don't know. I can't talk about it here." The last thing I needed was for my aunt and uncle to overhear. They'd either ground me for the rest of my natural life or rush me back to the psych ward.

"I'll come get you. Half an hour?"

"I'll be in my driveway."

3

I SHOWERED IN RECORD time, and twenty-four minutes
after I hung up the phone, I was clean, dry, clothed, and
wearing just enough makeup to hide the shock. But I was
still straightening my hair when I heard a car pull into
the driveway.

Crap. If I didn't get to him first, Uncle Brendon would
make Nash come in and submit to questioning.

I pulled the plug on the flatiron, raced back to my
room for my phone, keys and wallet then sprinted down
the hall and out the front door, shouting "good morning"
and "goodbye" to my astonished uncle all in the same
breath.

"It's early for lunch. How 'bout pancakes?" Nash asked
as I slid into the passenger seat of his mother's car and closed
the door.

"Um…sure." Though with death on my conscience and

Nash in my sight, food was pretty much the last thing on my mind.

The car smelled like coffee, and Nash smelled like soap, toothpaste, and something indescribably, tantalizingly yummy. I wanted to inhale him whole, and I couldn't stop staring at his chin, smooth this morning where it had been deliciously rough the night before. I remembered the texture of his cheek against mine, and had to close my eyes and concentrate to banish the dangerous memory.

I'm not a conquest, no matter how good he smells. Or how good he tastes. And the sudden, overwhelming need to know what his lips would feel like made me shiver all over, and scramble for something safe to say. Something casual, that wouldn't hint at the dangerous direction my thoughts had taken.

"I guess the car started," I said, pulling the seat belt across my torso. Then cursed myself silently for such a stupid opening line. Of course the car had started.

His brief gaze seemed to burn through me. "I have un-reasonably good luck."

I could only nod and clench the door grip while I forced my thoughts back to Heidi Anderson to keep them off Nash and…thoughts I shouldn't have been thinking.

When he glanced my way again, his focus slid down my throat to the neckline of my tee before jerking back to the road as he clenched his jaw. I counted my exhalations to keep them even.

We wound up at a booth in Jimmy's Omelet, a locally

owned chain that served breakfast until three in the afternoon. Nash sat across from me, his arms resting on the table, his sleeves pushed up halfway to his elbows.

Once the waitress had taken our orders and moved on, Nash leaned forward and met my gaze boldly, intimately, as if we'd shared much more than a rhyme in a dark alley and an almost-kiss. But the teasing and flirtation were gone; he looked more serious than I'd ever seen him. Somber. Almost worried.

"Okay…" He spoke softly, in concession to the crowd talking, chewing, and clanking silverware around us. "So last night you predicted this girl's death, and this morning she showed up on the news, dead."

I nodded, swallowing thickly. Hearing it like that—so matter-of-fact—made it sound both crazy and terrifying. And I wasn't sure which was worse.

"You said you've had these premonitions before?"

"Just a few times."

"Have any of them ever come true?"

I shook my head, then shrugged and picked up a napkin-wrapped bundle of silverware to have something to do with my hands. "Not that I know of."

"But you only know about this one because it was on the news, right?" I nodded without looking up, and he continued. "So the others could have come true too, and you might never have known about it."

"I guess." But if that were the case, I wasn't sure I wanted to know about it.

When I drew my focus from the napkin I'd half peeled from the knife and fork, I found him watching me intently, as if my every word might mean something important. His lips were pressed firmly together, his forehead wrinkled in concentration.

I shifted on the vinyl-padded bench, uneasy under such scrutiny. Now he probably really thought I was a freak. A girl who thinks she knows when someone's going to die—that might be interesting in certain circles; it definitely presented a certain morbid cachet.

But a girl who really could predict death? That was just scary.

Nash frowned, and his focus shifted back and forth between my eyes, like he was looking for something specific. "Kaylee, do you know why this is happening? What it means?"

My heart thumped painfully, and I clutched the shredded napkin. "How do you know it means anything?"

"I...don't." He sighed and leaned back in the booth, dropping his gaze to the table as he picked up a mini-jar of strawberry preserves from the jelly carousel. "But don't you think it should mean something? I mean, we're not talking about lottery numbers and horse-race winners. Don't you want to know why you can do this? Or what the limits are? Or—"

"No." I looked up sharply, irritated by the familiar, sick dread settling into my stomach, killing what little appetite

I'd managed to hold on to. "I don't want to know why or how. All I want to know is how to make it stop."

Nash leaned forward again, pinning me with a gaze so intense, so thoroughly invasive, that I caught my breath. "What if you can't?"

My mood darkened at the very thought. I shook my head, denying the possibility.

He glanced down at the jelly again, spinning it on the table, and when he looked back up, his gaze had gone soft. Sympathetic. "Kaylee, you need help with this."

My eyes narrowed and a spike of anger and betrayal shot through me. "You think I need counseling?" Each breath came faster than the last as I fought off memories of brightly colored scrubs, and needles and padded wrist restraints. "I'm not crazy." I stood and dropped the knife on the table, but when I tried to march past him, his hand wrapped firmly around my wrist and he twisted to look up at me.

"Kaylee, wait, that's not what I—"

"Let go." I wanted to tug my arm free, but I was afraid that if he didn't let go, I'd lose it. Four-point restraints or an unyielding hand, it was all the same if I couldn't get free. Panic clawed slowly up from my gut as I struggled not to pull against his grip. My chest constricted, and I went stiff in my desperation to stay calm.

"People are looking…" he whispered urgently.

"Then let me go." Each breath came short and fast

now, and sweat gathered in the crooks of my elbows.
"Please."

He let go.

I exhaled, and my eyes closed as sluggish relief sifted
through me. But I couldn't make myself move. Not yet.
Not without running.

When I realized I was rubbing my wrist, I clenched my
hands into fists until my nails cut into my palms. Distantly,
I noticed that the restaurant had gone quiet around us.

"Kaylee, please sit down. That's not what I meant." His
voice was soft. Soothing.

My hands began to relax, and I inhaled deeply.

"Please," he repeated, and it took every bit of self-
control I had to make myself back up and sink onto the
padded bench. With my hands in my lap.

We sat in silence until conversation picked up around
us, me staring at the table, him staring at me, if I had to
guess.

"Are you okay?" he asked finally, as the waitress set
food on the table behind me, and I felt the tension in my
shoulders ease as I leaned against the wooden back of the
booth.

"I don't need a doctor." I made myself look up, ready
to stand firm against his argument to the contrary. But it
never came.

He sighed, a sound heavy with reluctance. "I know.
You need to tell your aunt and uncle."

"Nash…"

"They might be able to help you, Kaylee. You have to tell someone—"

"They know, okay?" I glanced at the table to find that my fingers were tearing the shredded napkin into even smaller pieces. Shoving them to the side, I met Nash's gaze, suddenly, recklessly determined to tell him the truth. How much worse could he possibly think of me?

"Last time this happened, I freaked out and started screaming. And I couldn't stop. They put me in the hospital, and strapped me to a bed, and shot me full of drugs, and didn't let me out until we all agreed that I'd gotten over my 'delusions and hysteria' and wouldn't need to talk about them anymore. Okay? So I don't think telling them is going to do much good, unless I want to spend fall break in the mental-health unit."

Nash blinked, and in the span of a single second, his expression cycled through disbelief, disgust, and outrage before finally settling on fury, his brows low, arms bulging, like he wanted to hit something.

It took me a moment to understand that none of that was directed at me. That he wasn't angry and embarrassed to be seen out with the school psycho. Probably because no one else knew. No one but Sophie, and her parents had threatened her with social ostracism—total house arrest— if she ever let the family secret out of the proverbial bag.

"How long?" Nash asked, his gaze boring into mine so deeply I wondered if he could see right through my eyes and into my brain.

I sighed and picked at the label on a small bottle of sugar-free syrup. "After a week, I said all the right things, and my uncle took me out against doctor's orders. They told the school I had the flu." I was a sophomore then, and nearly a year away from meeting Nash, when Emma started dating a series of his teammates.

Nash closed his eyes and exhaled heavily. "That never should have happened. You're not crazy. Last night proves that."

I nodded, numb. If I'd misread him, I'd never be able to walk tall in my own school again. But I couldn't even work up any irritation over that possibility at the moment. Not with my secrets exposed, my heart laid open and latent terror lurking in the drug-hazy memories I'd hoped to bury.

"You have to tell them again, and—"

"No."

But he continued, as if I'd never spoken. "—if they don't believe you, call your dad."

"No, Nash."

Before he could argue again, a smooth, pale arm appeared across my field of vision, and the waitress set a plate on the table in front of me, and one in front of him. I hadn't even heard her approach that time, and based on Nash's wide eyes, he hadn't either.

"Okay, you kids dig in. And let me know if I can get you somethin' else, 'kay?"

We both nodded as she walked off. But I could only cut

my pancakes into neat triangles and push them around in the syrup. I had no appetite. Even Nash only picked at his food.

Finally, he put his fork down and cleared his throat until I looked up. "I'm not going to talk you into this, am I?"

I shook my head. He frowned, then sighed and worked up a small smile. "How do you feel about geese?"

AFTER A BREAKFAST I didn't eat, and Nash didn't enjoy, we stopped at a sandwich shop, where he bought a bag of day-old bread. Then we headed to White Rock Lake to feed a honking, pecking flock of geese, a couple of which were gutsy little demons. One snatched a piece of bread right out of my hand, nearly taking my finger with it, and another nipped Nash's shoe when he didn't pull food from the bag fast enough.

When the bread was gone, we escaped from the geese—barely—for a walk around the lake. The wind whipped my hair into knots and I tripped over a loose board in the pier, but when Nash took my hand, I let him keep it, and the silence between us was comfortable. How could it not be, when he'd now seen every shadow in my soul and every corner in my mind, and hadn't once called me crazy—or tried to feel me up.

And why not? I wondered, sneaking a glimpse at his profile as he squinted at the sun across the lake. Was I not pretty enough?

No, I didn't want to be the latest on his rumored list of conquests, but I wouldn't mind knowing I was worthy.

Nash smiled when he noticed me watching him. His eyes were more green than brown in the sunlight, and they seemed to be churning softly, probably reflecting the motion of the water. "Kaylee, can I ask you something personal?"

Like death and mental illness weren't personal?

"Only if I get to ask you something."

He seemed to consider that for a moment, then grinned, flashing a single deep dimple, and squeezed my hand as we walked. "You first."

"Did you sleep with Laura Bell?"

Nash pulled me to an abrupt halt and arched both brows dramatically over long, beautiful boy-lashes. "That's not fair. I didn't ask you who you've been with."

I shrugged, enjoying his discomfort. "Ask away." I wouldn't even need any fingers to tick off my list.

He scowled; he obviously had another question in mind. "If I say yes, are you going to get mad?"

I shrugged. "It's none of my business."

"Then why do you care?"

Grrr... "Okay, new question." I tugged him into step again, working up the nerve to ask something I wasn't sure I really wanted the answer to. But I had to know, before things went any further. "What are you doing here?" I held our joined hands up for emphasis. "What's in this for you?"

"Your trust, hopefully."

My head spun just a little bit at that, and I stifled a dazed grin. "That's it?" I blinked up at him as we stepped onto the pier. Even if that was true, that couldn't be all of it. I donned a mock frown. "You sure you're not trying to get laid?"

His grin that time was real as he pulled me close and pressed me gently against the old wooden railing, his lips inches from my nose. "You offering?"

My heart raced and I let my hands linger on his back, tracing the hard planes through his long-sleeved tee. Feeling him pressed against me. Smelling him up close. Considering, just for a single, pulse-tripping moment…

Then I landed back on earth with a fantasy-shattering thud. The last thing I needed was to be listed among Nash Hudson's past castoffs. But before I could figure out how to say that without pissing him off or sounding like a total prude, his eyes flashed with amusement and he leaned forward and kissed the tip of my nose.

I gasped, and he laughed. "I'm kidding, Kaylee. I just didn't expect you to think about it for so long." He grinned, then stepped back and took my hand again, while I stared at him in astonishment, my cheeks flaming.

"Ask your question before I change my mind."

His smile faded; the teasing was over. What else could he possibly want to know? What they served for lunch in the psych ward?

"What happened to your mom?"

Oh.

"You don't have to tell me." He stopped and turned to face me, backpedaling when he mistook my relief for discomfort. "I was just curious. About what she was like."

I pushed tangled strands of brown hair back from my face. "I don't mind." I wished my mother was still alive, of course, and I really wished I could live with my own family, rather than Sophie's. But my mom had been gone so long I barely remembered her, and I was used to the question. "She died in a car wreck when I was three."

"Do you ever see your dad?"

I shrugged and kicked a pebble off the pier. "He used to come several times a year." Then it was just Christmas and my birthday. And now I hadn't seen him in more than a year. Not that I cared. He had his life—presumably—and I had mine.

Judging from the flash of sympathy in Nash's eyes, he'd heard even the parts I hadn't said out loud. Then there was a subtle shift in his expression, which I couldn't quite interpret. "I still think you should tell your dad about last night."

I scowled and headed back down the pier with my arms crossed over my chest, pleased when the wind shifted to blow my hair away from my face for once.

Nash jogged after me. "Kaylee…"

"You know what the worst part of this is?" I demanded when he pulled even with me and slowed to a walk.

"What?" He looked surprised by my willingness to talk about it at all. But I wasn't talking about my dad.

My eyes closed, and when the wind died down, the sun felt warm on my face, in startling contrast to the chill building inside me. "I feel like I should have done something to stop it. I mean, I knew she was going to die, and I did nothing. I didn't even tell her. I just tucked my tail and ran home. I let her die, Nash."

"No." His voice was firm. My eyes flew open when he turned me to face him, wooden slats creaking beneath us. "You didn't do anything wrong, Kaylee. Knowing it was going to happen doesn't mean you could have stopped it."

"Maybe it does. I didn't even try!" And I'd been so caught up on what her death meant for me that I'd barely stopped to think about what I should have done for her.

His gaze bored into mine, his expression fierce. "It's not that easy. Death doesn't strike at random. If it was her time to go, there's nothing either of us could have done to stop that."

How could he be so sure? "I should have at least told her…."

"No!" His harsh tone startled us both, and when he reached out to grab my arms, I took a step back. Nash let his head dip and held his hands out to show that he wouldn't touch me, then shoved them in his pockets. "She wouldn't have believed you. And, anyway, it's dangerous to mess with stuff you don't understand, and you don't understand this yet. Swear that if this happens again and I'm not there, you won't do anything. Or say anything. Just turn around and walk away. Okay?"

"Okay," I agreed. He was starting to scare me, his eyes wide and earnest, the line of his beautiful mouth tight and thin.

"Swear," Nash insisted, irises flashing and whirling fiercely in the bright sunlight. "You have to swear."

"I swear." And I meant it, because in that moment, with the sun painting his face in a harsh relief of light and shadow, Nash looked both scared and scary.

But even worse, he looked like he knew exactly what he was talking about.

4

NASH TOOK ME HOME two hours before I had to be at
work, and when I walked through the door, the scent of
freesia gave me an instant headache. Sophie was home.

My cousin stood from the couch, where she'd obviously
been peeking through the curtains, and propped thin,
manicured hands on the hipbones poking out above low-
cut, skinny jeans. "Who was that?" she asked, though her
narrowed eyes said she already had a suspect in mind.

I smiled sweetly and walked past her into the hall. "A
guy."

"And his name would be…?" She followed me into my
room, where she sat on my unmade bed as if it were hers.
Or as if we were friends. Sophie only played that game
when she wanted something from me, usually money or
a ride. This time, she was obviously hunting information.

Gossip to fuel the rumor bonfire she and her friends kept burning bright at school.

But I wasn't about to fan her flames.

I turned my back on her to empty my pockets onto my dresser. "None of your business." In the mirror, I saw a scowl flit across her face, pulling her pixie features out of shape.

The problem with getting everything you want in life is that you're not prepared for disappointment when it comes.

I considered it my pleasure to acquaint Sophie with that concept.

"Mom said he's a senior." She pulled her legs onto my bed and crossed them beneath her, shoes and all. When I didn't answer, she glared at my reflection. "I can find out who he is in, like, two seconds."

"Then you obviously need nothing from me." I pulled my hair into a high ponytail. "Welcome to the party, Nancy Drew."

Tiny lines formed around her mouth when she frowned, and I crossed the room to pull my uniform shirt from a hanger, leaving it swinging on the closet rod. "Out. I have to go to work. So I can pay for my car insurance." Sophie wouldn't be eligible for her license for another five months, and it drove her nuts that I could drive and she couldn't.

My car was the best thing my father had ever given

me, even if it was used. And even if he'd never actually seen it.

"Speaking of cars, your mystery date's looked familiar. Little silver Saab, with leather upholstery, right?" Sophie stood, ambling toward the door slowly, narrow hips swaying, cocking her head as if in thought. "The backseat's pretty comfortable, even with that little rip on the passenger side."

Pain shot through my jaw, and I realized I was grinding my teeth.

"Say hi to Nash for me," she purred, one hand wrapped around my door. Then her expression morphed from vicious vixen to Good Samaritan, in the space of a single second. "I'm not trying to hurt your feelings here, Kaylee, but I think you should know the truth." Her pale green eyes went wide in faux innocence. "He's using you to get to me."

My temper flared and I slammed the door. Sophie yelped and jerked her hand out of the way just in time to avoid four broken fingers. My fist clenched my uniform shirt, and I tossed it over the dancer's-butt dent she'd left in my comforter.

She's wrong. But I studied my reflection anyway, trying to see myself as everyone else did. As Nash did. No, I didn't have Sophie's lean dancer's build, or Emma's abundant curves, but I wasn't hideous. Still, Nash could do much better than not-hideous.

Was that why he hadn't kissed me? Was I a convenience

between girlfriends? Or a pity date? Some kind of social outreach program for kindhearted jocks?

No. He wouldn't spend so much time talking to someone he had no real interest in, even if he was looking for a casual hookup. There were easier scores elsewhere.

But I could use a qualified second opinion. Phone in hand, I plopped down on the bed and held my breath while I typed, hoping Emma's mom had given her back her phone.

No such luck. Two very long minutes after I sent the text message—Can u talk?—the reply came.

She is still grounded. Talk to Emma at work.

She should never have taught her mother to text. I told her no good could come of that.

Em and I were scheduled for the same shift, so that afternoon I filled her in on my date with Nash as we sold tickets to the latest computer-animated cartoon and the inevitable romantic comedy. On our dinner break, we sat in one corner of the snack bar, sharing a soft pretzel and cheese fries while I told her about Heidi Anderson—what she hadn't heard from her sister—where no one could overhear.

Emma was fascinated by the accuracy of my prediction, and she agreed with Nash that I should tell my aunt and uncle, though her motive had more to do with shooting them a big I-told-you-so than with helping me figure out what to do with my morbid talent.

But again, I declined the advice. I had no interest in

any future meetings with Dr. Nelson—he of the medical restraints and the zombie pills. In fact, I was clinging to the hope that the next prediction—if there was another— would be months, or even years down the road. After all, there had been nearly nine months between the past two.

The last part of my shift dragged on at half the normal speed because less than fifteen minutes in, the manager moved Emma to the snack bar, leaving me alone in the ticket booth with an A&M computer science major whose undershirt—which he lifted his uniform to show me— read: *My other shirt is a storm trooper uniform.*

When the day was finally over, I clocked out and waited for Emma in the employee snack room. As I was zipping my jacket, Emma pushed through the door and stood with her body holding it open, a dark frown shadowing her entire face.

"What's wrong?" My hand hovered over the hook where her jacket still hung.

"Come on. You have to hear this." She pushed the door open wider and stood to the side, so I could pass through. But I hesitated. Her news obviously wasn't good, and I was all full up on creepy and depressing for the moment. "Seriously. This is weird."

I sighed, then shoved my hands into my jacket pockets and followed her over eight feet of sticky linoleum tile and across the theater lobby toward the snack counter.

Jimmy Barnes was busy with a customer, but once he

saw Emma waiting to talk to him, he rushed through the order so quickly he almost forgot to squirt butter on the popcorn. He had a bit of a crush on Emma.

He wasn't the only one.

"Back already?" Jimmy nodded at me, then leaned with both plump arms on the glass countertop, staring at Em as if the meaning of life lay buried in her eyes. His fingers were stained yellow with butter-flavored oil and he smelled like popcorn and the root beer he'd dribbled down the front of his black apron.

"Can you tell Kaylee what Mike said?"

Jimmy's goofy, puppy-love smile faded, and he stood, angling his body to face us both. "Creepiest thing I ever heard." He reached below the counter to grab a plastic-wrapped stack of sixteen-ounce paper cups, and began refilling the dispenser as he spoke.

"You know Mike Powell, right?" he asked.

"Yeah." I glanced at Emma with both brows raised in question, but she only nodded toward Jimmy, silently telling me to pay attention.

Jimmy pressed on an inverted stack of cups, which sank into a hole in the countertop to make room for more. "Mike took a shift at the snack bar at the Arlington branch today, filling in for some guy who got fired for spittin' in someone's Coke."

"Hey, can I get some popcorn over here?"

I looked up to see a middle-aged man waiting in front of the cash register, flanked by a little girl with her thumb in her mouth and an older boy with his gaze—and his thumbs—glued to a PSP.

"Will that be a jumbo, sir?" Jimmy held up one just-a-minute finger for us and veered toward the closest of several popcorn machines while I dug my phone from my pocket to check the time. It was after nine and I was starving. And not exactly eager for whatever weird, creepy story Jimmy had to tell.

When the customers left with a cardboard tray full of junk food and soda, Jimmy turned back to us. "Anyway, Mike called about half an hour ago, totally freaked out. He said some girl died right in front of his register this afternoon. Just fell over dead, still holding her popcorn."

Shock pinged through me, chilling me from the inside out. I glanced at Emma, and she gave me a single grim nod. As I turned back to Jimmy, a dark unease unfurled deep inside me, spiraling up my spine like tendrils of ice. "You're serious?"

"Totally." He twisted the end of the plastic sleeve around the remaining cups. "Mike said the whole thing was unreal. The ambulance took her away in a freakin' body bag, and the manager closed the place down and handed out vouchers to all the customers. And the cops kept asking Mike questions, trying to figure out what happened."

Emma watched me for my reaction, but I could only stare, my hands gripping the edge of the counter, unable to force my scattered thoughts into any logical order. The similarity to Heidi Anderson was obvious, but I had no concrete reason to connect the two deaths.

"Do they know how she died?" I asked finally, grasping at the first coherent thought to form.

Jimmy shrugged. "Mike said she was fine one minute, and flat on her back the next. No coughing, no choking, no grabbing her heart or her head."

A vague, heavy dread was building inside me, a slow simmer of foreboding, compared to the rapid boil of panic I'd felt when I saw Heidi's shadow-shroud. The deaths were connected. They had to be.

Emma was watching me again, and I must have looked as sick as I felt because she put one hand on my shoulder. "Thanks, Jimmy. See ya Wednesday."

On the way home, Emma loosened her seat belt and twisted in the passenger seat to frown at me in the dark, her face a mask of grim fascination. "How weird was that? First you predict that girl's death at Taboo. Then tonight, *another* girl falls down dead at the theater, just like last night."

I flicked on my blinker to pass a car in the right lane. "They're not the same," I insisted, in spite of my own similar thoughts. "Heidi Anderson was drunk. She probably died of alcohol poisoning."

"Nuh-uh." Emma shook her head, blond hair bouncing in the corner of my vision. "The news said they tested her blood. She was drunk, but not that drunk."

I shrugged, uncomfortable with the turn of the conversation. "So she passed out and hit her head when she fell."

"If she did, don't you think the cops would have figured that out by now?" When I didn't answer, Emma continued, shielding her eyes from the glare of a passing highway light. "I don't think they know what killed her. I bet that's why they haven't scheduled her funeral yet."

My hands tightened on the wheel, and I glanced at her in surprise. "What are you, spying on the dead girl?"

She shrugged. "Just watching the news. I'm grounded—what else is there to do? Besides, this is the weirdest thing that ever happened around here. And the fact that you predicted one of them is beyond bizarre."

I flicked on my blinker again and swerved off the highway at our exit, forcing my hand to relax around the wheel. I didn't even want to think about my premonition anymore, much less talk about it. "You don't know the deaths are connected. It's not like they were murdered. At least not the girl in Arlington. Mike *saw* her die."

"She could have been poisoned…." Emma insisted, but I continued, ignoring her as I slowed to make the turn onto her street.

"And even if they are connected, they have nothing to do with us."

"You knew the first one was going to die."

"Yeah, and I hope it never happens again."

Emma frowned but let the subject go. After I dropped

her off, I pulled into an empty lot down the street from her house and called Nash.

"Hello?" In the background, I heard gunfire and shouting, until he turned down the volume on his TV.

"Hey, it's Kaylee. Are you busy?"

"Just avoiding homework. What's up?"

I stared out the windshield at the dark parking lot, and my heart seemed to stumble over the next few beats while I worked up my nerve.

"Kaylee? You there?"

"Yeah." I closed my eyes and forced the next words out before my throat froze up. "Can I use your computer? I need to look something up, but I can't do it at home without Sophie snooping." And I did not want my aunt to bring me laundry without knocking—as was her habit— and see what I was looking up online.

"No problem."

But second thoughts came fast and hard. I should not be alone with Nash in his house—that whole willpower thing again.

He laughed as if he knew what I was thinking. Or heard it in my nervous silence. "Don't worry. My mom's here."

Relief and disappointment came in equal parts, and I fought to let neither leak into my voice. "That's fine." I started the engine, my headlights carving arcs of light across the dark gravel lot. "You hungry?"

"I was about to nuke a pizza."

"Interested in a burger?"

"Always."

Twenty minutes later, I parked on the street in front of his house and got out of the car, a fast-food bag in one hand, drink tray in the other. Again, his mother's Saab was in the driveway, but this time the door was closed.

I crossed the small, neat yard and stepped onto the porch, but Nash opened the front door before I could knock. "Hey, come on in." He took the drinks and held the door open, and I stepped past him into a clean, sparsely decorated living room.

Nash set the cups on an end table and stuffed his hands in his pockets while I looked around. His mother's furniture wasn't new or as upscale as Aunt Val's, but it looked much more comfortable. The hardwood floor was worn but spotless, and the entire house smelled like chocolate-chip cookies.

At first I assumed the scent was from a candle like the ones Aunt Val lit at Christmas, to give the impression that she knows how to bake. But then I heard an oven door creak open to the left of the living room, and that cookie-scent swelled. Mrs. Hudson was *actually* baking.

When my gaze returned to Nash, I found him looking at my shirt, but in amusement, rather than real interest. Which is when I realized I was still wearing my Ciné uniform. *Way to dress the part, Kaylee...*

Nash laughed when he saw my surprise, then gestured toward a narrow hallway branching off the living room.

"Come on…" But before he'd taken two steps, the swinging door into the kitchen opened, and a slim, well-proportioned woman appeared in the doorway, barefoot, in snug jeans and a blue-ribbed tee.

I'm not sure what I'd expected Nash's mom to look like, but this woman did *not* fit the bill. She was young. Like, thirty. But that couldn't be right, because Nash was eighteen. She wore her long, dark blond curls pulled into a simple ponytail, except for a few ringlets that had fallen to frame her face.

She could have been his older sister. His very hot older sister. *Aunt Val would* hate *her.…*

When Mrs. Hudson's eyes found mine, the world seemed to stop moving. Or rather, she stopped moving. Completely. As if she weren't even breathing. I guess I wasn't what she'd expected either. Nash's exes were all beautiful, and I bet none of them had ever come over in a shapeless purple polo with the Ciné logo embroidered on one shoulder.

Regardless, the intense way she stared at me unnerved me, like she was trying to read my thoughts in my eyes, and I had an unbearable urge to close them in case that's exactly what she was doing. Instead, I clutched the fast-food bag in both hands and returned her look with a frank one of my own, because she didn't look angry. Only very curious.

After several uncomfortable seconds, she flashed a beautiful, un-motherly smile and nodded, as if she approved of whatever she'd seen in me. "Hi, Kaylee, I'm Harmony." Nash's mom wiped her right hand on the front of her jeans, leaving a faint, palm-shaped smudge of flour, then stepped forward and reached out for mine. I shook her hand hesitantly. "I've heard so much about you."

She'd heard about me?

I glanced up to see Nash scowling at his mother, and had the distinct impression I'd just missed him shaking his head, or shooting her some other silent "shut up!" signal.

What was I missing?

"It's nice to meet you too, Mrs. Hudson." I suppressed the urge to wipe residual flour onto my work pants.

"Oh, it's not Mrs." Her smile softened, though her eyes never left mine. "It's been just me and Nash for years now. What about you, Kaylee? Tell me about your parents."

"I…um…"

Nash's fingers folded around mine and I let him pull me close. "Kaylee needs to borrow my computer." He gestured to the grease-stained bag I still held in one hand. "We're gonna eat while we work."

For a moment, Ms. Hudson looked like she might object. Then she shot Nash a stern smile. "Leave the door open."

Nash mumbled a vague acknowledgment, then headed down the short, dim hallway with the drink tray. Still speechless, I followed him, the fast-food bag clutched to my chest.

Nash's room was casual and comfortable, and I liked it instantly. His bed was unmade, and his desk was cluttered with CDs, Xbox games, and junk-food wrappers. The TV was on, but he hit the power button as he passed it, and whatever he'd been watching flashed into a silent black screen.

His desk chair was the only one in the room, and the open can of Coke on the desk said he was sitting there. For a moment, I froze like a rabbit in the crosshairs, staring at the bed, the only other place to sit, while my pulse whooshed in my ears.

Nash laughed and pushed the door to within an inch of closed, waving toward the bed with his empty hand. "It's not gonna fold up into the wall."

I was more worried about it swallowing me whole. And I couldn't help wondering how many girls had sat there before me....

Finally embarrassed into action, I shoved aside an unopened chemistry book and sat on the edge of the bed, already digging in the paper bag. "Here." I handed him a burger and a carton of fries.

He set the food on the desk and sank into the chair, jiggling the mouse until his monitor flared to life. "What are we looking for?" he asked, then folded a fry into his mouth.

I unwrapped my own burger, considering how best to phrase my answer. But there was no good way to put what I had to say. "Another girl died tonight. At the Ciné in

Arlington. A guy I work with was there, and he said she just fell over dead, holding a bag of popcorn."

Nash blinked at me, frozen in mid-chew. "You're serious?" he asked after he swallowed, and I nodded. "You think it's connected to that girl in the West End?"

I shrugged. "I didn't predict this one, but it's even weirder than what happened at Taboo. I want details." So I could prove to myself that the two deaths weren't as similar as they sounded.

"Okay, hang on…" He typed something into the address bar, and a search engine appeared on the monitor. "Arlington?"

"Yeah," I said, around a bite of my burger.

Nash typed as he chewed, and links began filling the screen. He clicked on the first one. "Here it is." It was a Dallas news channel's Web site—the station that had aired the story about Heidi Anderson the day before.

I leaned closer to see over his shoulder, acutely aware of how good he smelled, and Nash read aloud. "Local authorities are perplexed by the death of the second metroplex teenager in as many days. Late this afternoon, fifteen-year-old Alyson Baker died in the lobby of the Ciné 9, in the Six Flags mall. Police have yet to determine her cause of death, but have ruled out drugs and alcohol as factors. According to one witness, Baker 'just fell over dead' at the concession counter. A memorial will be held tomorrow at Stephen F. Austin High School for Baker, who was a sophomore there, and a cheerleader."

Sipping from my straw, I scanned the article for a moment after he finished reading. "That's it?"

"There's a picture." He scrolled up to reveal a black-and-white yearbook photo of a pretty brunette with long, straight hair and dramatic features. "What do you think?"

I sighed and sank back onto the edge of the bed. Seeing the latest dead girl hadn't answered any of my questions, but it had given me a name and a face, and made her death infinitely, miserably more real. "I don't know. She doesn't look much like Heidi Anderson. And she's four years younger."

"And she wasn't drunk."

"And I had no idea this one was going to happen." No longer hungry, I wrapped the rest of my burger and dropped it into the bag. "The only thing they have in common is that they both died in public."

"With no obvious cause of death." Nash glanced at the bag in my lap. "Are you gonna finish that?"

I handed him the burger, but his words still echoed in my mind. He'd hit the nail on the head with that one— and driven it straight into my heart. Heidi and Alyson had both literally dropped dead with no warnings, no illness and no wounds of any kind. And I'd known Heidi's death was coming.

If I'd been there when Alyson Baker was ordering her popcorn, would I have known she was about to die?

And if I had, would telling her have done any good?

I scooted back on the bed and drew my knees up to my chest as my guilt over Heidi's death swelled within me like a sponge soaking up water. Had I *let* her die?

Nash dropped the empty burger wrapper into the bag and swiveled in the desk chair to face me. He frowned as he looked at my expression and leaned forward to gently push my legs down, so he could see my face. "There's nothing you could have done."

Were my thoughts that obvious? I couldn't summon a smile, even with his dimples and late-night stubble only inches away. "You don't know that."

His mouth formed a hard line for a moment, like he might argue, but then he smiled slyly, and his gaze locked onto mine. "What I *do* know is that you need to relax. Think about something other than death." His voice was a gentle rumble as he moved from the chair to sit next to me on the bed, and the mattress sank beneath his weight.

My breath hitched in anticipation, and my pulse raced. "What should I be thinking about?" My own voice came out lower, my words so soft I could barely hear them.

"Me," he whispered back, leaning forward so that his lips brushed my ear as he spoke. His scent enveloped me, and his cheek felt scratchy against mine. "You should be thinking about *me*." His fingers intertwined with mine in my lap, and he pulled away from my ear slowly, his lips skimming my cheek, deliciously soft in contrast to the sharp stubble. He dropped a trail of small kisses along my jaw, and my heart beat harder with every single one.

When he reached my chin, the kisses trailed up until his mouth met mine, gently sucking my lower lip between his. Teasing without making full contact. My chest rose and fell quickly, my breaths shallow, my pulse racing.

More...

He heard me. He must have. Nash pulled back just long enough to meet my gaze, heat blazing behind his eyes, and I realized that he was breathing hard too. His fingers tightened around mine and his free hand slid into the hair at the base of my skull.

Then he kissed me for real.

My mouth opened beneath his, and the kiss went deeper as I drew him in, suddenly ravenous for something I'd never even tasted. My fingers tightened around his, and my free hand found his arm, exploring the hard planes, reveling in the potential of such restrained strength.

Nash pulled back then and looked at me, deep need smoldering behind his eyes. The intensity of that need—the staggering depth of his longing—slammed into me like a wave on the side of a ship, threatening to knock me overboard. To toss me into that turbulent sea, where the current would surely carry me away.

His finger traced my lower lip, his gaze locked onto mine, and my mouth opened, ready for his again.

His hesitance was a terrible mercy. I could barely breathe with him touching me, so overwhelmed was I by...everything. But he smelled so good, and felt so good, I didn't want him to stop, even if I never breathed again.

This time I kissed him, taking what I wanted, delighted and astonished by his willingness to let me. My head was so full of Nash I wasn't sure I'd ever think about anything else again....

Until the bedroom door opened.

Nash jerked back so fast he left me gasping in surprise. I blinked, slowly struggling up from the wave of sensations I wanted to ride again. My cheeks flamed as I smoothed my ponytail.

"Dinner, huh?" Ms. Hudson stood in the doorway, arms crossed over her chest, a fresh smear of chocolate on the hem of her shirt. She frowned at us, but didn't look particularly angry or surprised.

Nash rubbed his face with both hands. I sat there, speechless, and more embarrassed than I'd ever been in my life. But at least we'd been caught by his mother, rather than my uncle. That, I would never have recovered from.

"Let's leave the door open for real this time, huh?" She turned to leave, but then her gaze caught on the computer screen, where Alyson Baker's picture still stared out at the room. Something dark flickered across her face—fear, or concern?—then her expression hardened as she leveled it at her son.

"What are you two doing?" she demanded softly, obviously no longer referring to our social interaction.

"Nothing." Nash's expression carried just as much weight as his mother's had, but I couldn't read anything specific in his, though the tension in the room spiked noticeably.

"I should go." I stood, already digging my keys from my pocket.

"No." Nash took my hand.

Ms. Hudson's expression softened. "You really don't have to," she said. "Stay and have some cookies. Just leave the door open." She eyed Nash on that last part, and tension drained from the air as her frown melted.

Nash rolled his eyes but nodded. Then they both turned to me, waiting for my answer.

"Thanks, but I have some homework to finish…." And Nash's mother had just caught us making out on his bed, which felt very much like the end of the night to me.

Nash walked me to my car and kissed me again, his body pressing mine into the driver's side door, our hands intertwined. Then I drove home in a daze and floated straight to my room, ignoring every less-than-subtle hint for information Sophie tossed my way. And only later would I realize that I had, in fact, forgotten all about the dead girls and was still thinking about Nash when I fell asleep.

5

"INSIDE OR OUT?" Nash set his tray on the nearest table and dug in his pocket. Coins jingled, barely audible over the clatter of silverware and the buzz of several dozen simultaneous conversations, and he pulled out a handful of change, already turning toward the soda machine.

The autumn morning had dawned clear and cool, but by third period, it was warm enough for my biology teacher to open the windows in the lab and vent the acrid scent of chemical preservatives. "Out." Lunch in the quad sounded good to me, especially considering the swarm of student bodies in the cafeteria, and the dozen or so people who had already noticed his fingers curled around mine in the pizza line.

Including his latest ex, who now glared at me from within a cocoon of hostile cheerleader clones.

I glanced over my shoulder at Emma, who nodded. "I'll

get a table." She turned and dodged a freshman carrying three ice-cream bars, who almost knocked her tray from her hands.

"Sorry," he mumbled, then stopped to watch her, his expression a blend of blatant lust and longing. Emma didn't even notice.

Nash pulled two Cokes from the machine and set one on my tray, then we wove our way around two tables to the center aisle, headed straight for the exit. I could practically feel the eyes of my classmates trained on my back, and it was everything I could do not to squirm beneath their scrutiny. How could he stand people watching him all the time?

We were two feet from the double doors leading into the quad when they swung open, only inches from smacking into my tray. A gaggle of slim girls in matching letterman jackets brushed past us, several pausing to smile at Nash. One even ran her fingers down his sleeve, and I was startled by the sudden, irrational urge to slap her hand away. Which proved unnecessary when he walked past her with nothing but a distracted nod.

Sophie was the only one who even glanced my way, and her expression could hardly be considered friendly. Until it landed on Nash. She let her arm brush his as she passed, glancing up into his eyes, a carnal smile turning up one corner of her perfectly made-up mouth in blatant, unspoken invitation.

Seconds later, the dancers were gone, leaving behind

a cloud of perfume strong enough to burn my eyes. I stomped through the still-open doors and down the steps. Nash jogged to catch up with me. He carried his tray in one hand, and his opposite arm snaked around my waist, fingers curling around my hip with an intimate familiarity that made my pulse spike. "She's just trying to piss you off."

"She says she's been in your backseat." I couldn't keep suspicion from my tone. Yes, his hand on my hip made a very public statement, and that—along with his silence on the matter of my mental health—finally put to rest my stubborn fear that he'd planned a quick hookup over the weekend, and would be done with me by Monday.

But Nash had never even tried to deny the rumors of his past exploits, and I couldn't stand the thought that Sophie had been one of them.

"What?" He stopped in the middle of the quad, frowning down at me in obvious confusion.

"The back of your car. She says there's a rip in your backseat and wants me to think she's seen it up close."

Nash chuckled softly and started walking again as he spoke, so that I had no choice but to follow. "Um… yeah. She put it there. She was wrecked the night I took her home, and she threw up all over the front floorboard. I put her in the back, and she got some stupid buckle on her shoe caught in the stitching and ripped it loose."

I laughed, and my anger melted like Sophie's makeup in July. In fact, I almost felt sorry for her—but not too sorry to dangle that little nugget of information in front of my cousin the next time she flirted with Nash in front of me.

The quad was actually a long rectangle, surrounded on three sides by various wings of the school building, with the cafeteria entrance on the end of one long wall. The fourth side opened up to the soccer and baseball practice fields at the rear of the campus.

Emma had claimed a table in the far corner, mostly sheltered from the wind by the junction of the language and science halls. I sat on the bench opposite her, and Nash slid in next to me. His leg touched mine from hip to knee, which was enough to keep me warm from the inside out, in spite of the chilly, intermittent breeze at my back.

"What's with the dance team?" Emma asked as I bit the point off my slice of pizza. "They came through here a minute ago, squealing and bouncing around like someone poured hot sauce in their leotards."

I laughed and nearly choked on a chunk of pepperoni. "They won the regional championship on Saturday. Sophie's been insufferable ever since."

"So how long will they be squeaking like squirrels?"

Holding up one finger, I chewed and swallowed another bite before answering. "The state championship is next month. After that, there will either be more irrepressible squealing, or inconsolable tears. Then it's over until May, when they audition for next year's team." Regardless, I would mourn the end of the competition season right along with Sophie. Dance-team practices took up most of her spare time for several months of the year, giving me some much-coveted peace and quiet while she was out of the house.

And, as spoiled and arrogant as she was, Sophie was totally dedicated to the team. She gave the other dancers more respect than she'd ever seen fit to waste on me, and the dedication and punctuality she showed them were the only evidence I'd seen in thirteen years that she had a single responsible bone in that infuriatingly graceful body.

Plus, most of her teammates could drive, and someone always seemed willing to give her a ride. After the state championship, Sophie would go back to daily ballet classes, and now that I had a car, I was fairly certain her parents would make me drive her to and from. Like I had nothing better to do with my time. And my gas money.

"Well, here's hoping we all go deaf either way." Emma held her bottled water aloft, and Nash and I clinked our cans into it. "So…" She screwed the lid back on her bottle. "Heard anything new about that girl from Arlington?"

Nash frowned, his brows lowered over eyes more brown than green at the moment.

"Yeah." I dropped the remains of my pizza onto my tray and picked up a bruised red apple. "Her name was Alyson Baker. Happened just like Jimmy said. She fell over dead, and the cops have no idea what killed her."

"Was she drinking?" Emma asked, obviously thinking about Heidi Anderson.

"Nope. She wasn't on anything either." Nash gestured with the crust of his first slice. "But she has nothing to do with the first, right?" He glanced my way, brows raised now in question. "I mean, you didn't predict this one. You never even saw her, right?"

I nodded and took the first bite out of my apple. He was right, of course.

But there *was* an obvious connection between the two girls: they were both dead with no apparent cause. The local news knew that. Emma knew it. I knew it. Only Nash seemed oblivious. Or at least uninterested.

Emma pointed at him with the business end of a plastic fork, her porcelain face twisted into an equally beautiful mask of disbelief. "So you don't think it's weird that two girls have dropped dead in the past two days?"

He sighed and pulled the tab from his empty soda can, watching it, rather than either of us. "I never said it wasn't weird. But I don't get this morbid obsession you two have with those poor girls. They're gone. You didn't know either of them. Let them rest in peace."

I rolled my eyes and peeled the vendor's sticker from my apple. "We're not disturbing their rest."

"And it's not obsession—it's caution," Emma countered, aiming her water bottle at him like a conductor's baton. "No one knows how they died, and I'm not buying the co-incidence angle. That could be either one of us tomorrow."

Her gaze turned my way, clearly including me among the potential victims of…um…dropping dead for no reason. "Or any one of *them*." She nodded toward the cafeteria, and I turned to see Sophie and several of her friends bounce down the steps in the company of half a dozen jocks in matching green-and-white jackets.

"You're totally overreacting." Nash pushed his tray away and twisted on the bench to face us both. "It's just a weird coincidence that has nothing to do with us."

"What if it's not?" I demanded, and even I recognized the pain in my voice. I couldn't let go of the possibility that I could have helped. Could maybe have saved Heidi, if I'd only said something. "No one knows what happened to those girls, so you can't possibly know it won't happen again."

Nash closed his eyes, as if gathering his thoughts. Or maybe his patience. Then he opened them and looked at first Emma, then me. "No, I don't know what happened to either of them, but the cops will figure it out sooner or later. They probably died of totally different, completely unrelated illnesses. An aneurism, or a freak teenage heart attack. And I'll bet you my Xbox that they have nothing to do with each other."

His eyes narrowed on mine then, and he took my hand in both of his. "And they have nothing to do with you."

"Then how did she know it was going to happen?" Emma stared at us both, brown eyes wide. "Kaylee knew that first girl was going to die. I'd say that makes her pretty deeply involved."

"Okay, yes." Nash turned from me to glare at her. "Kaylee knew about Heidi. That's weird, and creepy, and sounds like the plot from some cheesy horror movie—"

"Hey!" I elbowed Nash, and he shot me a dimpled grin.

"Sorry. But she asked. My point is that your premonition is the only weird part of this. The rest is just coincidence. A total fluke. It's not going to happen again."

I pulled my hand from his grasp. "What if you're wrong?"

Nash frowned and ran his fingers through his artfully mussed hair, but before he could answer, a hand dropped onto my shoulder and I jumped.

"Trouble in paradise?" Sophie asked, and I looked up to find her beaming at Nash over my head.

"Nope. We're all shiny and happy here, thanks," Emma said when I couldn't unclench my teeth long enough to reply.

"Hey, Hudson." A green-sleeved arm slid around Sophie's shoulders, and I found myself staring at Scott Carter, the first-string quarterback and my cousin's current plaything. "Makin' new friends?"

Nash nodded. "You know Emma, right?"

Carter's jaw tightened as his eyes settled on my best friend. He knew her, all right. Emma had turned him down cold over the summer, then dumped a Slushie on his shirt at the Cinemark when he refused to take the hint. If anyone other than Jimmy had been working with her, she'd probably have been reported and fired.

Nash's hand curled around mine. "And this is Kaylee."

Carter's eyes turned my way, for probably the first time ever, and his smile returned as his gaze traveled from my face to the front of my shirt. Which he could probably see straight down, since he was standing. "Sophie's sister, right?"

"Cousin," Sophie and I said in unison. It was the only thing we agreed on.

"Hey, we're taking my dad's boat out on White Rock Lake Friday night. You two should come."

"She can't." Sophie sneered at me, curling her arm through Carter's. "She has to *work*."

As if it were a dirty word. Though personally, after what Emma had to say about him, I'd rather spend all night scraping gum from the underside of theater chairs than spend one minute on Carter's father's boat.

"We'll catch you next time," Nash said, and Carter nodded as Sophie tugged him toward a table at the front of the quad, already swarming with green-and-white jackets.

"Wow." Emma whistled softly. "He is such a dick. He just looked down your shirt with Sophie and Nash both standing there. That's a jock for you."

"We're not all bad," Nash said, but he looked distinctly

unamused by both Carter's optical invasion and Emma's commentary on it.

Without his teammates around, it was easy to forget that Nash played football. Baseball too. What could he possibly want with me, while girls like Sophie were standing in line to drool all over him?

"Don't you usually sit over there?" I asked, nodding toward the green-and-white bee swarm. We'd sat with the jocks earlier in the year, when Emma was going out with one of the linebackers, but honestly, the noise and constant posturing got on my nerves.

"You two are much better company." Nash grinned, pulling me closer, but for once, I barely noticed. Something in that crowd of matching jackets had snagged my attention. Something felt...wrong.

Nooo...! It couldn't happen again! Nash had said it wouldn't!

But already the first tendrils of panic were prickling the inside of my flesh.

The edges of my vision went dark, as if death hovered just out of sight. My heart hammered. My skin tingled, and my hands curled into fists. Nash flinched and pulled his hand from mine. I'd forgotten I was holding it and had drawn blood from his palm.

"Kaylee?" His voice was thick with concern, but I couldn't look away from the green-and-white crowd. Couldn't concentrate on him while panic thundered through my head and guilt clawed at my heart. Someone

was going to die. I could feel it, but I couldn't tell who
yet. The jackets blended into one another, like a herd of
Technicolor zebras, individuals hiding among the min-
gling multitude.

But social camouflage wouldn't work. Death would
find the one it wanted, and I couldn't warn the victim if
I couldn't find him. Or her.

And it was a her. I could feel that much.

"She's doing it again."

I heard Emma as if she were speaking from far away,
though I knew dimly that she'd moved to sit next to me. I
couldn't look at her. I had eyes only for the crowd hiding
the soon-to-be-dead girl. I needed to see who she was. I
had to see....

Then the crowd parted and the applause began. Music
played; someone had brought out a small stereo. Girls were
tossing their jackets onto a pile on the ground. They lined
up in the grass, forming a zigzag formation I recognized
from the competitions my aunt and uncle had dragged me
to. The dance team was doing a demonstration. Showing
off the routine that had captured the regional trophy.

And then I saw her. Second from the left, three down
from Sophie. A tall, slender girl with honey-brown hair
and heavily lashed eyes.

Meredith Cole. The team captain. Shrouded in a
shadow so thick I could barely make out her features.

As soon as my eyes found her, my throat began to burn,
like I'd inhaled bleach fumes. Devastation drenched me,

threatening to pull me beneath the surface of despair. And that familiar dark knowledge left me shivering where I sat. Meredith Cole would die very, very soon.

"Kaylee, come on." Nash stood, tugging on my arm, trying to pull me up. "Let's go."

My throat tightened, and my breaths grew short. My head swam with the bitter chaos building inside me, and my heart felt swollen and heavy with grief. But I couldn't go. I had to tell her. I'd let Heidi die, but I could save Meredith. I could warn her, and everything would be okay.

My mouth fell open, but the words didn't come. Instead, a scream clawed at my throat, announcing its arrival with the usual burst of panic, and this time there was nothing I could do to stop it. I couldn't speak; I could only scream. But that wouldn't be enough. I needed *words* to warn Meredith, not inarticulate shrieking. What good was my "gift" if I couldn't use it? If all I could do was scream uselessly?

The keening began deep in my throat, so low it felt like my lungs were on fire. Yet the sound was soft at first. Like a whisper I felt more than heard. I clamped my jaws shut in horror as Nash's eyes widened, his irises seeming to churn again in the bright sunlight.

My vision darkened and went dull, as if that same foggy gray filter had been draped over the entire world. The day was dimmer now, the shadows thicker, the air hazy. My own hands looked fuzzy, as if I couldn't quite bring them into focus. Tables, students, and the school building itself were suddenly leached of their vibrancy, like someone had opened a drain at the base of a rainbow and let all the color out.

I stood and clamped a hand over my mouth, begging an oddly faded-looking Nash with my eyes for help. The keening sound rolled up my throat now and stuck there, like a growl, offering no release.

Nash wrapped one arm around my waist and nodded for Emma to take my other side. "Calm down, Kaylee," he whispered into my ear, his breath warm against my neck, stirring the fine hairs there. "Just relax and listen to—"

My legs collapsed, even as my gaze was drawn back to Meredith, now dancing between Sophie and a petite blonde I knew only by sight.

Nash scooped me into his arms and held me tight to his chest, still whispering something in my ear. Something familiar. Something that rhymed. His words fell on me with an almost physical presence, soothing me everywhere they touched me, like a balm I could hear.

Yet still the scream raged inside me, demanding a way out, and apparently willing to forge an exit itself, if I offered no alternative.

Emma walked ahead of us to the end of the English hall and around the corner, out of sight of the quad. No one else noticed; they were all watching the dance squad.

Nash put me down against the short wall at the end of the building, next to a door that only worked as an exit.

He sat beside me again, and this time he wrapped his arms around me while Emma knelt next to us. Nash was warm at my back, and the only sounds I could hear were his whispers and my own soft keening, persisting in spite of my struggle to suppress it.

I stared over his shoulder and past Emma's concerned face, at the weirdly gray field house in the distance, concentrating on my efforts to speak without screaming. Something rushed across the left edge of my vision, and my gaze homed in on it automatically, trying to bring it into focus. But it moved too fast, leaving me with only a vague impression of a human silhouette, out of proportion in no way I could explain with so short a glimpse. The figure was misshapen, somehow. Odd-looking. And when I blinked, I could no longer be sure of where I'd seen it.

A teacher, probably, rendered unrecognizable by the weird gray fog that had overlaid my vision. I squeezed my eyes shut to avoid any future distractions.

Then, as swiftly as it had struck, the panic faded. Tension drained from my body like air from a beach ball, leaving me limp with relief and fatigue. I opened my eyes to see that color and clarity had returned to the world. My hands relaxed, and the scream died in my throat. But an instant later it tore through the air, and it actually took me a second to realize that the shriek hadn't come from me.

It had come from the quad.

I knew what had happened without even looking.

Meredith had collapsed. My urge to scream died the moment she did.

Again, I'd known someone was going to die. And again, I'd let it happen.

My eyes closed as a fresh wave of shock and grief rolled over me, followed immediately by guilt so heavy I could hardly lift my head. *My fault.* I should have been able to save her.

More shouts came from the quad, and someone yelled for someone else to call an ambulance. Doors squealed open, then crashed into the side of the brick building. Sneakers pounded on concrete steps.

Tears of shame and frustration poured down my face. I buried my head in Nash's shoulder, heedless as my tears soaked into his shirt. I might as well have killed her myself, for all the good my warning had done.

Around the corner, the buzz of chaos rose, each terrified voice blending into the next. Someone was crying. Someone else was running. And above it all, Mrs. Tucker, the girls' softball coach, blew her whistle, trying ineffectively to calm everyone down.

"Who is it?" Emma asked, still kneeling beside us, eyes wide in shock and understanding as she brushed back a strand of my hair so she could see my face.

"Meredith Cole," I whispered, wiping tears on my sleeve.

Nash squeezed me tighter, wrapping his arms around mine, where they clutched at my stomach.

Emma stood slowly, her expression a mixture of disbelief and dread. She backed away from us, legs wobbling. Then she turned carefully and peeked around the corner. "I can't see anything. There're too many people."

"Doesn't matter," I said, mildly surprised by the dazed quality of my own voice. "She's already dead."

"How do you know?" Her hand gripped the corner of the building, nails digging into the rough mortar outlining the brown bricks. "Are you sure it's Meredith?"

"Yes." I sighed, then rose and pulled Nash up, wiping more tears from my cheeks. He stood to my left, Emma to my right. Together, we turned the corner and entered the chaos.

6

EMMA WAS RIGHT—THERE were people everywhere. Several classroom doors had opened into the quad, and students were pouring out in spite of protests from their teachers. And since there were still ten minutes left in second lunch, the cafeteria was now emptying its usual crowd onto the grass too.

I saw at least twenty students on cell phones, and the snatches of conversation I caught sounded like 911 calls, though most of the callers didn't actually know what had happened, or who was involved. They only knew someone was hurt, and there had been no gunfire.

Coach Tucker loomed on the edge of the green-and-white central throng, her sneakers spread wide for balance, pulling kids out of the way one at a time even as she shouted into a clunky, school-issue, handheld radio. Finally the crowd parted for her, revealing a motionless female form lying on the brown grass, one arm thrown out at her side. I couldn't see her face because one of the football players—number fourteen—was performing CPR.

But I knew it was Meredith Cole. And I could have told number fourteen that his efforts were wasted; he couldn't help her.

Coach Tucker pulled the football player away from the dead girl and dropped to her knees beside the body, shouting for everyone to move back. To go back into the building. Then she bent with her face close to Meredith's to see if she was breathing. A moment later, Coach Tucker tilted the dancer's head back and resumed CPR where number fourteen had left off.

Seconds later, the dance team's faculty sponsor—Mrs. Foley, one of the algebra teachers—raced across the quad from an open classroom, stunned speechless for several seconds by the chaos. After a quick word with a couple of students, she gathered her remaining dancers into a teary huddle several feet from Meredith and the softball coach. The other students stared at them all in astonishment, some crying, some whispering and others standing in silent shock.

As we watched from the fringes of the mayhem, three more adults jogged down the cafeteria steps: the principal, who looked too prim in her narrow skirt and heels to even make a dent in the pandemonium; her assistant, a small balding man who clutched a clipboard to his narrow chest like a life raft; and Coach Rundell, the head football coach.

The principal stood on her toes and whispered something into Coach Rundell's ear, and he nodded curtly. Coach wore a whistle and carried a megaphone.

He needed neither, but he used them both.

The shriek of the whistle pierced my eardrums like a railroad spike, and everyone around us froze. Coach Rundell lifted the megaphone to his mouth and began issuing orders with a speed and clarity that would have made any drill sergeant proud.

"We are now on lockdown! If you do not have second lunch, return to your classroom. If you do have second lunch, take a seat in the cafeteria."

At some signal from the principal, her assistant scuttled off to make the necessary lockdown announcements and arrangements. Teachers started herding their students inside in earnest now, and one by one, the doors closed and a tense quiet descended on the quad. Mrs. Foley, looking overwhelmed and on the verge of tears herself, gathered her sobbing dancers and led them into the building through a side entrance. The principal began ushering the lunch crowd back into the cafeteria, and when her assistant showed up again, he helped.

Nash, Emma and I fell into the stream of students right behind the huddle of green-and-white football jackets, and as we passed the last picnic table, I looked to the right, where Coach Rundell had now taken over CPR from

Coach Tucker. Even sick with guilt and numb with shock, I had to see for myself. Had to prove to my head what my heart knew all along.

And there Meredith lay, long brown hair fanned out across the dead grass, her face visible only when the coach sat up for a round of chest compressions.

My eyes watered and I sniffed back more tears, and Nash stepped up on my right, blocking my view as we climbed the broad concrete steps into the building. Inside, the lights were all off because of the lockdown. But the cafeteria windows—a virtual wall of glass—had no shades and were too big to cover, so daylight streamed in, casting deep shadows and lighting the long room in a washed-out palette of colors, in contrast to the bright light usually cast from the fluorescent fixtures overhead.

At the far end of the room, the jocks had gathered in a silent, solemn huddle around one of the round tables. Several sat with their elbows propped on wide-set knees, heads either hanging or cradled in both hands. Number fourteen—who'd tried valiantly to save Meredith—held his girlfriend on his lap, her face streaked with tears and mascara, his arm around her waist, his chin resting on her shoulder.

Other students sat grouped around the rest of the tables. A few whispered questions no one had answers for, a few more cried softly, and everyone looked stunned to the point of incomprehension. There had been no warning, no violence, and no obvious cause. This lockdown didn't fit with the drills we practiced twice a semester, and everyone knew it.

The tables were all occupied, and several small groups of students sat on the floor against the long wall, holding backpacks, purses, and short stacks of textbooks. Emma looked shaken and pale as we made our way toward an empty corner, and I could feel my legs wobbling, left almost totally numb by the accuracy of my second prediction in three days. Only Nash seemed relatively steady, his bruising grip on my hand the sole indication that he might not be as calm as he looked.

We sat in a row on the floor, Em on my left, Nash still clutching my right hand, each too stunned to speak. My thoughts were chaotic, a never-ending furor of guilt, shock, and utter incredulity. A private cacophony in absolute contrast to the hushed, somber room around me. And I couldn't make it stop. Could not slow the torrent long enough to wallow in any single emotion, or puzzle out any one question.

I could only sit, and stare, and wait.

Minutes later, sirens blared to life down the street, warbling softly at first, but growing in volume with each passing second. The ambulance came to an earsplitting halt at the front of the school, but by the time it rolled carefully around the building and past the cafeteria windows, the electronic screeching had gone silent, though it still echoed in my head, a fitting sound track to the mayhem within.

The ambulance stopped out of sight of the windows,

but its lights flashed an angry red against the dull brown brick, declaring an optimistic urgency I knew to be unnecessary.

Meredith Cole was dead, and no matter how long they worked on her, she wasn't coming back. That bitter certainty ate at me, consuming me from the inside out until I felt hollow enough to echo with each aching thump of my heart.

While the medics worked outside, teachers came and went from the cafeteria, occasionally answering questions from anyone brave enough to speak up, and at some point, the senior guidance counselor pulled up a chair at the jocks' table and began speaking softly to those who'd been close enough to actually see Meredith fall.

Eventually, the vice principal came over the intercom and declared that the school day had been officially suspended, and that we would all be dismissed individually, once our legal guardians had been contacted. By that time, the red lights had stopped flashing, and though no one had yet made the announcement, it echoed around us like all-important truths, unvoiced, and unwanted, and unavoidable.

After that, the first group of students was called to the office and Emma leaned against me while I leaned against Nash, letting his scent and his warmth soothe me as I settled in for the wait. But minutes later, Coach Tucker stopped in the cafeteria doorway and scanned the faces until her gaze landed on me. I sat up as she navigated the maze of tables, heading right for us, and stood when she reached out a hand to pull me up, barely sparing a glance for Nash and Emma when they rose. "The dancers are understandably upset, and we're calling their parents first. Sophie's not taking it well. Her sponsor spoke to your mother, and they'd like you to go ahead and take your sister home."

I sighed, grateful when Nash's hand slid into mine again. "She's my cousin."

Coach Tucker frowned, as if details like that shouldn't matter under the circumstances. She was right, but I couldn't bring myself to apologize.

"Don't worry about your books." She eyed me sternly now. "Just get her home."

I nodded, and the coach headed back through the cafeteria, motioning for me to follow. "I'll talk to you guys later," I said, glancing from Emma to Nash as I squeezed his hand. She smiled weakly, and he nodded, digging his phone from his pocket.

I'd just stepped into the hall, heading toward the office, when my own phone buzzed. A glance at the screen showed a blinking text message icon. It was from Nash.

Don't tell anyone. Will explain soon.

A moment later, a follow-up message arrived. It was one word: Please.

I didn't reply, because I didn't know what to say. No one would believe me if I tried to explain what had happened. But the premonitions were real, and they were accurate.

Silence no longer seemed like an option, especially if there was any chance I could stop the next one from coming true.

If I could at least give the next victim a warning—and maybe a fighting chance—wasn't I morally obligated to do just that?

Besides, hadn't Nash suggested I tell my aunt and uncle the day before?

"Kaitlin! Over here." I glanced up to find Mrs. Foley waving me forward from the atrium outside the front office. Sophie sat on the floor behind her, beneath the foliage of a huge potted plant, surrounded by half a dozen other red, mascara-smeared faces.

"It's Kaylee," I muttered, coming to a stop in front of the stunned dancers.

"Of course." But the sponsor didn't look like she cared what my name was. "I've spoken to your mother—" but I didn't bother to tell her that would be impossible without a Ouija board "—and she wants you to take Sophie straight home. She's going to meet you there."

I nodded, and ignored the sympathetic hand the dance-team sponsor placed momentarily on my shoulder, as if to thank me for sharing some venerable burden. "You ready?" I asked in my cousin's general direction, and to my surprise, she bobbed her head in assent, stood with her purse in hand, and followed me across the quad without betraying a single syllable of malicious intent.

She must have been in shock.

In the parking lot, I unlocked the passenger's side door, then went around to let myself in. Sophie slid into her seat and pulled the door closed, then turned to face me slowly, her normally arrogant expression giving way to what could only be described as abject grief.

"Did you see it?" she asked, full lower lip quivering, and for once absent of lip gloss. She must have wiped it all off, along with the tears and most of her makeup. She looked almost... normal. And I couldn't help the pang of sympathy her misery drew from me, in spite of the bitch-itude she radiated every other day of my life. For now, she was just scared, confused, and hurting, looking for a compassionate ear.

Just like me.

And it kind of stung that I couldn't totally let my guard down with her, because I had no doubt that once her grief had passed, Sophie would go all *Mean Girls* on me again, and use against me whatever I'd shown her. "See what?" I sighed, adjusting the rearview mirror so I could watch her indirectly.

My cousin rolled her eyes, and for a moment her usual intolerance peeked through the fresh layer of raw sorrow. "Meredith. Did you see what happened?"

I turned the key in the ignition, and my little Sunfire hummed to life, the steering wheel vibrating beneath my hands. "No." I felt no great loss over having missed the show; the preview was quite enough to deal with.

"It was horrible." She stared straight out the windshield

as I buckled my seat belt and pulled the car from the parking lot, but she obviously saw nothing. "We were dancing, just showing off for Scott and the guys. We'd made it through all the hard parts, including that step where Laura usually skips a beat in practice...."

I had no idea what step she was talking about, but I let her ramble on, because it seemed to make her feel better without putting me on the figurative chopping block.

"...and were nearly done. Then Meredith just...collapsed. She crumpled up like a doll and fell flat on the ground."

My hands clenched the steering wheel, and I had to force them loose to flick on my blinker. I turned right at the stoplight, exhaling only once the school—and thus the source of my latest premonition—was out of sight. And still Sophie prattled on, airing her grief in the name of therapy, completely oblivious to my discomfort.

"I thought she'd passed out. She doesn't eat enough to keep a hamster alive, you know."

I hadn't known, of course. I didn't typically concern myself with the eating habits of the varsity dance squad. But if Meredith's appetite was anything like my cousin's—or my aunt's, for that matter—Sophie's assumption was perfectly plausible.

"But then we realized she wasn't moving. She wasn't even breathing." Sophie paused for a moment, and I treasured the silence like that first gulp of air after a deep dive. I didn't want to hear any more about the death I'd been unable to prevent. I felt guilty enough already. But she wasn't done. "Peyton thinks she had a heart attack. Mrs. Rushing told us in health last year that if you work your body too hard and don't fuel it up right, your heart will eventually stop working. Just like that." She snapped her fingers, and the glitter in her nail polish flashed in the bright sunlight. "Do you think that's what happened?"

It took me a moment to realize her question wasn't rhetorical. She was actually asking my opinion about something, and there was no sarcasm involved.

"I don't know." I glanced in the rearview mirror as I turned onto our street, and wasn't surprised to see Aunt Val's car on the road behind us. "Maybe." But that was an outright lie. Meredith Cole was the third teenage girl to drop dead with no warning in the past three days, and while I wasn't about to voice my suspicions out loud— at least not yet—I could no longer tell myself the deaths weren't connected.

Nash's coincidence theory had hit an iceberg and was sinking fast.

I parked in the driveway, and Aunt Val drove past us into her spot in the garage. Sophie was out of the car before I'd even turned the engine off, and the minute she saw her mother, she burst into tears again, as if her inner floodgates couldn't withstand the assault of sympathetic eyes and a shoulder to cry on.

Aunt Val ushered her sobbing daughter through the garage and into the kitchen, then guided her gently to a stool at the bar. I came behind them both, carrying Sophie's purse, and punched the button to close the garage bay door. Inside, I dropped my cousin's handbag on the counter while Sophie sniffed, and blubbered, and hiccupped, spitting out half-coherent details as she wiped first her cheeks, then her already reddened nose with a tissue from the box on the counter.

But Aunt Val didn't seem very interested in the specifics, which she'd probably already heard from the dance-team sponsor. While I sat at the table with a can of Coke and a wish for silence, she bustled around the kitchen making hot tea and wiping down countertops, and only once she'd run out of things to do did she settle onto the stool next to her daughter. Aunt Val made Sophie drink her tea slowly, until the sobs slowed and the hiccupping stopped. But even then Sophie wouldn't stop talking.

Meredith's death was the first spear of tragedy to pierce my cousin's fairy tale of a world, and she had no idea how to deal with it. When she was still sobbing and dripping snot into her lukewarm tea twenty minutes later, Aunt Val disappeared into the bathroom. She came back carrying a small brown pill bottle I recognized immediately: leftover zombie pills from my last visit with Dr. Nelson, from the mental-health unit.

I twisted in my chair and arched my brows at my aunt, but she only smiled half regretfully, then shrugged. "It will calm her down and help her sleep. She needs to rest."

Yes, but she needed a natural sleep, not the virtual coma

induced by those stupid sedatives. Not that either of them would have listened to me, even if I'd offered my opinion on the subject of chemical oblivion.

For a moment, I envied my cousin her innocence, even as I watched it die. I'd learned about death early in life, and as inconsolable as Sophie was at the moment, she'd had fifteen years to prance around in her plastic-wrapped, padded, gaily colored, armor-plated existence, where darkness dared not tread. No matter what happened next, no one could take away her happy childhood.

Aunt Val watched Sophie swallow a single, tiny white pill, then walked her daughter down the hall into her room, where the bedsprings soon creaked beneath her slight weight. Ten minutes later, she was snoring obnoxiously enough to leave no doubt in my mind that my cousin had inherited just as much from her father as from her mother.

While my aunt put Sophie to bed, I grabbed a second Coke from Uncle Brendon's shelf in the fridge—the one realm Aunt Val's sugar-free, nonfat, tasteless regime had yet to conquer—and took it into the living room, where I checked the local TV station. But there was no news on at two-thirty in the afternoon. I'd have to wait for the five o'clock broadcast.

I turned off the TV, and my thoughts wandered to the Coles, whom I'd only met once, at a dance-team competition the year before. My eyes watered as I imagined Meredith's mother trying to explain to her young son that his big sister wouldn't be coming home from school. Ever.

Glass clinked in the kitchen, momentarily pulling me from the mire of guilt and grief I was sinking into, and I twisted on the couch to see my aunt pouring hot tea into a huge latte mug. My brows furrowed in confusion for a moment—maybe Aunt Val needed a sedative too?—until she stood on her toes to open the top cabinet. Where she and Uncle Brendon kept the alcohol.

My aunt pulled down a bottle of brandy and unscrewed the lid. Then she dumped a generous shot into her mug. And left the bottle on the countertop, clearly planning on a second helping.

She took a sip of her "tea," then turned toward the living room, remote control in hand. The moment her gaze met mine, she froze, and her cheeks flushed.

"It hasn't hit the news yet," I said, and couldn't help noticing how tired and heavy her steps looked as she crossed the tiles into the living room. Aunt Val and Mrs. Cole had been gym buddies for years. Maybe Meredith's death had hit her harder than I'd realized. Or maybe she was unnerved by how upset Sophie was. Or maybe she'd connected Meredith's death to Heidi Anderson's—to my knowledge, she hadn't yet heard about Alyson Baker—and had started to suspect something was wrong. As I had.

Either way, her skin was pale and her hands were shaking. She looked so fragile I hesitated to add to her troubles.

But the premonitions had gone too far. I needed help, or advice, or…something.

What I really needed was for someone to tell me what good premonitions of death were if they didn't help me warn people. What was the point of knowing someone was going to die, if I couldn't stop it from happening?

Aunt Val wouldn't know any of that, but neither would anyone else. And in the absence of my own parents, I had no one else to talk to.

My fingers tangled around one another in my lap as she sank wearily onto the other end of the couch, her knees together, ankles crossed primly. The frown lines around her mouth and the tremor in her hand said she was not as composed as she clearly wanted to appear.

That, and the not-tea scent wafting from her mug.

The last time I'd tried to tell her I knew someone was going to die, she and Uncle Brendon had driven me straight to the hospital and left me there. Of course, at the time, I'd been screaming hysterically in the middle of the mall and lashing out at anyone who tried to touch me.

Presumably, they'd had no choice.

Surely it would go better this time, because I was calm and rational, and not currently in the grip of an irrepressible screaming fit. And because she was already one shot into a bottle of brandy.

My nerves pinged out of control, and I reached absently for the scent diffuser on the end table to my left, stirring the vanilla-scented oil with a thin wooden reed. "Aunt Val?"

She jumped, sloshing "tea" onto her lap. "Sorry, hon." She set her mug on a coaster on the end table, then rushed into the kitchen to blot at her pants with a clean, wet rag. "This thing with Meredith has me on edge."

I knew exactly how she felt.

I exhaled smoothly, then took a deep breath as my aunt returned to the living room, the wet spot on her slacks now covering half of one slim thigh. "Yeah, it was pretty...scary."

"Oh?" She stopped several feet from her chair, eyes narrowed at me in concern laced with...suspicion? "Were you there?" Had she already guessed what I was going to say?

Maybe Nash was right. Maybe I should keep my secret a little longer....

I shook my head slowly, and my gaze flicked back to the sticks protruding from the tiny oil bottle. "No, I didn't actually see it—" she exhaled in relief, and I almost hated to ruin it with the rest of what I had to say "—but... You know the girl who died at Taboo the other day?"

"Of course. How sad!" She returned to her chair and took a slow sip from her tea, eyes closed, as if she were thinking. Or maybe praying. Then she took a much longer drink and lowered her mug, eyes wide and wary. "Kaylee, that girl had nothing to do with what happened today. According to the news, she was drunk, and may have been on something stronger than alcohol."

I hadn't heard that last tidbit, but I got no chance to question it because she was talking again. Like mother, like daughter.

My aunt gestured with her mug as she spoke, but nothing sloshed out this time. It was already empty. "Sophie said Meredith collapsed while she was dancing. That poor child ate almost nothing and lived on caffeine. It was really only a matter of time before her body cried 'enough.'"

"I know, and Sophie may be right." I let go of the scent sticks and bent the tab on my Coke can back and forth, carefully working it free from its anchor to avoid seeing the pity and skepticism surely lurking behind her cautious sympathy. "The way they died may have nothing to do with anything." Though I certainly had my doubts. "But, Aunt Val, I think *I'm* the connection between them."

"What?"

I made myself look up just in time to see my aunt's eyes narrow in confusion. But then her forehead actually relaxed, tension lines smoothing as if she'd just figured out what I was talking about, and it came as a relief.

If the return of my "delusions" put her at ease, what on earth had she expected me to say?

Her expression softened, and the familiar, patronizing mask of sympathy stung my pride. "Kaylee, is this about your *panic attacks?*" She leaned forward and whispered that last part, as if she were afraid someone would overhear.

Anger zinged through me like tiny bolts of lightning, and I made myself set down my half-empty drink can before I crushed it. "It's not a joke, Aunt Val. And I'm not crazy. I knew Meredith was going to die before it happened."

For an instant—less than a single breath—my aunt looked terrified. Like she'd just seen her own ghost. Then she shook her head—literally shaking off her fear of my relapse—and donned a stoic, determined mask. I'd been right all along. She wasn't going to listen. Ever.

"Kaylee, don't do this again," she begged, a frown etching deep lines around her mouth as she stood and carried her empty mug into the kitchen. I followed her, watching in mounting irritation as she lifted the teakettle from the stove. "I know you're upset about Meredith, but this won't bring her back. This isn't the way to deal with your grief."

"This has nothing to do with grief," I insisted through gritted teeth, dropping my half-full can into the recycling bin. It landed with a thud, followed by the fizz and gurgle of the contents emptying into the plastic tub.

I read frustration in my aunt's narrowed gaze. Desperation in the death grip she had on the teakettle. She probably wished she could knock me out as easily as she had Sophie. And some part of me knew that talking to her would do no more good than trying to warn Meredith had. But another, more stubborn part of me refused to give up. I was done with secrets and sympathetic looks. And I was definitely done with hospitals and those little white pills. I was not going to let anyone else call me crazy. Not ever again.

Aunt Val must have seen my determination, because she set the teakettle back on the stove, then planted both palms flat on the countertop, eyeing me from across the bar. "Think about Sophie. She's already traumatized. What do you think a selfish, attention-seeking story like this would do to her?"

My jaw tightened, and tears burned behind my eyes. "Screw Sophie!" My fists slammed into the bar, and the blow reverberated up my arms like a bruising shock wave of anger.

My aunt flinched, and I felt a momentary surge of satisfaction. Then I stepped deliberately back from the bar, my hands propped on my hips. "I'm sorry," I said, well aware that I didn't sound very sorry. "But this isn't about her. I'm trying to tell you I have a serious problem, and you're not even listening!"

Aunt Val closed her eyes and took a deep breath, like she was practicing yoga. Or searching for patience. "We all know you have problems, Kaylee," she said when her eyes opened, and her quiet, composed tone infuriated me. "Calm down and—"

"I knew, Aunt Val." I planted both hands on the countertop again and stared at the granite. Then I looked up and made myself say the rest of it. "And I knew about the girl at Taboo too."

My aunt's eyes narrowed drastically, showcasing two sets of crow's feet, and her voice dropped dramatically. "How could you, unless you were there?"

I shrugged and crossed my arms over my chest. "I snuck in." I wasn't about to rat on Emma or her sister. "Ground me if you want, but that won't change anything. I was there, and I saw Heidi Anderson. And I knew she was going to die. Just like I knew about Meredith."

Aunt Val's eyes closed again, and she turned to stare out the window over the sink, gripping the countertop with white-knuckled hands. Then she exhaled deeply and turned back to me. "Okay, this other girl aside..." Though we both knew she'd readdress the clubbing issue later. "If you knew Meredith was going to die, why didn't you tell someone?"

A fresh pang of guilt shuddered through me like a psychological aftershock, and I sank onto one of the cushioned bar stools facing her, my arms crossed on the countertop. "I tried." Tears filled my eyes, blurring my aunt's face, and I swiped at them with my sleeve before they could fall. "But when I opened my mouth, all I could do was scream. And it happened so fast! By the time I could talk again, she was dead." I looked up, searching her face for some sign of understanding. Or belief. But there was nothing I recognized in her expression, and that scared me almost as badly as listening to Meredith die.

"I'm not even sure that saying something would have

helped," I said, feeling my courage flounder. "But I swear I tried."

Aunt Val rubbed her forehead, then picked up her mug and started to take a drink—until she realized she hadn't poured one. "Kaylee, surely you know how all this sounds."

I nodded and dropped my gaze. "I sound crazy." I knew that better than anyone.

She shook her head and leaned across the bar for my hand. "Not crazy, hon. Delusional. There's a difference. You're probably just really upset about what happened to Meredith, and your brain is dealing with that by making up stories to distract you from the truth. I understand. It's scary to think that anyone anywhere can just drop dead with no warning. If it could happen to her, it could happen to any of us, right?"

I pulled my hand from hers, gaping at my aunt in disbelief. What would it take to make her believe me? Proof was pretty hard to come by when the premonitions only came a few minutes in advance.

I slid off the stool and backed up a step, eager to put a little space between us. "I barely knew Meredith. I'm not scared because I think it can happen to me. I'm scared because I knew it was going to happen to her, and I couldn't stop it." I sucked in a deep breath, trying to breathe beyond the guilt and grief threatening to suffocate me. "I almost wish I *were* going crazy. At least then I wouldn't feel so guilty about letting someone die. But I'm not crazy. This is real."

For several seconds, my aunt just stared at me, her expression a mixture of confusion, relief, and pity, like she wasn't sure what she should feel.

I sighed, my shoulders fell. "You still don't believe me."

My aunt's expression softened, and her posture wilted almost imperceptibly. "Oh, hon, I believe that you believe what you're saying." She hesitated, then shrugged, but the gesture looked more calculated than casual. "Maybe you should take a sedative too. It will help you sleep. I'm sure everything will make more sense when you wake up."

"Sleep won't help me." I sounded acerbic, even to my own ears. "Neither will those stupid pills." I grabbed the bottle from the bar where she'd left it and hurled it at the refrigerator as hard as I could. The plastic cracked and the lid fell off, scattering small white pills all over the floor.

Aunt Val jumped, then stared at me like I'd just broken her heart. When she knelt to clean up the mess, I jogged down the hall and into my room, then slammed the door and leaned against it. I'd done the best I could with my aunt; I'd try again with Uncle Brendon when he came home.

Or maybe not.

Maybe Nash knew what he was talking about when he said not to tell anyone.

7

FOR SEVERAL MINUTES, I stood still in my room, so angry, and scared, and confused, I didn't know whether to scream, or cry, or hit something. I tried to read the novel on my nightstand to distract myself from the disaster my life had become, and when that didn't work, I turned on the TV. But nothing on television held my attention and all the songs on my iPod only seemed to magnify my anger and frustration.

My mind was so full of chaos, my thoughts coming much too fast for me to grasp, that no matter what I did or where I stood, I couldn't escape the miserable roar of half-formed thoughts my head spun with. I was starting to seriously reconsider that sedative—desperate to just be *nowhere* for a little while—when my phone buzzed in my pocket.

Another text message from Nash. U OK?

Fine. I lied. U? I almost told him he'd been right. That I shouldn't have told my aunt. But that was a lot of information to fit into a text.

Yeah. With Carter, he replied. Call U soon.

I thought about texting Emma, but she was still grounded. And knowing her mother, she stood no chance of a commuted sentence, even after practically seeing a classmate drop dead.

Frustrated and mentally exhausted, I finally fell asleep in the middle of the movie I wasn't really watching in the first place. Less than an hour later, according to my alarm clock, I woke up and turned the TV off. And that's when I realized I'd almost slept through something important.

Or at least something interesting.

In the sudden silence, I heard my aunt and uncle arguing fiercely, but too softly to understand from my room at the back of the house. I eased my bedroom door open several inches, holding my breath until I was sure the hinges wouldn't squeal. Then I stuck my head through the gap and peered down the hall.

They were in the kitchen; my aunt's slim shadow paced back and forth across the only visible wall. Then I heard her whisper my name—even lower in pitch than the rest of the argument—and I swallowed thickly. She was probably trying to convince Uncle Brendon to take me back to the hospital.

That was *not* going to happen.

Angry now, I eased the door open farther and slipped into the hall. If my uncle gave in, I'd simply step up and tell them I wasn't going. Or maybe I'd just jump in my car and leave until they came to their senses. I could go to Emma's. No, wait. She was grounded. So I'd go to Nash's.

Where I wound up didn't matter, so long as it wasn't the mental-health ward.

I inched down the hall, grateful for my silent socks and the tile floor, which didn't creak. But I froze several feet from the kitchen doorway when my uncle spoke, his words still low but now perfectly audible.

"You're overreacting, Valerie. She got through it last time, and she'll get through it this time. I see no reason to bother him while he's working."

While I appreciated my uncle standing up for me, even if he didn't believe in my premonitions either, I seriously doubted Dr. Nelson would consider himself "bothered" by a phone call about a patient. Not considering what he was probably getting paid.

"I don't know what else to do." Aunt Val sighed, and a chair scraped the floor as my uncle's shadow stood. "She's really upset, and I think I made it worse. She knows something's going on. I tried to get her to take a sedative, but she busted the bottle on the refrigerator."

Uncle Brendon chuckled, from across the kitchen now. "She knows she doesn't need those damn pills."

Yeah! I was starting to wonder if my uncle wore chain mail beneath his clothes, because he sounded eager to slay the dragon Skepticism. And I was ready to ride into battle with him....

"Of course she doesn't," Aunt Val conceded wearily, and her shadow folded its arms across its chest. "The pills are a temporary solution, like sticking your finger in a crack in a dam. What she really needs is your brother, and if you're not going to call him, I will."

My father? Aunt Val wanted him to call my dad? Not Dr. Nelson?

My uncle sighed. "I hate to start all this now if we could possibly put it off a while longer." The refrigerator door squealed open, and a soda can popped, then hissed. "It was just coincidence that this happened twice in one week. It may not happen for another year, or even longer."

Aunt Val huffed in exasperation. "Brendon, you didn't see her. Didn't *hear* her. She thinks she's losing her mind. She's already living on borrowed time, and she should not have to spend whatever she has left of it thinking she's crazy."

Borrowed time?

A jolt of shock shot through me, settling finally into my heart, which seemed reluctant to beat again for a moment. What did that mean? I was sick? Dying? How could they not have told me? And how could I be dying if I felt fine? Except for knowing when other people are going to die...

And if that were true, wouldn't I know if I were going to die?

Uncle Brendon sighed, and a chair scraped across the floor again, then groaned as he sank into it. "Fine. Call him if you want to. You're probably right. I just really hoped we'd have another year or two. At least until she's out of high school."

"That was never a certainty." Aunt Val's silhouette shrank as it came closer, and I scuttled toward my room, my spine still pressed against the cold wall. But then she stopped, and her shadow turned around. "Where's the number?"

"Here, use my phone. He's second in the contacts list."

My aunt's shadow elongated as she moved farther away, presumably taking the phone from my uncle. "You sure you don't want to do it?"

"Positive."

Another chair scraped the tiles as my aunt sat, and her shadow became an amorphous blob on the wall. A series of high-pitched beeps told me she was already pressing buttons. A moment later she spoke, and I held my breath, desperate to hear every single word of whatever they'd been keeping from me.

"Aiden? It's Valerie." She paused, but I couldn't hear my father's response. "We're fine. Brendon's right here. Listen, though, I'm calling about Kaylee." Another pause, and this time I heard a low-pitched, indistinct rumble, barely recognizable as my father's voice.

Aunt Val sighed again, and her shadow shifted as she slumped in her chair. "I know, but it's happening again." Pause. "Of course I'm sure. Twice in the last three days. She didn't tell us the first time, or I would have called sooner. I'm not sure how she's kept quiet about it, as it is."

My father said something else I couldn't make out.

"I did, but she won't take them, and I'm not going to force her. I think we've moved beyond the pills, Aiden. It's time to tell her the truth. You owe her that much."

He owed me? Of course he owed me the truth—whatever that was. They all owed me.

"Yes, but I really think it should come from her father." She sounded angry now.

My father spoke again, and this time it sounded like he was arguing. But I could have told him how futile it was to argue with Aunt Val. Once she'd made up her mind, nothing could change it.

"Aiden Cavanaugh, you put your butt on a plane today, or I'll send your daughter to you. She deserves the truth, and you're going to give it to her, one way or another."

I SNUCK BACK TO MY room, shocked, confused, and more than a little proud of my aunt. Whatever this mysterious truth was, she wanted me to have it. And she didn't think I was losing my mind. Neither of them did.

Though they apparently thought I was dying.

I think I'd rather be crazy.

I'd never really contemplated my own death before, but I would have thought the very idea would leave me too frightened to function. Especially having very nearly witnessed someone else's death only hours earlier. Instead, however, I found myself more numb than terrified.

There was a substantial fear building inside me, tightening my throat and making my heart pound almost audibly inside my chest. But it was a very distant fear, as if I couldn't quite wrap my mind around the concept of my own demise. Of simply not existing one day.

Maybe the news just hadn't sunk in yet. Or maybe I couldn't quite believe it. Either way, I desperately needed to talk it through with someone who wasn't busy keeping vital secrets from me. So I texted Emma, in case her mother had lifted the cell phone ban.

Ms. Marshall replied a few minutes later, telling me that Emma was still grounded, but she'd see me the next day for Meredith's memorial, if I was planning to go.

I wrote back to tell her I'd be there, then dropped my phone on my bed in disgust. What good is technology if your friends are always grounded from it? Or hanging out with teammates?

For lack of anything better to do, I turned the TV on again, but I couldn't concentrate because what I'd just overheard kept playing through my mind. I analyzed every word, trying to figure out what I'd missed. What they'd been keeping from me.

I was sick; that much was clear. What else could "living on borrowed time" mean? So what did I have? What kind of twisted illness had "premonitions of death" as the primary symptom, and death itself as the eventual result?

Nothing, unless we were still considering adolescent dementia. Which we were not, based on the fact that they didn't think I needed the zombie pills.

So what kind of illness could make me *think* I was crazy?

Ignoring the television now, I slid into my desk chair and fired up the Gateway notebook my father had sent me for my last birthday. Each second it took to load sent fresh waves of agitation through me, fortifying my unease until that fear I'd expected earlier finally began to take root in earnest.

I'm going to die.

Just thinking the words sent terror skittering through me. I couldn't sit still, even for the few minutes it took Windows to load. When my leg began to jiggle with nerves, I stood in front of my dresser to peer in the mirror. Surely if I were ready to kick the proverbial bucket, I would know the minute I saw myself. That's how it seemed to work when someone else was going to die.

But I felt nothing when I looked at my reflection, except the usual fleeting annoyance that, unlike my cousin, my skin was pale, my features completely unremarkable.

Maybe it didn't work with reflections. I'd never seen Heidi in the mirror, nor Meredith. Holding my breath, and barely resisting the absurd urge to cross my fingers, I glanced down at myself, unsure whether I was more afraid of feeling the urge to scream, or of not feeling it.

Again, I felt nothing.

Did that mean I wasn't dying, after all? Or that my gruesome gift didn't work on myself? Or merely that my death wasn't yet imminent? *Aaagggghhh! This was pointless!*

My computer chimed to tell me it was up and running, and I dropped into my desk chair. I pulled up my Internet browser and typed "leading cause of death among teenagers" into the search engine, my chest tight and aching with morbid anticipation.

The first hit contained a list of the top ten causes of death in individuals fifteen through nineteen years of age. Unintentional injury, homicide, and suicide were the top three entries. But I had no plans to end my own life, and accidents couldn't be predicted. Neither could murder, unless my aunt and uncle were planning to take me out themselves.

Lower on the list were several equally scary entries, like heart disease, respiratory infection, and diabetes, among others. However, those all included symptoms I couldn't possibly have overlooked.

That left only the fourth leading cause of death for people my age: malignant neoplasms.

I had to look that one up.

The description from a separate, respected medical site was dense and nearly impossible to comprehend. But the layman's definition under that was too clear for comfort. "Malignant neoplasm" was doctor-talk for cancer.

Cancer.

And suddenly every hope I'd ever harbored, every dream I'd ever entertained, seemed too fragile a possibility to survive.

I had a tumor. What else could it be? And it had to be brain cancer to affect the things I felt and knew, didn't it? Or the things I thought I knew.

Did that mean the premonitions weren't real? Were brain tumors giving me delusions? Some sort of sensory hallucinations? Had I imagined predicting Heidi's and Meredith's deaths, after the fact?

No. It couldn't be. I refused to believe that any mere illness—short of Alzheimer's—could rewrite my memories.

Hovering on the sharp, hot edge of panic now, I returned to the search engine and typed "symptoms of brain cancer." The first hit was an oncology Web site that listed seven kinds of brain cancer along with the leading symptoms of each. But I had none of them. No nausea, seizures, or hearing loss. I had no impaired speech or motor function, and no spatial disorders. I wasn't dizzy, had no headaches, and no muscle weakness. I wasn't incontinent—thank goodness—nor did I have any unexplained bleeding or swelling, nor any impaired judgment.

Okay, some might say sneaking into a nightclub was a sign of impaired judgment, but I was pretty sure my decision-making skills were right on target for someone my age, and miles above the judgment of others. Such as certain spoiled, vomit-prone cousins, who shall remain nameless.

I was tempted to rule out brain cancer based on the symptoms alone, until I noticed the section on tumors in the temporal lobe. According to the Web site, while temporal-lobe "neoplasms" sometimes impaired speech and caused seizures, they were just as often asymptomatic.

As was I.

That was it. I had a tumor in my temporal lobe. But if so, how did Aunt Val and Uncle Brendon know? More important, how long had they known? And how long did I have?

My fingers shook on the keys, and a nonsense word appeared in the address bar. I pushed my chair away from the desk and closed my laptop without bothering to shut it down. I had to talk to someone. Now.

I shoved my chair aside and crawled onto my bed on my hands and knees, snatching my phone from the comforter on the way to my headboard. At the top of the bed, I leaned back and pulled my knees up to my chest. My eyes watered as I scrolled through my contacts for Nash's number. I was wiping tears from my face with my sleeves by the time he answered.

"Hello?" He sounded distracted, and in the background, I heard canned fight sounds, then several guys groaned in unison.

"Hey, it's me." I sniffed to keep my nose from running.

"Kaylee?" Couch springs creaked as he sat up—I had his attention now. "What's wrong?" He switched to an urgent whisper. "Did it happen again?"

"No, um… Are you still at Scott's?"

"Yeah. Hang on." Something brushed against the phone, and dimly I heard Nash say, "Here, man, take over for me." Then footsteps clomped, and the background noise gradually softened until a door creaked closed, and the racket stopped altogether. "What's up?"

I hesitated, rolling onto my stomach on my bed. He hadn't signed on for this kind of drama. But he hadn't run from the death predictions, and I had to talk to someone, and it was either Nash or Emma's mother. "Okay, this is going to sound stupid, but I don't know what else to think. I heard my aunt and uncle arguing, then my aunt called my dad" I swallowed back a sob and wiped more moisture from my face. "Nash…I think I'm dying."

There was silence over the line, then engine noise as a car drove past him. He must have been in Scott's front yard. "Wait, I don't get it. Why do you think you're dying?"

I folded my lumpy feather pillow in half and lay with one cheek on it, treasuring the coolness against my tear-flushed face. "My uncle said he thought I'd have more time, then my aunt told my dad that he needed to tell me the truth, so I wouldn't think I was crazy. I think it's a brain tumor."

"Kaylee, you're adding two and two and coming up with seven. You must have missed something." He paused and footsteps clomped on concrete, like he was on the sidewalk. "What did they say, exactly?"

I sat up and made myself inhale slowly, trying to calm down. The words weren't coming out right. No wonder he had no idea what I was talking about. "Um…Aunt Val said I was living on borrowed time, and that I shouldn't have to spend any of it thinking I was crazy. She told my dad it was time to tell me the truth." I stood and found myself pacing nervously back and forth across my fuzzy purple throw rug. "That means I'm dying, right? And she wants him to tell me?"

"Well, they obviously have *something* important to tell you, but I seriously doubt you have a brain tumor. Shouldn't you have some symptoms, or something, if you're sick?"

I dropped into my desk chair again and ran my finger over the mouse pad to wake up the monitor. "I looked it up, and—"

"You researched brain tumors? This afternoon?" Nash

hesitated, and the footsteps paused. "Kaylee, is this because of Meredith?"

"No!" I shoved off against the desk so hard my wheeled chair hit the side of the bed. "I'm not a hypochondriac! I'm just trying to figure out why this is happening to me, and nothing else makes sense." Frustrated, I scrubbed one hand over my face and made myself take another deep breath. "They don't think I'm crazy, so it's not psychological." And my relief at knowing that was big enough to swallow the Pacific Ocean. "So it has to be physical."

"And you think it's brain cancer...."

"I don't know what else to think. There's one kind of brain cancer that sometimes doesn't have any symptoms. Maybe I have that kind."

"Wait..." He paused as a gust of wind whistled over the line. "You think you have a tumor because you have *no* symptoms?"

Okay, I still wasn't making any sense. I closed my eyes and let my head fall against the back of the chair. "Or maybe the premonitions are my symptom. Some kind of hallucination."

Nash laughed. "You're not hallucinating, Kaylee. Not unless Emma and I have tumors too. We both saw you predict two deaths, and we saw one of them actually happen. You weren't imagining that."

I sat up in my chair, and this time my long, soft exhalation was in relief. "I was seriously hoping you'd say that."

It helped—albeit a tiny little bit—to know that if I was dying, at least I was going out with my mind intact.

"Glad I could help." I could hear the smile in his voice, which drew one from me in response.

I swiveled in my chair and propped my feet up on my nightstand. "Okay, so maybe I'm having premonitions because of the tumor. Like, it's activating some part of my brain most people can't access. Like John Travolta in that old movie."

"Saturday Night Fever?"

"Not that old." My smile grew a little, in spite of what should have been a very somber conversation. I loved how easily Nash calmed me, even over the phone. His voice was hypnotic, like some kind of auditory tranquilizer. One I could easily get hooked on. "The one where he can move stuff with his mind, and learn whole languages by reading one book. And it all turns out to be because he has brain cancer and he's dying."

"I don't think I've seen that one."

"He gets all kinds of freaky abilities, then he dies. It's tragic. I don't want to be tragic, Nash. I want to be alive." And suddenly the tears were back. I couldn't help it. I'd had more than enough of death in the past few days, without adding my own to the list.

"Okay, you're going to have to trust me on this, Kaylee." The footsteps were back, and then a door closed, cutting off the bluster of wind on his end of the call. Then his voice got softer. "Your premonitions don't come from brain cancer. Whatever your aunt and uncle were talking about, that's not it."

"How do you know?" I blinked the moisture from my eyes, irritated with how emotional I was becoming. Wasn't that another symptom of brain cancer?

Nash sighed, but he sounded more worried than exasperated. "I have to tell you something. I'll pick you up in ten minutes."

8

SEVEN MINUTES LATER, I sat on the living-room couch,
my keys in my pocket, my phone in my lap, my fingernails rasping anxiously across the satin upholstery. I was
angled to face both the television—muted, but tuned to
the local evening news—and the front window, hoping
no one would realize I was expecting company. "No one,"
meaning my aunt and uncle. Sophie was still out cold,
and I was starting to wonder how many of those pills her
mother had given her.

Aunt Val was in the kitchen, banging pots, pans, and
cabinet doors as she made spaghetti, her favorite comfort
food. Normally she wouldn't indulge in so many carbs in
a single meal, but she was obviously having a rough day.
A very rough day, if the scent of garlic bread was any indication.

"Hey, Kay-Bear, how you holdin' up?"

I glanced up to find my uncle leaning against the plaster column separating the dining room from the living room. He hadn't called me that in nearly a decade, and the fact that he was using my old nickname probably meant he thought I was… fragile.

"I'm not crazy." I met his clear green eyes, daring him to argue.

He smiled, and the resulting smile lines somehow made him look even younger than usual. "I never said you were."

I huffed and shot a glare toward the kitchen, where Aunt Val was stirring noodles in a huge aluminum pot. "She thinks I am." I knew better than that now, of course, but wasn't about to let on that I'd heard their argument.

Uncle Brendon shook his head and crossed the eggshell carpet toward me, arms folded over the faded tee he'd changed into after work. "She's just worried about you. We both are." He sank into the floral-print armchair opposite me. He always sat there, rather than on the solid white chair or sofa, hoping that if he spilled something, Aunt Val would never notice the stain on such a busy pattern.

"Why aren't you worried about Sophie?"

"We are." He paused, then seemed to consider his answer. "But Sophie's…resilient. She'll be fine once she's had a chance to grieve."

"And I won't?"

My uncle raised one brow at me. "Val said you barely

knew Meredith Cole." And just like that, he'd sidestepped the real question—that of my future well-being.

And we both knew it.

Before I could answer—and I was in no hurry—an engine purred outside, and I glanced through the sheers to see an unfamiliar blue convertible pull into the driveway beside my car, glittering in the late-afternoon sun. Behind the wheel was a very familiar face, crowned by an equally familiar head of thick brown hair.

I stood, stuffing my phone into my empty pocket.

"Who's that?" Uncle Brendon twisted to look out the window.

"A friend. I gotta go."

He stood, but I was already halfway across the room. "Val's making dinner!" he called after me.

"I'm not hungry." Actually, I was starving, but I had to get out of the house. I couldn't possibly suck down spaghetti like it was a regular Monday night. Not knowing that my entire family had been lying to me for who knows how long.

"Kaylee, get back here!" Uncle Brendon roared, following me through the front door onto the porch. I'd rarely heard him raise his voice, and had never heard him yell like that.

I took off at a trot, slid into the passenger seat, then slammed the door and locked it.

"Is that your uncle?" Nash asked, right hand hovering over the gearshift. "Maybe I should meet—"

"Go!" I shouted, louder than I'd meant to. "I'll introduce you later." Assuming I lived that long.

Nash slammed the car into Reverse and swerved backward out of the driveway, twisting in his seat to peer out the rear windshield. As we pulled away from the house, I took one last look at my uncle, who stared after us from the middle of the driveway, thick arms crossed over his chest. Behind him, Aunt Val stood on the porch holding a dishrag, her perfect mouth hanging open in surprise.

When we turned the corner, I let myself melt into the car seat, only then noticing how posh it was. "Please tell me you didn't pick me up in a stolen car."

Nash laughed and glanced away from the road to smile at me, and my pulse sped up when our gazes met, in spite of the circumstances. "It's Carter's. I've got it till midnight."

"Why would Scott Carter let you take his car?"

He shrugged. "He's a friend."

I just blinked at him. His questionable choice of companions aside, Emma was my best friend, and I would never let her take my car. And I didn't drive a brand-new Mustang convertible.

Nash grinned when I didn't seem convinced, and his next glance lingered longer than it should have, then roamed south of my face. "He might be under the impression that you…um…need some serious comfort."

My heart leaped into my throat, and I had to speak around it. "And you think you're up for the challenge?"

Flirting should have felt weird, considering the day I'd had. But instead, it made me feel alive, especially with the possibility of my own death hanging over me like a black cloud, casting its malignant shadow over my life. Over everything but Nash, and the way I felt when he looked at me. Touched me…

Nash shrugged again. "Carter offered to pick you up himself…."

Of course he had. Because he was Nash's best friend, and Sophie's boyfriend. And my cousin had seriously bad taste in guys. As, apparently, did Nash. "Why do you hang out with him?"

"We're teammates."

Ahhh. And if blood was thicker than water, then football, evidently, would congeal in one's veins.

"And that makes you friends?" I twisted to peer briefly into the tiny backseat, which was empty and still smelled like leather. And like Sophie's freesia-scented lotion.

Nash shrugged and frowned, like he didn't understand what I was getting at. Or like he wanted to change the subject. "We have stuff in common. He knows how to have a good time. And he goes after what he wants."

He could easily have been describing my father's German shepherd. As could I, when I replied, "Yeah, but once he gets it, he'll just want something else."

Nash's hands tightened around the wheel, and he glanced at me with his eyes wide in comprehension, his forehead furrowed in disappointment. "Is that what you think I'm doing?"

I shrugged. "Your record kind of speaks for itself." And why else had he put up with so much from me? Why would a guy like Nash Hudson stick around through freaky death premonitions and possible brain cancer, if he didn't want something?

Or even if he did, for that matter? He could have put in a lot less work for a lot more payoff somewhere else.

"This isn't like that, Kaylee," he insisted, and I wasn't sure I wanted to know what "that" was. "This is… We're different." He didn't look at me when he said it, but I felt myself flush anyway.

"What does that mean?"

He sighed, and his hands loosened around the wheel. "You hungry?"

HALF AN HOUR LATER, we sat in Scott Carter's car with the front seats pushed back as far as they would go. The setting sun took up the entire windshield, painting White Rock Lake a dozen deep hues of red and purple.

I was well into a six-inch turkey sub, and Nash was half done with some combination of provolone, ham, pepperoni, and a couple of meats I didn't recognize. But it smelled good.

I'd already dripped mustard on Carter's gearshift, and vinegar on the front seat. Nash had just laughed and helped me mop it all up.

If I was dying, I'd decided to spend every single day I had left eating at least one meal with Nash. Talking to him made me feel good, even when everything else in my life was totally falling apart.

I swallowed a big bite, then washed it down with a gulp from my soda. "Promise me that if I do have a brain tumor, you'll bring me sandwiches in the hospital."

He eyed me almost sternly, peeling paper away from his bread. "You don't have cancer, Kaylee. At least, that's not why you're having premonitions."

"How do you know?" I bit another chunk from my sandwich, chewing as I waited for an answer he seemed reluctant to provide.

Finally, after three more bites and two false starts, Nash wrapped the remains of his sandwich and stuffed it between our drinks on the console, then took a deep breath and met my gaze. His forehead was wrinkled like he was nervous, but his gaze held steady. Strong.

"I have to tell you something, and you're not going to believe me. But I can prove it to you. So don't freak out on me, okay? At least not until you've heard the whole thing."

I swallowed another bite, then wrapped the rest of my sandwich and set it in my lap. This didn't sound like the kind of news I should get with food in my mouth. Not unless I wanted to check out earlier than I'd expected, with a chunk of turkey wedged in my throat.

"Okaaay... Whatever it is, it can't be worse than brain cancer, right?"

"Exactly." He ran his fingers through deliberately messy hair, then met my gaze with an intensity that was almost frightening. "You're not human."

"What?" Confusion was a calm white noise in my head, where I'd expected fear or even anger to rage. I'd been prepared to hear something weird. I was intimately acquainted with weird. But I had no idea what to say to "not human."

"Either your aunt and uncle don't know, or they don't want you to know for some reason, which is why I didn't tell you yesterday at breakfast. But you're killing me with this whole brain cancer thing." He was watching me carefully, probably judging from my expression how close I was to flipping out on him.

And honestly, if I'd had any idea what he was talking about, I might have been pretty close.

"I think if they knew you thought you were dying, they'd tell you the truth," he continued. "It sounds like they're going to tell you soon anyway, but I didn't want you to think I was lying to you too." He flashed deep dimples with a small grin. "Or that you have cancer."

For a moment, I could only stare at him, struck numb and dumb by an outpouring of words that contained no real information. And I have to admit there were a couple of seconds there when I wondered if maybe I wasn't the one in need of a straitjacket.

But he'd believed me when I told him about Heidi, as crazy as the whole thing sounded, and had talked me through two different premonitions. The least I could do was hear him out.

"What am I?" The very question—and my willingness to ask it—made my heart pound so hard and so fast I felt like the car was spinning. My arms were covered in goose bumps.

Fading daylight cast shadows defining the planes of his face as he squinted through the windshield into the sun, now a heavy scarlet ball on the edge of the horizon. But his focus never left my eyes. "You're a *bean sidhe,* Kaylee. The death premonitions are normal. They're part of who you are."

Another moment of stunned silence, which I clung to—a brief respite from the madness that each new word seemed to bring. Then I forced the pertinent question to my lips, fighting to keep my jaw from falling off my face as my mouth dropped open. "Sorry, what?"

He grinned and ran one hand over the short stubble on his jaw. "I know, this is the part where you start thinking I'm the crazy one."

As a matter of fact…

"But I swear this is the truth. You're a *bean sidhe.* And so are your parents. At least one of them, anyway."

I shook my head and pushed my hair back from my face, trying to clear away the confusion and make sense of what he'd said. "Banshee? Like, from mythology?" We'd done a mythology unit in sophomore English the year before, but it was mostly Greek and Roman stuff. Gods, goddesses, demigods, and monsters.

"Yeah. Only the real thing." He took a drink from his cup, then set it in the holder. "There's a bunch they don't teach you in school. Things they don't even know about, because they think it's all just a bunch of old stories."

"And you're saying it's not?" I found myself scooting closer to the door, until the handle cut into my back, trying to put some space between myself and the only guy in the world who could make me sound normal.

"No. Kaylee, it's you!" He watched me intently, expectantly, and while I wanted to wallow in denial, I couldn't. Even if Nash was one grape short of a bunch, there was something compelling about him. Something irresistible, even beyond the sculpted arms, gorgeous eyes, and adorable dimples. He made me feel…content. Relaxed. Like everything would be okay, one way or another. Which was quite a feat, considering his claim that I was unqualified to run in the human race.

"Think about it," he insisted. "What do you know about *bean sidhes?*"

I shrugged. "They're women in long, wispy gowns who walk around during funerals, wailing over the dead. Sometimes they wail over the dying, announcing that the end is near." I sipped watered-down soda, then gestured with my cup. "But, Nash, banshees are just stories. Old European legends."

He nodded. "Most of it, yes. They spell it wrong, for starters. The Gaelic is B-E-A-N S-I-D-H-E. Two words. Literally, it means 'woman of the faeries.'"

My eyebrows shot halfway up my forehead as I dropped my cup back into the drink holder. "Wait, you think I'm a faerie? Like, with little glittery wings and magic wands?"

Nash frowned. "This isn't Disney, Kaylee. 'Faerie' is a very broad term. It basically means 'other than human.' And forget about the wispy gowns and following funerals. All that went out of style a long time ago. But the rest of it? Women as death heralds? Sound familiar?"

Okay, there was a *slight* similarity to my morbid predictions, but… "There's no such thing as *bean sidhes,* no matter how you spell it."

"There are no premonitions either, right?" His hazel eyes sparkled in the fading light when he grinned, refusing to be derailed by my cynicism. "Okay, let's see how much of this I can get right. Your dad… He looks really young, right? Too young to have a sixteen-year-old daughter? Your uncle too. They're brothers, right?"

Unimpressed, I rolled my eyes and folded one leg beneath me on the narrow leather car seat. "You saw my uncle an hour ago—you know he's young. And I haven't seen my dad in a year and a half." Though as a child, I'd always thought he looked young and handsome. But that was a long time ago….

"I know your uncle looks young, but that means nothing to a *bean sidhe*. He could be a hundred."

That time I laughed. "Right. My uncle's a senior citizen." Wouldn't it piss Aunt Val off to think he could be more than twice her age and still look younger!

Nash frowned at my skepticism, his face darkening as the last rays of daylight slowly bled from the sky. "Okay, what about the rest of your family? Your ancestors are Irish, right?"

I rolled my eyes and crossed my arms over my chest. "My name's Cavanaugh. That's not a big leap." Plus, he already knew my dad lived in Ireland.

"*Bean sidhes* are native to Ireland. That's why the stories all stem from old Irish folktales."

Oh. Now that was quite a coincidence. But nothing more. "Got anything else, Houdini?"

Nash reached across the center console and took my hand again, and this time I didn't pull away. "Kaylee, I knew what you were the minute you told me Heidi Anderson was going to die. But I probably would have known earlier if I'd been paying attention. I just never expected to run into a *bean sidhe* at my own school."

"How would you have known earlier?"

"Your voice."

"Huh?" But my heart began to beat harder, as if it knew something my head hadn't quite caught on to.

"Last Friday at lunch, I heard you and Emma talking

about sneaking into Taboo, and couldn't get you out of my head. Your voice stuck with me, like after I truly heard you that first time, I couldn't stop hearing you. Your voice carries above everything else. I can find you in a crowd even if I can't see you, so long as you're talking. But I didn't know why. I just knew I needed to talk to you outside of school, and that you'd be at the club on Saturday night."

Suddenly I couldn't catch my breath. My lungs seemed too big for my chest, and I couldn't make them fully expand. "You followed me to Taboo?" His admission made my head spin, questions and confessions both battling for the right to speak first. But I couldn't think clearly enough to focus on them.

"Yeah." He sounded so matter-of-fact, as if it should be no big surprise that a hot, out-of-my-league guy would go to a club on a Saturday night just to see me. "I wanted to talk to you."

I swallowed thickly and stared at my hands. I could hardly believe what I was about to tell him. "When you talk to me, I feel like everything's okay, even when things are really falling apart. Why?" I looked up then and met his gaze, searching for the truth even if I wouldn't understand it. "What did you do to me?"

"Nothing. Nothing on purpose, anyway." He squeezed my hand, threading his fingers through mine. "We truly hear each other because we're the same. I'm a *bean sidhe,*

Kaylee. Just like my mom and dad, and at least one of your parents. Just like you."

Just like me. Was it possible? My instinct was to say no. To shake my head and squeeze my eyes shut until I was sure the crazy dream was over. Really, though, was being a *bean sidhe* any weirder than being plagued with premonitions of death?

But even if it was true, something didn't fit….

"In the stories there are no male *bean sidhes*."

"I know." Nash scowled and let go of my hand to cross his arms over his chest. "The stories come from what humans know about us, and they only seem to know about the ladies. You girls are pretty hard to miss, with all the screaming and wailing."

"Ha ha." I started to shove him, then froze in the act of raising my arm. I'd just defended—albeit jokingly—a species I claimed not to belong to. Or even believe in.

And that's when it hit me. When the whole thing sank in.

Yes, it sounded crazy. But it felt *right*. And little pieces of it actually made sense, in a way that was more intuitive than logical.

My throat felt swollen, and my eyes began to burn with tears of relief. Being not-human was better than being crazy. And infinitely better than dying of cancer. But most important, having answers—even weird answers—was better than not knowing. Than doubting myself.

"I'm a *bean sidhe?*" Two tears fell before I could banish them, and I wiped the rest away with my sleeve. Nash nodded solemnly, and I repeated it, just to get used to the idea. "I'm a *bean sidhe.*"

Saying it out loud helped that last little bit of certainty slip into place, and I felt my chest loosen. One long breath slipped from my throat, and I sank into the car seat, staring out the windshield at a sunset I barely noticed. A tension I hadn't even felt began to ease through my body.

Nash had given me one answer, but he'd brought to mind dozens of others, and I needed more information. Immediately.

"So why doesn't anyone know about male *bean sidhes?* And if you're a guy, wouldn't that make you more of a male *sidhe?*"

He reached for his drink, and the muscles in his arm shifted beneath skin tinted red in the last rays of sunlight. "Unfortunately, the term was coined by humans, who don't know male *bean sidhes* exist, because we don't wail. We don't get the premonitions."

I frowned. "So what makes you a *bean sidhe?* I mean, how are you different from…humans?" Even having accepted my new identity, it felt weird to refer to myself as other than human.

He leaned against Carter's car-door handle and took another long drink before answering. "We have other abilities. But what I can do won't make much sense to you until you know what you can do."

I shook my head, uncomprehending. "I thought I was a death herald."

"That's what you are, not what you can do. At least, that's not all you can do."

9

I LEANED FORWARD, angling my knee to avoid the gearshift, more curious than I wanted to admit as I waited for the rest of it. But he twisted to peer out his window. "My legs are getting stiff. Let's walk." He pushed his door open without waiting for my reply.

"What?" I demanded, leaning over the console to watch as he stretched in the parking lot, muscles bunching and shifting as he pulled both arms over his head. "You're going to keep me in suspense?"

"No, just in motion." I groaned with impatience, and he ducked into the car to grin at me. "What, you can't walk and talk at the same time?" Then his grin widened and he slammed the door in my face. I had no choice but to follow.

Automatic lights flared to life as I stepped onto the concrete, bathing the entire lot, the adjacent, deserted playground, and part of the pier in a soft yellow glow. I circled the car and gave him my hand when he reached for it. "Fine, I'm walking. Start—"

Nash kissed me, one hand gripping the curve of my left hip, and the rest of my sentence was lost forever. When he finally pulled away, he left me breathing hard and craving things I could barely conceptualize. His gaze met mine from inches away, and I noticed that his irises were still swirling in the soft yellow light overhead. Or maybe they were swirling again.

Suddenly his eyes didn't seem so strange. And neither did my fascination with them. "So…your eyes?" I whispered when I could speak again, making no move to step back. "Is that part of what male *bean sidhes* do?"

"My eyes?" He frowned and blinked. "The colors are swirling, aren't they?"

"Yeah." I leaned closer for a better look, and since I was so close, anyway, I kissed him back, sucking lightly on his lower lip, then delving deeper. Exhilaration shot through me when he groaned and gripped my waist with both hands. His hands started to slide lower, and I only stepped back when I got scared by the realization that I didn't want him to stop.

"Um…" I cleared my throat and shoved my hands in my pockets, then finally looked up to find him watching me. "Your eyes are beautiful," I said, desperate to bring the conversation back on track. "But don't they kind of clue people in? That you're…not human?"

"Nah." He brushed a chunk of dark hair from his forehead and grinned. "It only happens when I'm experiencing something…um…really intense." I felt myself flush, but he continued as if he hadn't noticed. "A *bean sidhe's* eyes are like a mood ring you can't take off. But you can't read your own, and humans can't see it at all. Just other *bean sidhes*." His held my gaze with an intense look of his own. "Yours are doing it too. More shades of blue than the ocean, swirling like a Caribbean whirlpool."

Oh, lovely. My flush deepened until I thought my cheeks would combust. He could see what I was thinking—what I wanted—in my eyes. But I could see what he wanted too….

"Tell me the rest of it." I turned toward the park with my hands still in my pockets. I wanted to know everything—but mostly I wanted to change the subject.

Nash stepped over a parking bumper and caught up with me in two strides. "Human lore says that when a *bean sidhe* wails, she's mourning the dead, or the soon-to-be dead, but that's not the whole story." He glanced up to study my profile. "I've seen you hold back your wail twice. What do you remember about the time you let it go?"

I flinched at the memory, reluctant to revisit the event that landed me in the hospital. "It was horrible. Once I let it go, I couldn't pull it back. And I couldn't think about anything else. There was this feeling of total despair, then this awful noise that felt like it just erupted from my throat." I stepped over a landscape timber, then onto the thick bed of wood chips carpeting the playground, and Nash followed. "The scream was in control of me, rather than the other way around. People were staring, and dropping purses and shopping bags to cover their ears. This little girl started crying and clinging to her mom, but I couldn't make it stop. It was the worst day of my life. Seriously."

"My mom says the first time's always rough. Though it doesn't usually get you locked up."

That's right; his mother was a *bean sidhe* too. No wonder she'd stared at mc. She probably knew I had no idea what I was.

When we got to the heart of the playground—a massive wooden castle full of towers, and tunnels, and slides— Nash stepped beneath a piece of equipment and reached up for the first monkey bar beam. "Were you watching the pre-departed when he actually…departed?"

I raised an eyebrow in dark amusement, trying not to stare at the triceps clearly displayed beneath the snug, short sleeves of his tee. "Pre-departed?"

He grinned. "It's a technical term."

"Aah. No, I wasn't looking at anything." I sank onto a low tire swing held up by three chains, rocking back and forth slowly, trying to forget the words even as I spoke them. "I was trying to make the screeching stop. Mall Security called my aunt and uncle, and when I couldn't stop crying, they took me to the hospital."

Nash let go of the bar and settled onto the rubber-coated steps of a nearby slide, watching me from a couple of feet away. "Well, if you'd looked at the other guy, you would have seen the deceased's soul. Hovering."

"Hovering?"

"Yeah. Souls are fundamentally attracted to a *bean sidhe's* wail, and as long as it lasts, they can't move on. They just kind of hang there, suspended. You remember sirens in mythology? How their song could draw a sailor to his death?"

"Yeah…?" And that image did nothing to ease the apprehension now swelling inside me like heartburn.

"It's like that. Except the people are already dead. And they aren't usually sailors."

"Wow." I put my feet down to stop the tire from rocking. "I'm like flypaper for the soul. That's…weird. Why would anyone want to do that? Suspend some poor guy's soul?"

Nash shrugged and stood to pull me up. "Lots of reasons. A *bean sidhe* who knows what she's doing can hold on to a soul long enough for him to prepare for the afterlife. Let him make his peace."

I frowned, unable to picture it. "Okay, but how peaceful can it possibly be, with me screaming bloody murder?"

He laughed again, and I followed him up the steps to a wobbly bridge made of wooden planks chained loosely together. "It doesn't sound like screaming to the soul. Or to me either. Your wail is beautiful to male *bean sidhes*." Nash turned to look at me from the top step, his gaze soft, and almost reflective. "More like a wistful, haunting song. I wish you could hear it the way we hear it."

"Me too." Anything would be better than the earsplitting screech I heard. "What else can I do? Tell me the parts that don't make me want to dig my own ears out of my skull."

Nash pulled me onto the bridge, which rocked beneath us until I sat in the middle with my legs dangling over the side. "You can keep a soul around long enough for him to hear the thoughts and condolences of his friends. Or say goodbye to his family, though they can't hear him."

"So I'm...useful?" My pitch rose in earnest hope.

"Totally." He settled onto the next plank, facing my profile with one leg hanging over the edge of the bridge and the other arching behind me.

My smile swelled, as did the warmth spreading throughout my chest, slowly overtaking my unease at the very thought of suspending a human soul. I wasn't sure whether this blossoming peace stemmed from my newfound purpose in life—and in death—or from the way Nash watched me, like he'd do anything to make me smile.

"So what can you do?"

"Well, my vocal cords aren't as powerful as yours, but a male *bean sidhe's* voice does carry a kind of...Influence. A strong power of suggestion, or projection of emotion." He shrugged and draped one arm over the rope railing, leaning back to see me better. "We can project confidence, or excitement. Or any other emotion. A bunch of us together can urge groups into action, or pacify a mob. That one was big during the witch trials, and public panics of old." He grinned. "But mostly, we just relax people when they're nervous, or upset." Nash shot me a meaningful look, and I sucked in a startled breath so big I nearly choked on it.

"You calmed me, didn't you? In the alley behind Taboo."

"And behind the school, this afternoon. With Meredith…"

How could I not have realized? I'd never been able to control the panic before, without putting distance between myself and…the pre-deceased.

I blinked back grateful tears and started to thank him, but he spoke before I could get the words out. "Don't worry about it. It was cool to finally get to show off."

"And there's more, other than the Influence?"

He nodded, and the bridge rocked as he leaned forward, eyeing me dramatically. "I can direct souls."

"What?" Chill bumps popped up beneath my sleeves, in spite of the unseasonably warm evening.

Nash shrugged, like it was no big deal. "You can suspend a soul, and I can manipulate it. Tell it where to go."

"Seriously? Where do you send it?" I couldn't wrap my mind around the concept.

"Nowhere." He leaned back against the rope and frowned. "That's the problem. Your skills are useful. Altruistic, even. Mine…? Not so much."

"Why not?"

"Because there's only one place to send a disembodied soul."

"The afterlife?" I folded one leg beneath the other and twisted to face him, trying not to be completely overwhelmed by the possibilities he was throwing at me.

He shook his head as a cicada's song began in the distance. "A soul doesn't need me for that."

And suddenly I understood. "You can put it back! Into the *body*." I sat up straight and the bridge swayed. "You can bring someone back to life!"

Nash shook his head, still somber in spite of my growing enthusiasm, and stood to pull me up. "It takes two of us. A female to capture the soul, and a male to reinstate it." His hand found my hip again, and the heat behind his gaze nearly scorched me. "We could be amazing together, Kaylee."

My cheeks blazed.

Then the reality of what he was saying truly hit me, like a blast of cold air to the face.

"We can save people? Reverse death? You should have told me that part first!" A tingly exhilaration blossomed in my chest, and at first I didn't understand when he shook his head.

But then my excitement withered, replaced by a cold, heavy feeling of regret. Of mounting guilt. "So not only did I fail to warn Meredith, I let her die, when we could have saved her. Why didn't you tell me?" I couldn't stop the flash of anger that realization brought. Meredith would still be alive if I'd known how to help her!

"No, Kaylee." Nash tilted my chin up until I saw the dark regret swirling in his eyes. "We can't just go around shoving souls back into dead bodies. It doesn't work like that. You can't even warn someone of his own death. It's physically impossible, because you can't do anything else while you're singing a soul's song. Right?"

I nodded miserably. "It's completely consuming…." Though I still couldn't imagine that horrible screech sounding like the song he'd described. "But there has to be a way around that." I sidestepped him on the wobbly bridge and took the steps two at a time. My mind was racing and I needed to move. "We could work out some kind of signal or something. When I get a premonition, I could point, and you could go warn the…um…pre-deceased."

Nash caught up with me, already shaking his head again. He caught my arm and pulled me to a halt, but let go when I stiffened. "Even if you could warn someone, it wouldn't change anything. It would just make the poor guy's last moments terrifying." I started to shake my head, but he rushed on. "That's what I've been trying to tell you, Kaylee. You can't stop death."

"But you just said we could." I leaned against the side of a green plastic twisty-slide, frowning up at him. "Together, we could have saved Meredith. Maybe even

Heidi Anderson. Doesn't it bother you that we didn't even try?"

"Of course it does, but saving Meredith wouldn't have stopped her death. It would only have prolonged her life. And reanimating someone whose time has come carries serious consequences. And believe me, the price isn't worth paying."

"What does that mean?" How could saving someone not be worth the price?

Nash's gaze burned into me, as if to underline the importance of what he was going to say. "A life for a life, Kaylee. If we'd saved Meredith, someone else would have been taken instead. Could be one of us, or anyone nearby."

Ouch.

I sank onto the rubber mat at the base of the slide, my eyes closed in horror. Okay, that was a high price. And even if I'd been willing to pay it myself, I had no right to make that decision for an innocent bystander. Or for Nash. Yet I couldn't let the issue go. No matter what he said, no matter how logical the arguments, letting Meredith die felt wrong, and I couldn't stand the thought of ever having to do that again.

Nash sighed and sank onto the mat with me, his arms propped on his knees. "Kaylee, I know how you feel, but that's the way death works. When someone's time comes, he has to go, and you'll only drive yourself crazy looking for loopholes in the system. Trust me." The anguish in

Nash's voice resonated in my heart, and I ached to touch him. To ease whatever grief lent such pain to his words.

"You've tried, haven't you?" I whispered. He nodded, and I leaned over to let my mouth meet his, lingering when the contact shot sparks through my veins. I wanted to hold him, to somehow make it all better. "Who was it?"

"My dad."

Stunned, I leaned back to see his face, and the hurt I found there seemed to leach through me, leaving me cold with dread. "What happened?"

Nash exhaled slowly and leaned back against the side of the slide. Light from the streetlamp above played on his hand when he rubbed his forehead, as if to fend off the memory. "He fell off a ladder trying to paint the shutters on a second-story window and hit his head on some bricks bordering my mom's flower bed. She was pruning the bushes when he fell, so she saw it happen."

"Where were you?" I spoke softly, afraid he'd stop talking if my voice shattered his memories.

"In the backyard, but I came running when she screamed. When I got there, she was crying, holding his head on her lap. There was blood all over her legs. Then my dad stopped breathing, and she started singing.

"It was beautiful, Kaylee." His words grew urgent and he sat straighter, like he was trying to convince me. "Eerie and sad. And there was his soul, just kind of hanging above them both. I tried to guide it. I didn't really know what I was doing, but I had to try to save him. But he made me stop. His soul… I could hear it. He said he had to go, and I should take care of my mom. He said she would need me, and he was right. She felt guilty because she'd asked him to paint the shutters. She hasn't been the same since."

I didn't realize I was holding my breath until I had to take the next one. "How old were you?"

"Ten." His eyes closed. "My dad's was the first soul I ever saw, and I couldn't save him. Not without killing someone else, and he wouldn't let me risk my own life. Or my mom's." He opened his eyes to stare at me intently. "And he was right about that too, Kaylee. We can't take an innocent life to spare someone who's supposed to die."

He'd get no argument from me there. But… "What if Meredith wasn't supposed to die? What if it wasn't her time?"

"It was. That's how it works." Nash's voice held the conviction of a child professing belief in Santa Claus. He was a little too sure, as if the strength of his assertion could make up for some secret doubt.

"How do you know?"

"Because there are schedules. Official lists. There are people who make sure death is carried out the way it's supposed to be."

I blinked at him, eyes narrowed in surprise. "Are you serious?"

"Unfortunately." A breeze of bitterness swept across his

face, but it was gone before I was even sure it was there in the first place.

"That sounds so…bureaucratic."

He shrugged. "It's a very well-organized system."

"Every system has flaws, Nash." He started to disagree, but I rushed on. "Think about it. Three girls have died in the same area in the past three days, each with no known cause. They all just fell over dead. That's not the natural order of things. It's the very definition of 'unnatural.' Or at least 'suspicious.'"

"It's definitely unusual," he admitted. Nash rubbed his temples again and suddenly sounded very tired. "But even if they weren't supposed to die, there's nothing we can do about it without getting someone else killed."

"Okay…" I couldn't argue with that logic. "But if someone isn't meant to die, does the penalty for saving him still apply?"

Nash looked shocked suddenly, as if that possibility had never occurred to him. "I don't know. But I know someone who might."

10

"So who's this Tod?" I slurped the last of my soda, watching as passing headlights briefly illuminated his features, then abandoned him to short stretches of shadow. It was like rediscovering him with each beam of light that found his face, and I couldn't stop watching.

"He works second shift at the hospital." Nash flicked his blinker on as he made a left-hand turn.

"Doing what?"

"Tod's…an intern." He took another left, and Arlington Memorial lay before us on the right, the mirrored windows of the new surgical tower reflecting the streetlights back at us.

I gathered the wrappers from our meal and shoved them into the paper sack on the floorboard between my feet. "I didn't know interns had set schedules."

Nash turned into the dimly lit parking garage and

glanced in both directions, looking for an empty spot near the entrance. But he was also obviously avoiding my eyes. "He's not exactly a medical intern."

"What is he, then? Exactly."

An empty space appeared at the end of the first level, and he pulled into it, taking more care with Carter's car than he had with his mother's. Then he shifted into Park and killed the engine before turning to face me fully. "Kaylee, Tod isn't human either. And he's not exactly a friend, so he may not be eager to answer our questions."

I crossed my arms over my chest and tried to look irritated, which wasn't easy, considering that every time he looked at me like that, like there was nothing else in the world worth looking at, my heart beat harder and my breath caught in my throat. "A non-human non-friend? Who works at the hospital as a non-medical intern?" At least it wasn't another football player. "Now that we're clear on what he's *not,* care to tell me what he *is?*" ·

Nash sighed, and I knew from the sound that I wasn't going to like whatever he had to say. "He's a grim reaper."

"He's a what?" Surely I'd heard him wrong. "Did you just say Tod's the Grim Reaper?"

Nash shook his head slowly, and I exhaled in relief. *Bean sidhes* were one thing—we could actually help people—but I was not ready to face the walking, talking personification of Death. Much less ask him questions.

"He's not *the* Grim Reaper," Nash said, watching me

closely. "He's only *a* reaper. One of thousands. It's just a job."

"Just a job? Death is just a job! Wait…" I sucked in a deep breath and closed my eyes. Then I counted to ten. When that wasn't enough, I counted to thirty. Then I met Nash's gaze, hoping panic didn't show in the probably swirling depths of mine. "So…when you said you can't stop death, what you really meant is that you can't stop Tod?"

"Not him specifically, but yes, that's the general idea. Reapers have a job to do, just like everyone else. And as a whole, they're not very fond of *bean sidhes.*"

"Do I even want to know why not?"

Nash smiled sympathetically and took my hand, and my pulse jumped at even such small contact. *Crap.* I could already see that any future anger at him was going to be very hard to sustain. "Most reapers don't like us because we have the potential to seriously screw up their workday. Even if we don't actually restore a person's soul, a reaper can't touch it so long as you hold it. So every second you spend singing means a one-second delay in the delivery of that soul. In a busy district, that could throw him disastrously behind schedule. Also, it just plain pisses them off. Reapers don't like anyone else playing with their toys."

Great. "So not only am I not-human, but Death is my arch foe?" *Who, me? Panic?* "Anything else you want to tell me, while we're confessing?"

Nash tried to stifle a chuckle, but failed. "Reapers aren't

our enemies, Kaylee. They just don't particularly enjoy our company."

Something told me the feeling would be mutual. I gave him a shaky nod, and Nash opened the driver's side door and stepped into the dark parking garage. I got out on the other side, and as I closed the door, he clicked a button on Carter's key chain to lock the car. Both sounds reverberated around us, and by all appearances, we were alone in the garage. Which was good, considering the discussion we were in the middle of.

"So what does Tod look like? Whitewashed skeleton skulking around in a black cape and hood? Carrying a scythe? 'Cause I'm thinking that would cause mass panic in the hospital."

He took my hand as we made our way down the aisle toward the garage entrance, footsteps echoing eerily. "Do you chase after funeral processions in a long, dirty dress, hair trailing behind you in the wind?"

I shot him a mock frown. "Have you been following me again?"

Nash rolled his eyes. "He looks normal—not that it matters. You can't see a reaper unless he wants to be seen."

A warm, late-September wind blew through the garage entrance, fluttering flyers stuck to windshields and fast-food wrappers scattered across the concrete. "Will Tod want us to see him?"

"Depends on what kind of mood he's in." Nash walked

past the huge revolving door in favor of the heavy glass pane, which he pulled open for me to pass through into the tiny vestibule. I held the next door for him, and we stepped into a small, quiet lobby lined with empty, uncomfortable-looking armchairs. The warmth of the building was a relief, and my goose bumps faded with each step we took away from the door.

Nash ignored the volunteer at the help desk—not that it mattered; she was asleep at her post—and guided me toward a bank of elevators at the end of the hall.

My shoes squeaked on the polished floor, and each breath brought with it a whiff of antiseptic and pine-scented air freshener. Either would have been bad enough on its own, and together they threatened to overwhelm both my nose and my lungs. Fortunately the elevator on the left stood empty and open.

Inside, Nash pushed the button for the third floor. When the doors closed, the "welcome" scent faded, replaced immediately by the generic hospital smell, a combination of stale air, cafeteria meat loaf, and bleach.

Tod works on the third level?" I asked as gears grinded overhead and the elevator began to rise.

"He works all over the hospital, but Intensive Care is on three, and that's where we're most likely to find him. Assuming he wants to be found."

A new chill went through me as his statement sank in. We were most likely to find Tod in Intensive Care—where people were most likely to be dying.

My palms began to sweat, and my heart pounded so hard I was sure Nash could hear it echo in the elevator. What were the chances I'd make it through the ICU without finding a soul to sing for?

Slim to none, I was betting. And since we were already in the hospital, if I freaked out this time, they'd probably put me on the express gurney to the mental-health ward. Do not pass Go. Do not collect two hundred dollars.

I was *not* going back there.

My hand clenched Nash's, and he stroked my fingers with his thumb. "If you feel it starting, just squeeze my hand and I'll get you out." I started to shake my head, and he ran the fingers of his free hand down the side of my face, staring into my eyes. "I promise."

I sighed. "Okay." He'd already helped me through two panic attacks—I couldn't stop thinking of them as such—and I had no doubt he could do it again. And, anyway, I didn't really have any choice. I couldn't help the next victim of an untimely death without finding Tod-the-reaper, and I couldn't find Tod without checking all his favorite haunts.

The elevator dinged, and the door slid open with a soft *shhh* sound. I glanced at Nash, bolstering my courage as I straightened my spine. "Let's get this over with."

The third floor stretched out to either side of us, and one long, sterile white hall opened up directly across from the elevator doors, where a man and a woman in matching blue scrubs sat behind a big circular nurses' station. The man looked up when my shoes squeaked on the floor, but the woman didn't notice us.

Nash nodded toward the left-hand hallway, and we headed that way, walking slowly, pretending to read the names written on disposable nameplates outside each door. We were just two kids hoping to pay respects to our grandfather one last time. Except that we didn't "find" him on the chosen hallway, or anywhere else on the third floor, which was almost a letdown after my initial fear of entering the ICU. Fortunately, Arlington wasn't that big of a town, and only three of the beds in Intensive Care were actually occupied. And none of those occupants was in any immediate danger of meeting a reaper.

Tod was also absent from the fourth, fifth, and sixth floors, at least as far as we could tell. The only places left to look were the surgical tower, the emergency room on the first floor, and the maternity ward, on two.

I did *not* want to find a grim reaper—even if he didn't carry a scythe—in the maternity ward, and we would definitely be noticed in the surgical tower. So we checked the ER first.

During my one previous trip to Arlington Memorial, my aunt and uncle had called ahead, and the mental-health ward had been expecting us, which meant we didn't have to stop in the ER. So I'd never seen one in person until Nash and I crossed the front lobby and pushed through the double doors into the emergency waiting area. I have, however, spent plenty of time in the psychiatric unit, which is no trip to Disneyland. It's populated with nurses who look at you with either pity or contempt, and patients in slippers who either won't meet your eyes or won't look away. But the ER holds its own special brand of misery.

Far from the energetic rush of adrenaline I'd expected based on certain television hospital dramas, the actual emergency room was quiet and somber. Patients waited in thinly cushioned chairs lining the walls and grouped in the middle of the long room, their faces twisted into grimaces of pain, fear, or impatience.

One old woman languished in a wheelchair beneath a threadbare blanket, and several feverish children shivered in their mothers' arms. Men in work clothes pressed crusted gauze bandages to wounds seeping blood, or ice packs to purple lumps on their heads. At the far end of the room near the triage desk, a teenager moaned and clutched one arm to her chest as her mother thumbed through an old tabloid, blatantly ignoring her.

Every few minutes, employees in scrubs entered through one end of the room, crossed the faded, dingy vinyl tile, and pushed through a set of double doors on the other end. Those alone read from charts or stared straight ahead, while those in pairs broke the grim near-silence with incongruous snatches of casual conversation. Regardless, the employees went out of their way to avoid eye contact with the people waiting, while the patients eyed them in hope so transparent it was uncomfortable for me to watch.

"Do you see him?" I whispered to Nash, skipping

over the sick women and children to scan the faces of the men.

"No, and we won't until he's ready to be seen."

I stuffed my hands in my pockets, physically resisting the urge to take his hand for comfort, just because the ER creeped me out. If I couldn't handle the huddled masses staring into space like zombies, how could I hope to face the Grim Reaper? Or even *a* grim reaper? "So how are we supposed to find him?"

"The plan was for him to find us," he whispered back. "Two *bean sidhes* walking around while he's trying to work should have drawn him out pretty quickly, if for no other reason than to run us off."

"Then I'm guessing he's decided not to show."

"Looks that way." Nash's gaze settled on a sign on the wall, which pointed the way to the gift shop, the cafeteria, and the radiology lab. "You thirsty?"

"Not really." I'd polished off a thirty-two-ounce soda in the car, and would have to find a bathroom soon as it was.

"Then come sit with me. If we make it clear we have all night to wait, he'll probably show up to hurry us along."

"But we don't have all—"

"Shh." Smiling, he slid one arm around my waist and whispered into my ear. "Don't tip our hand." Pleasant chills rushed down my neck and throughout my body, originating where his breath brushed my earlobe.

We followed the signs down the hall, around the corner,

and into the cafeteria, which was still serving dinner at seven-thirty in the evening. Nash bought a huge slice of chocolate cake and a school-size carton of milk. I got a Coke. Then we chose a small square table in one corner of the nearly empty room.

Nash sat with his back to the wall, eating as if nothing were wrong. As if he went looking for an agent of death every evening. But I couldn't sit still. My gaze roamed the room, skimming over a custodian emptying a trash can and a woman in a hairnet inspecting the salad bar for wilted lettuce. My feet bounced on the floor, my knees hitting the underside of the table over and over. Nash's milk sloshed with each impact, but he didn't seem to notice.

He was halfway through his cake—minus the bite or two I'd found room for—when a shadow fell across our table. I looked up to find a young man standing in front of the empty chair on my right. He wore faded, baggy jeans and a short-sleeved white tee with no sign of a coat, in spite of the temperature outside. And his fierce expression did nothing to harden cherubic lips and bright blue eyes, crowned by a mop of blond curls.

Nash didn't even look up.

I glanced at the blond guy, then followed his gaze to the disposable salt-and-pepper shakers in the center of the table. Assuming he wanted to borrow them, I was reaching for the salt when he pulled the empty chair out and dropped into it, crossing bare forearms on the table in front of him.

"What do you want?" he growled in a pitch so low and gravelly I would have sworn it could never have come from such an angelic face.

Nash took his time chewing, then finally swallowed and pushed his plate back. "Answers."

I frowned, gaping at the blond in disbelief. "You're the grim reaper?"

Tod glanced at me for the first time, his frown practically etched into place. "You were expecting someone older? Taller? Maybe kind of gaunt and skeletal?" Contempt dripped from his words like acid, and his focus snapped back to Nash in annoyance. "See? That's the problem with the old title. I should start calling myself a 'collections agent' or something like that."

"Then they'd just make you wear a suit and tie," I said, amused by the mental image.

The corner of Nash's mouth twitched.

"Who's the sidekick?" Tod tossed his head my way, but his attention—and irritation—remained focused on Nash.

"We need to know about the exchange rate," Nash said, cutting me off before I could introduce myself.

Tod's brows gathered low over shadowed blue eyes, and in the gleam from the fluorescent bulbs overhead, I noticed a short, pale goatee on the end of his strong, square chin. "Do I look like the information desk to you?"

"You look…bored." A mischievous look spread over Nash's face as Tod's scowl deepened, and I wondered what I was missing. "The hospital not keeping you busy? Hey, I hear there's an opening at Colonial Manor. You liked it there, didn't you?"

"The nursing home?" I asked, but neither of them even glanced at me; they were too busy glaring at each other. "Why would a nursing home hire someone to kill its patients? For that matter, why would a hospital?"

Nash chuckled and ran one hand through his head full of messy brown spikes, but Tod's eyes flicked my way, and his jaw tightened. "Does she come with a mute button?"

"He doesn't work *for* the hospital," Nash said, ignoring the reaper's hopefully rhetorical question. "He works *in* the hospital. And at this rate, he'll be stuck here for the next century, at least. Right, Tod?"

The reaper didn't answer, but I could hear his teeth grinding.

"You know, if you keep bottling up your anger like that, you're not going to be anywhere a century from now, much less still working full-time." Wait, was I needling an agent of death? *Probably not the best idea, Kaylee…*

"Reapers don't age," Tod snapped at me, while still glaring at Nash. "It's one of the fringe benefits."

"Like us, right?" I glanced at Nash just in time to see him flinch, and knew I'd said something wrong. And when I looked at Tod again, I found him staring at me in surprise, an impish grin highlighting his angelic features like light from above.

"Where'd you find her?"

"We do age," Nash said, but the last word was clipped short, like he'd almost said my name, then left it out at the last minute. And that's when I understood: he didn't want Tod to know who I was.

I was fine with that. The very idea of Death knowing my name made my skin crawl. Even if this particular Death was only one of many, and almost too pretty to look at.

"We just age very slowly," Nash continued.

By then I was blushing furiously; I'd just painted myself as a complete fool. What kind of idiot doesn't know the lifespan of her own species?

Nash hooked his foot around my ankle beneath the table, rubbing my leg in sympathy and comfort. I shot him a grateful smile and made myself meet Tod's eyes boldly. The best way to even the playing field was to knock him down a peg. "Why are you stuck here?" I asked, hoping I'd correctly assessed that as his sore spot.

"Because he's a rookie." Nash smirked. "And there isn't much opportunity for advancement in a line of work where the employees never die."

"You're a rookie?" I looked at Tod again, and again his jaw bulged with irritation. "How old are you?" I'd assumed, based on that "ageless" comment, that he was much older than he looked.

"He's seventeen," Nash said, his smirk still firmly in place.

"I was seventeen when I started this job," the reaper snapped. "But that was two years ago."

"You've been doing this for two years and you're still a rookie?"

Tod looked insulted, and I wasn't sure whether to laugh or apologize. "Yeah, well, my recruiter wasn't very concerned with truth in advertising. And your boyfriend here is right about the turnover rate—it's nonexistent. The senior reapers in this district are edging up on two hundred years old. If we hadn't lost one last year, I'd still be sitting in the TV room at Colonial Manor, waiting for old men to keel over into their oatmeal."

"Wait, how do you lose a reaper?" I couldn't help but ask. "Freak sickle accident?" But no one else looked amused by my joke.

"The less you know about reaper business, the better," Nash whispered, and Tod nodded arrogantly.

Oh. I held both hands up in defense and leaned back in my chair. "Sorry. So...old men keeling into their oatmeal...?"

Tod shrugged. "Yeah. But at least here I get the occasional gunshot victim or unexpected relapse. Life's all about the surprises, right?"

"I guess." But surprises had kind of lost their novelty for me with the discovery that I wasn't human. Except for that whole fatal premonition thing. I'd love to be caught off guard by death again, like normal people.

Well, not by my own death, of course.

"Speaking of surprises…" Twisting the lid off my Coke, I glanced at Nash for a signal, and he nodded, telling me to continue. Evidently I wasn't imagining Tod's willingness to talk to me, rather than to him. "We need your help avoiding a really nasty one."

Tod made a show of glancing at his wrist, conspicuously absent of a watch. "You two have already wasted my whole break. I have an aneurism on the fourth floor in ten minutes, and I can't be late. I hate the ones that linger."

"This won't take long." I pinned him with my gaze, refusing to break contact once I saw him hesitate. "Please."

The reaper sighed, running one hand through his mop of short curls. "You have five minutes."

I breathed softly in relief. Until the reality of the situation sank in.

Had I just begged for an audience with Death?

11

"THIS IS ABOUT the exchange rate?" the reaper asked, drawing me out of my own head, where shock over the events of the past couple of hours was finally catching up with me.

When I didn't answer, Nash nodded.

The reaper shrugged and slouched back into his chair. "You know as much as I do about that. A life for a life."

Nash glanced at me with both brows raised, to ask if I was okay. I nodded, drawing my thoughts back into focus, and he leaned forward with his arms crossed on the table. "But that's the penalty for saving someone on your list, right? Someone who's *supposed* to die."

"You're not 'saving' anyone." Tod scowled—we'd obviously found his hot button. "You're stealing souls, which only delays the inevitable. And throws my whole shift off schedule. And hurls my boss into all new realms of pissed-off. And you don't even want to know about the paperwork involved in even a simple, equal exchange."

"I'm not—" Nash started, but Tod cut him off.

"But beyond all that, it's illegal. Thus the penalty."

I screwed the lid back onto my bottle and pushed it toward the middle of the table. "But does the penalty still apply if we save someone who wasn't supposed to die?"

Tod's forehead wrinkled in confusion, then his expression went suddenly blank, leaving a cold comprehension shining in his eyes. "Shit like that doesn't happen here—"

"Come off it, Tod." Nash eyed the reaper intently, old pain etched into the lines of his frown. "You owe me the truth."

But Tod went on as if he hadn't been interrupted. "—and even if it did, you'd never know it, because no reaper could afford to admit he accidently took the wrong soul."

"We're not talking about an accident." I glanced up when the cafeteria doors flew open and a woman entered with three kids in tow, reminding me for the first time since Tod had joined us that we were discussing very odd things in a very public place.

"What about the list? Wouldn't that prove it if someone wasn't supposed to die?" Nash whispered now in concession to our new company.

Tod scrubbed his face with both hands, clearly frustrated and losing patience with our questions. "Probably, but you'd never get your hands on the list. And even if you could, it'd be too late. The penalty would already have been applied."

"Are you seriously saying a reaper would take an innocent life in exchange for a soul he shouldn't have claimed in the first place?" Indignation burned hot in my veins. If any process in the world was free from corruption, it should have been death. After all, wasn't death the great equalizer?

Or was that taxes?

"No, you're right." Tod gave me a halfhearted nod. "In theory, the penalty shouldn't apply in a case like that. But theory and reality don't always coexist where death is concerned. So even if you could get your hands on the right list, and even if you were right about the reaper's… mistake, chances are that an innocent soul would already have been taken. Or one of your own."

I couldn't help noticing he didn't put us in the "innocent" category.

"So we're screwed either way." Exasperated, I tossed my hands into the air and leaned back in my chair, closing my eyes.

"What's this about, anyway?" Tod asked, and I opened my eyes to find him watching me in…was that interest? "Who are you trying to save?"

"We don't know. Probably no one." Nash poked at the last bite of cake with his fork, smearing chocolate frosting across the paper plate. "Several girls have died in our area recently, and Ka—" He stopped, omitting my name from the sentence at the last second. "She—" he nodded in my direction "—thinks their deaths are suspicious."

"'She' does, huh?" A grin tugged at the corner of the young reaper's mouth, and I could practically hear the gears turning in his head. "What's suspicious about them?"

"They were all teenagers. They were all very pretty. They all died the same way. They were all in good health. They each died a day apart." I ticked the facts off on my fingers as I spoke, and when I'd used up one hand, I showed it to him. "Take your pick. But either way, that's too many coincidences. There's *no* way all three of them were supposed to die, and I don't care whose list they were on."

The gleam of interest in Tod's eyes told me I'd recaptured his attention. "You think they were killed?"

I tapped one foot on the sticky floor, trying to sort out my thoughts. "I don't know. Maybe, but if so, I have no idea how. All but the first one died in front of witnesses, who saw nothing suspicious. Other than a beautiful girl keeling over with no warning."

"There are ways to make that happen, of course." Tod half stood and walked his chair closer to the table, then sank back into it. "But even if they were killed, that doesn't change anything. Murder victims are on the master list every day. I've only had one in two years, but the senior reapers get them on a weekly basis."

I felt my eyes go wide, and a heavy, tight feeling gripped my chest. "You mean people are *supposed* to be killed?" For a moment, true horror eclipsed the determination and fear already warring inside me. How could murder be a part of the natural order?

Tod shook his head. "People are supposed to die, and the specifics vary widely. Including murder."

I turned on Nash, blinking back the angry tears burning my eyes. "So what's the point of all this? If I can't change it, why do I have to know about it?"

Nash took my hand. "She's having trouble letting them go," he said, and Tod nodded as if he understood.

"What do you know about it?" I snapped, beyond caring that none of this was the reaper's fault. Or that I probably should have been scared of him. "You take lives for a living." As ironic as that sounded… "Death is an everyday occurrence for you."

Nash huffed, and a satisfied look hovered on the edge of his expression. "Yeah, and you'd never know from listening to him now that he had so much trouble with it at first."

"Watch it, Hudson," Tod growled, bright blue eyes going icy.

A new look flitted across Nash's features—some combination of amusement and mischief. "Tell her about the little girl."

"Do you have some kind of disorder? Some synapse misfiring up there—" he gestured vaguely toward Nash's head "—that makes you incapable of keeping your mouth shut? Or are you just a garden-variety fool?"

"What girl?" I ignored both the reaper's outburst and the *bean sidhe*'s satisfied half smile.

"It'll help her understand," Nash said when it became clear that Tod wasn't going to respond.

"Understand what?" I demanded, glancing from one to the other. And finally Tod sighed, still glaring at Nash.

"He's just trying to make me look like an idiot," the reaper snapped. "But I have stories that make him look even worse, so keep that in mind, soul snatcher, next time you go shooting off your mouth."

Nash shrugged, obviously unbothered by the threat, and Tod twisted in his chair to face me fully. "At first, I wasn't too fond of my job. The whole thing seemed pointless and sad, and just plain wrong at times. Once I actually refused an assignment and nearly got myself terminated. I'm guessing that's what he wants you to hear."

Nash nodded on the edge of my vision, but I kept my focus on the reaper. "Why would you refuse an assignment?"

Tod exhaled in frustration. Or maybe embarrassment. "I was working at the nursing home, and this little girl came with her parents to visit her grandmother. She choked on a peppermint her grandma's roommate gave her, and she was supposed to die. She was on the list—all official. But when the time came, I couldn't do it. She was only three.

So when a nurse showed up and gave her the Heimlich, I let her live."

"What happened?" My heart ached for the little girl, and for Tod, whose job conflicted with every ounce of compassion in my body. And in his, evidently.

"My boss got pissed when I came back without her soul. He took her grandmother's instead, and when a shift opened up at the hospital, he passed me over and gave it to someone else." Anger darkened his eyes. "I was stuck at the nursing home for nearly three more years before he finally moved me over here. And there's no telling how long it'll be before I move up again."

"But don't you think it was worth it?" I couldn't help asking. "The grandmother had already lived her life, but the little girl was just starting. You saved her life!"

The reaper shook his head slowly, blond curls glimmering in the light overhead. "It wasn't an even exchange. From the moment she was supposed to die, that little girl was living on borrowed time. Her grandmother's time. When you make an exchange, what you're really doing is trading one person's death date for another's. That little girl died six months later, on the day her grandmother was originally scheduled to go."

That time I couldn't stop the tears. "How can you stand it?" I wiped at my eyes angrily with the napkin Nash handed me, glad I wasn't wearing much mascara.

Tod glanced at Nash, then his expression softened when he turned back to me. "It's easier now that I'm used to it.

But at the time, I had to learn to trust the list. The master list is like the script from a play—it shows every word spoken by every actor, and the show keeps going so long as no one deviates from it."

"But that does happen, right?" I wadded the napkin into a tight ball. "Even if the list is infallible, the people aren't. A reaper could deviate from the list, like you did with the little girl, right?"

Nash shifted in his seat, drawing our attention before Tod could answer. "You think those girls died in place of people who were actually on the list? That they were exchanges?"

I shook my head. "Three in three days? It's still too much of a coincidence. But if Tod can deviate by not taking a soul, couldn't another reaper deviate by taking an extra one? Or three?"

"No." Tod shook his head firmly. "No way. The boss would notice if someone turned in three extra souls."

I arched one brow at him. "What makes you think he turned them in?"

The reaper's scowl deepened. "You don't know what you're talking about. It's impossible."

"There's a way to find out." Nash eyed me somberly before turning his penetrating gaze on Tod. "You're right—we can't get our hands on the list. But you can."

"No." Tod shoved his chair back and stood. Across the cafeteria, the mother and children looked up, one little boy smeared from ear to ear with chocolate ice cream.

"Sit down!" Nash hissed, glaring up at him.

Tod shook his head and started to turn away from us, so I grabbed his hand. He froze the minute my flesh touched his and turned back to me gradually, as if every movement hurt. "Please." I begged him with my eyes. "Just hear him out."

The reaper slowly pulled his fingers from my grasp, until my hand hung in the air, empty and abandoned. He looked both angry and terrified when he sank back into his seat, now more than a foot from the table.

"We don't need to see the whole thing," Nash began. "Just the part from this weekend. Saturday, Sunday, and today."

"I can't do it." He shook his head again, blond curls bouncing. "You don't understand what you're asking for."

"So tell us." I folded my hands on the table, making it clear that I had time for a long story. Even if I didn't.

Tod exhaled heavily and aimed his answer at me, pointedly ignoring Nash. "You're not talking about just one list. 'Master list' is a misnomer. It's actually lots of lists. There's a new master for every day, and my boss splits that up into zone, then shift. I only see the part for this hospital, from noon to midnight. There's another reaper who works here the other half of the day, and I never see anything on his lists, much less the lists for other zones. It's not like I can just walk up to a coworker and ask to see his old lists. Especially if he's actually reaping 'independently.'"

"He's right. That's too complicated." Nash sighed, closing his eyes. Then he opened them again and looked at me resolutely. "We need the master list."

Tod groaned and opened his mouth to argue, but I beat him to it. "No, we don't. We don't even need to see it."

"What?" Nash frowned, and I raised one finger, asking him silently to wait as I turned back to the reaper.

"I understand that you don't work off the master list, but you've seen it, right? You said there are murder victims on it every week...?"

"Yeah, I see it every now and then." Tod shrugged. "It's all digital now, and my boss keeps it running on his computer all the time, in case he has to adjust anything. I glance at it when I go in his office."

"Okay, that's good." I couldn't resist a small smile. "We don't need to see it. We just need you to look at it and tell us whether or not these three names were there."

Tod leaned forward with his elbows on his knees, cradling his head in his hands. He rubbed his forehead, then took a deep, resigned breath and finally looked up at me. "Where did they die?"

"The first one was in the West End, at Taboo. Heidi...?" Nash glanced at me with his brows arched.

"Anderson," I supplied. "The second was Alyson Baker, at the Cinemark in Arlington, and the third was at East Lake High School, just this afternoon."

"Wait, those are all in different zones." Tod frowned, and the well-defined muscles of his arms tensed as he leaned against the table. "If you really think none of them were supposed to die, you're talking about three different reapers involved in this little conspiracy. Which is starting to sound pretty complicated, by the way."

"Hmm…" I didn't know enough about reapers to know how far-fetched a theory we were talking about, but I did know that the more people who were in on a secret, the harder it was to keep quiet. Tod was right. So…maybe we were only looking for one reaper, after all. "Is there anything keeping one of you guys from operating in someone else's zone?"

"Other than integrity and fear of being caught? No."

Grim reaper integrity…?

"So if a reaper has neither integrity nor fear, there's nothing to stop him from taking out half the state of Texas next time he gets road rage in rush hour traffic?" I heard my pitch rising, and made myself lower my voice as I screwed the lid off my Coke. "Don't you guys have to turn in your…um…death ray, or whatever, when you're off the clock?"

Tod's perfect lips quirked up in a quick smile. "Um, no. There's no death ray, though that would be really cool. Reapers don't use any equipment. All we have is an ability to extinguish life and take possession of the soul. But trust me, that's more than enough."

With that, his expression darkened. "In theory, you should never find a reaper without integrity. It's not like we apply for this job to satisfy some kind of massive power hunger. We're recruited, and screened for every psychological condition known to man. No one capable of something like you're talking about should ever find work as a reaper."

"You sound less than confident in the system," I said, watching his face carefully.

He shrugged. "You said it yourself. People aren't infallible, and the system is run by people."

"So can you get a look at the lists?" Nash said, watching Tod almost as closely as I did.

Tod bit his lower lip in thought. "You're talking about three different zones, for three different days—and none of them on the current master list."

"So can you do it?" I repeated, leaning forward in anticipation.

Tod nodded slowly. "It won't be easy, but I like a challenge. So long as it pays off." His blue-eyed gaze zeroed in on me, and something told me he was no longer talking about poking around in his boss's office. "I'll get you what you want to know—in exchange for your name."

"No." Nash didn't even hesitate. "You'll do it because if you don't, we'll hang out here and she'll suspend every soul you try to take until you're so far behind schedule your boss sends you back to the nursing home. If you're lucky."

"Right." Tod smirked now as his gaze shifted from me to Nash. "She's so green her roots are showing. I bet she's never even seen a soul."

"He's right," I said. Nash snatched my hand from the table and squeezed it hard, begging me silently not to give Tod what he wanted. But I saw no reason not to. My name would be easy to figure out, which made it a cheap price for the information we needed. "My first name is Kaylee. You can have my last name when you give us what we want."

"Deal." Tod stood, beaming as if his face gave off its own glow. "I'll let you know what I find out, but I can't promise it'll be tonight. I'm already late for that aneurism."

I nodded, disappointed but not really surprised.

"Now, if you'll excuse me, I have to go make some poor woman a widow." And with that, he disappeared.

There was no chiming of bells, no twinkling of light. No signal at all that he was about to vanish. He was simply there one moment, and gone the next, with no special—or sound—effects of any kind.

"You didn't tell me he could do that!" I glanced at Nash to find him frowning at the table. "What's wrong?"

"Nothing." He stood and picked up the paper plate still holding his last bite of cake. "Let's go." We threw our trash away on our way out of the cafeteria, and I followed him across the hospital and through the parking garage in silence. *Guess he* really *didn't want Tod to know my name...*

When we reached the car, Nash followed me to the passenger's side door, where he unlocked and opened it for me. But instead of getting in, I turned to face him and put one hand flat on his chest. "You're mad at me." My heart beat so hard my chest ached. I could feel his heart thumping beneath my palm, and for one horrifying moment, I was sure I'd never get to feel it again. That he would simply drive me home, then vanish from my life like Tod had vanished from the cafeteria.

But Nash shook his head slowly. He was backlit by an overhead light near the entrance, and his dark hair seemed to glow around the edges. "I'm mad at him. I should have come by myself, but I didn't think he'd be interested in you."

My eyebrows shot up and I stepped to the side to see him better. "Because I'm a shrieking hag?"

Nash pulled me close again and pressed me into the car, then kissed me so deeply I wasn't sure if I was actually breathing. "You have no idea how beautiful you are," he said. "But Tod's been hung up on someone else for a long time, so I thought you'd be safe. I should have known better."

"Why didn't you want him to know my name?"

Nash leaned back to see me better, and the line of his jaw went hard. "Because he's Death, Kaylee. No matter how innocent he looks, or how desperately he clings to the notion that he's some kind of afterlife hero, carting helpless souls from point A to point B, he's still a reaper. One day he might find your name on his list. And while I know that keeping your name a secret won't save you if that happens, I'm not just going to hand over your identity to one of Death's gophers."

"He knows your name." I let my hand trail from his chest down his arm until my fingers curled around his.

"I knew him before he was a reaper."

"You did?" It hadn't occurred to me until then that Tod might have had a normal life once. What were reapers like before they surrounded themselves with death and the dying?

Nash nodded, and I opened my mouth to ask another question, but he laid one finger against my lips. "I don't want to talk about Tod anymore."

"Fair enough," I mumbled against his finger. Then I removed his hand and stepped up on my toes. "I don't want to talk about him either." I kissed him, and my pulse went crazy when he responded. His tongue met mine briefly, then his lips trailed over my chin and down my neck.

"Mmm…" I murmured into his hair, as his tongue flicked in the hollow of my collarbone. Chill bumps popped up on my arms, and my hands went around his back. My fingers splayed over the material of his shirt. "That feels good."

"You taste good," he whispered against my skin. But before I could respond, an engine growled to life a row away, and light washed over us both, momentarily blinding me. Nash straightened, moaning in frustration as the car across the aisle pulled toward us before turning toward the exit. "I guess I should take you home," he said, shading his face with one hand while the other remained on my arm.

I blinked, trying to clear floating circles of light from my eyes. "I don't want to go home. My entire family has been lying to me my whole life. I don't have anything to say to them."

"Don't you want to know why they've been lying to you?"

I blinked at him, taken by surprise for a moment. I hadn't considered simply confronting them with the truth. They'd *never* see that coming.

A slow smile spread across my face, and I saw it reflected in Nash's. "Let's go."

12

"You're coming in, right?" I asked when Nash shifted into Park but left the engine running.

There wasn't enough light in the driveway for me to truly see his eyes, but I knew he was watching me. "You want me to?"

Did I?

A slim silhouette appeared in the front window: Aunt Val, one hand on her narrow hip, the other holding an oversize mug. They were waiting to talk to me. Or more likely *at* me, because they probably had no intention of telling me the truth, since they didn't know someone else already had.

"Yeah, I do."

It wasn't that I needed him to fight my battles. I was actually looking forward to demanding some long-overdue answers, now that the big lie—aka my entire life—had been exposed.

But I could certainly have used a little moral support.

Nash smiled, his teeth a dim white wedge among shadows, and twisted the key to shut down the engine.

We met at the front of the car and he took my hand, then leaned forward to brush a kiss against the back of my jaw, just below my left ear. Even as I stood in my driveway, knowing my aunt and uncle were waiting, his touch made me shiver in anticipation of more.

I'm not crazy. I knew that now. And I wasn't alone— Nash was like me. Even so, dread was a plastic spork slowly digging out my insides as I pulled open the front door, then the screen. I stepped into the tiled entry and tugged Nash in after me.

My aunt stood in the middle of the floor, a frail mask of reproach poorly disguising whatever stronger, more urgent sentiment peeked out around the edges. My uncle rose from the couch immediately, taking us both in with a single glance. To his credit, the first expression to flit across his features was relief. He'd been worried, probably because I hadn't answered any of the twelve messages he'd left on my silenced cell.

But his relief didn't last long. Now that he knew I was alive, he looked ready to kill me himself.

Uncle Brendon's anger lingered on me, then more than a bit of it transferred when his focus shifted to Nash.

"It's late. I'm sure Kaylee will see you at the memorial tomorrow."

Aunt Val only sipped her coffee—or maybe "coffee"—offering me no help.

Nash looked to me for a decision, and my tight grip on his hand demonstrated my resolve. "Uncle Brendon, this is Nash Hudson. I need to ask you some questions, and he's going to stay. Or else I go with him."

My uncle's dark brows drew low and his gaze hardened—but then his eyes went wide in surprise. "Hudson?" He studied Nash more carefully now, and sudden recognition lit his face. "You're Trevor and Harmony's boy?"

What? My gaze bounced between them in confusion. On my left, Aunt Val coughed violently and pounded on her own chest. She'd choked on her "coffee."

"You know each other?" I asked, but Nash looked as clueless as I felt.

"I knew your parents years ago," Uncle Brendon said to Nash. "But I had no idea your mother was back in the area." He shoved both hands into the pockets of his jeans, and the uncertain gesture made my uncle look even younger than usual. "I was so sorry to hear about your father."

"Thank you, sir." Nash nodded, his jaw tense, both his motion and words well practiced.

Uncle Brendon turned back to me. "Your friend's father was…" And that's when it hit him. His face flushed, and his expression seemed to darken. "You told her."

Nash nodded again, holding his gaze boldly. "She has a right to know."

"And obviously neither of you were going to tell me."

Aunt Val sank into the nearest armchair and drained her mug, then almost dropped it onto a coaster.

"Well, I can't say this is entirely unexpected. Your dad's already on his way here to explain everything." My uncle's hands hovered at his sides, as if he didn't quite know what to do with them. Then he sighed and nodded to himself, like he'd come to some kind of decision. "Sit down. Please. I'm sure you both have questions."

"Can I get anyone a drink?" Aunt Val rose unsteadily, her empty mug in hand.

"Yeah." I gave her a saccharine smile. "I'll have whatever you're having."

She frowned—for once unconcerned with the wrinkles etched into her forehead—then made her way slowly into the kitchen.

"I'd love some coffee," Uncle Brendon called after her as he sank into the floral-print armchair, but his wife disappeared around the corner with no reply.

I dropped onto the sofa and Nash sat next to me, and in the sudden silence I realized my cousin hadn't come out to interrogate me or flirt with him. And no music came from her room. No sound at all, in fact. "Where's Sophie?"

Uncle Brendon sighed heavily and seemed to sink deeper into the chair. "She doesn't know about any of this. She's asleep."

"Still?"

"Again. Val woke her up for dinner, but she hardly ate anything. Then she took another of those damned pills and went back to bed. I ought to flush the rest of them." He mumbled the last part beneath his breath, but we both heard him.

And I agreed with him wholeheartedly on that one, if on little else at the moment.

Fueling bravado with my smoldering anger, I pinned my uncle with the boldest stare I could manage. "So I'm not human?"

He sighed. "You never were one to beat around the bush."

I only stared at him, unwilling to be distracted by pointless chatter. And when my uncle began to speak, I clutched Nash's hand harder than ever.

"No, technically we're not human," he said. "But the distinction is very minor."

"Right." I rolled my eyes. "Except for all the death and screaming."

"So you're a *bean sidhe* too, right?" Nash interjected, oiling the wheels of discourse with more civility than I could have mustered in that moment. At least one of us was calm….

"Yes. As is Kaylee's father, my brother." Uncle Brendon met my eyes again then, and I knew what he was going to say from the cautious sympathy shining in his eyes. "As was your mother."

This wasn't about my mom. So far as I knew, she'd never lied to me. "What about Aunt Val?"

"Human." She answered for herself, stepping into the living room with a steaming cup of coffee in each hand. She crossed the carpet cautiously and handed one mug to my uncle before sinking carefully into the armchair across from his. "And so is Sophie."

"Are you sure?" Nash frowned. "Maybe she just hasn't had an opportunity for any premonitions yet."

"She was there with Meredith this afternoon," I reminded him.

"Oh, yeah."

"We've known from the moment she was born," my aunt said, as if neither of us had spoken.

"How?" I asked, as she slowly, carefully crossed one leg over the other.

Aunt Val lifted the mug to her lips, then spoke over it. "She cried." She sipped her coffee, her eyes not quite focused on the wall over my head. "Female *bean sidhes* don't cry at birth."

"Seriously?" I glanced at Nash for confirmation, but he only shrugged, apparently as surprised as I was.

Uncle Brendon eyed his wife in mounting concern, then turned back to us. "They may have tears, but a *bean sidhe* never truly screams until she sings for her first soul."

"Wait, that can't be right." I'd cried plenty as a child, hadn't I? Surely at my mother's funeral…?

Okay, I couldn't actually remember much from that

age, but I knew for a fact that I'd screamed bloody murder
when I rode my bike off the sidewalk and into a rose bush,
at eight years old. And again at eleven, when I accidentally ripped a hoop earring through my earlobe with a
hairbrush. And again when I'd been dumped for the first
time, at fourteen.

How long had I been making fatal predictions, without even knowing it? Had I thrown inconsolable fits in
preschool? Or had my youth largely kept me away from
death? How long had they been treating me like I was
crazy, when they knew what was wrong with me all
along?

My spine stiffened, and I felt my cheeks flush in anger.
Every answer my uncle provided only brought up more
questions, about things I should have known all along.
"Why didn't you tell me?" I demanded, teeth clenched to
keep me from yelling and waking Sophie up. I'd missed so
much. Wasted countless hours doubting my own sanity.

When what I really should have been doubting was my
humanity!

"I'm so sorry, Kaylee. I wanted to." Uncle Brendon
closed his eyes as if he were gathering his thoughts, then
met mine again, and to my surprise, I realized I believed
him. "I started to tell you last year, when you were…in the
hospital. But your dad asked me not to. The damage was
already done, and he hoped we could wait a little longer.
At least until you finished high school."

That's what they'd hoped I'd have more time for! Not

life, but a normal, human adolescence. A noble thought, but somewhat lacking in the execution…

"I'm surprised your little farce held up this long!" I found myself on the edge of the couch as I spoke, Nash's hand still grasped in mine. He was the only thing keeping me seated as I vented the geyser of anger and resentment threatening to burst through the top of my skull. "How long did you think it would be before I'd run into someone on the verge of death?"

Uncle Brendon shrugged miserably but held my gaze. "Most teenagers never see anyone die. We were hoping you'd be that fortunate, and we could wait and let your dad explain all this… later. When you were ready."

"When I was ready? I was ready last year, when I saw a bald kid in a wheelchair being pushed through the mall in his own private death shroud! You were waiting for *him* to be ready." For my father to finally step up and earn his title.

"She's right, Brendon," Aunt Val slurred, now slumped in her chair, her linen-clad legs splayed gracelessly. I watched her, waiting for more, but turned back to my uncle when she lifted her mug to her mouth instead of speaking.

"Why keep it a secret in the first place?"

"Because you—" Aunt Val began again, gesturing in grand sweeps with her half-empty mug. But my uncle cut her off with a stern look.

"That's for your father to explain."

"It's not like he hasn't had time!" I snapped. "He's had sixteen years."

Uncle Brendon nodded, and I read regret on his face. "I know—we all have. And considering how you wound up figuring it out—" he glanced apologetically at Nash "—I think we were wrong to wait so long. But your dad will be here in the morning, and I'm not going to step on his toes with the rest of it. It's his story to tell."

There was a story? Not just a simple explanation, but an actual story?

"He's really coming?" I'd believe that when I saw him. Yet my chest tightened, shot through with a jolt of adrenaline at the thought: my dad had answers no one else seemed willing to give me. But I might have known it would take an all-out catastrophe to get him stateside again. He wasn't coming to see me. He was coming to do damage control, before my aunt reversed the charges.

Uncle Brendon frowned at my obvious skepticism—he could probably see it swirling in my eyes. "We called him this afternoon—"

"*I* called him," Aunt Val corrected. "I told him to put his ass on a plane, or I'd…"

"You've had enough." My uncle was on his feet before I could blink, and an instant later he held his wife's mug. She slouched in her chair, eyes wide in sluggish surprise, hand still curved, as if around the cup handle. "I'll get you some fresh coffee." He stopped in the threshold between the living room and dining room, Aunt Val's mug gripped so tightly his knuckles were white. "I'm sorry," he said to Nash. "My wife isn't taking any of this well. She's worried about the girls, and she's a friend of Meredith Cole's mother."

Yeah, but she and Mrs. Cole were gym buddies, not conjoined twins. And I'd hardly ever seen my aunt drink more than a single glass of wine at a time—she said alcohol had too many calories.

Nash nodded. "My mother would be upset too."

Yeah, but I bet she wouldn't be drowning in brandy....

"How is your mother?"

"She still misses him." Nash glanced at our entwined hands, obviously uncomfortable talking about his own family.

Uncle Brendon's expression softened in sympathy. "Of course she does." Then he turned into the kitchen and let the subject rest.

For a moment, we stared at the carpet in silence, not quite sure what to say next. We'd hit a lull in the single most awkward conversation of my life, and I wasn't exactly eager to pick it back up.

But Aunt Val obviously was. "She wouldn't have liked this." Her gaze was focused on the floor several feet in front of her chair, her arms draped over the sides, hands dangling. I'd never seen her look so...aimless. Limp.

"My mom?" Nash asked, confused, but I knew what she meant. She was talking about *my* mother.

"Wouldn't have liked what?" I asked, curious in spite

of my lingering anger. No one ever seemed willing to talk about my mom in front of me.

"If it had gone the other way, she would have told you the truth. But Aiden couldn't face it. He was never as strong as she was." Aunt Val's gaze found me, and I was startled by the sudden clarity in her eyes. The unexpected intensity shining through a glaze of intoxication. "I never met anyone stronger than Darby. I wanted to be just like her until—"

"Valerie!" Uncle Brendon stood frozen in the doorway, a fresh—presumably un-spiked—mug of coffee in one hand.

"Until what?" I glanced from one to the other.

"Nothing. She doesn't know what she's saying." He set the mug on the nearest end table—without a coaster—and crossed the room in a blur of denim, practically exhaling frustration and anxiety. Uncle Brendon lifted his wife from her chair with an arm around her shoulders, and she tottered unsteadily, lending credence to his claim.

Yet despite her wobbly legs, her eyes were steady when they met his, and his silent censure did not escape her notice. But neither did it make her retract her statement. Whatever had just passed between them, it was crystal clear that Aunt Val did in fact know what she was saying.

Uncle Brendon half carried his wife toward the hallway. "I'm going to get her settled in for the night. It was good to meet you, Nash, and please give my best to your mother." He glanced pointedly at me, then at the door.

Evidently visiting hours were over.

"Uncle Brendon?" I had one question that couldn't wait for my father, and I wanted to be holding Nash's hand when I heard the answer, just in case.

My uncle hesitated in the doorway, and Aunt Val laid her head on his shoulder, her eyes already closed. "Yeah?"

I took a deep breath. "What did Aunt Val mean when she said I'm living on borrowed time?"

Comprehension washed over him like waves smoothing out sand on the beach. "You heard us this afternoon?"

I nodded, and my hand tightened around Nash's.

A pained look chased his smile away, and he pulled Aunt Val straighter against him. "That's part of your father's story. Have a little patience and let him tell it. And try to trust me—Val really doesn't know what she's talking about."

I exhaled in disappointment. "Fine." That was the best I was going to get; I could already tell. Fortunately, my father would be there in the morning, and this time I wouldn't let him leave without answering every one of my questions.

"Get some sleep, Kaylee. You too, Nash. With the memorial, tomorrow probably won't be any easier than today was."

We both nodded, and Uncle Brendon lifted Aunt Val into his arms—she was snoring lightly now—and carried her down the hall.

"Wow." Nash whistled as I fell back against the arm of the couch facing him. "How much has she had?"

"No telling. She doesn't drink much, though, so it probably doesn't take much to lay her out cold, and she started this afternoon."

"My mom just bakes when she gets upset. Some weeks I live on brownies and chocolate milk."

I grinned. "Trade ya." Aunt Val would rather shoot herself than touch a stick of real butter, much less a bag of chocolate chips. Her theory was that not knowing how to bake saved her thousands of calories a month.

My theory was that for all the brandy she'd had in the past eight hours, she could have had a whole pan of brownies.

"I like brownies. You're stuck with your aunt."

"Yeah, I figured."

Nash stood, and I followed him to the door, my arm threaded through his. "I gotta get Scott's car back before he calls the cops," he said. I walked him out, and when we stopped by the driver's side door, I wrapped my arms around his waist as his went around my back. He felt sooo good, and the thought that I could touch him anytime I wanted sent a whole flock of butterflies fluttering around in my stomach.

I leaned back against the car, and Nash leaned into me. His mouth met mine, and my lips opened, welcoming him. Feeding from him. When his kisses trailed down my chin to my neck, I let my head fall back, grateful for the night air cooling the heat he brought off me in waves. His lips were hot, and the trail of his kisses burned down my throat and over my collarbone.

Each breath came faster than the last. Every kiss, every flick of his tongue against my skin, scalded me in the most delicious way. His fingers trailed up from my waist as his lips dipped lower, pushing aside the neckline of my shirt.

Whoa… "Nash." I put my hands on his shoulders.

"Mmm?"

"Hey…" I pushed against him, and he rose to meet my own heated gaze, his irises churning furiously in the light from the porch. Was this because we were two of a kind? This irresistible urge to touch each other?

My racing pulse slowed as my heart began to ache. Was it really me he wanted, or did our mutual species throw our hormones into overdrive? Would he want me if I were human?

Did that even matter? I *wasn't* human. Neither was he.

"You want me to pick you up for the memorial?"

His eyes narrowed in confusion over my abrupt subject change. Then he inhaled deeply, slowed the churning in his eyes, and settled against the car next to me. "What about your dad?"

"He can drive himself."

Nash rolled his eyes. "I didn't think you'd want to go, with your dad in town."

"I'm going. And I'm going to drag my dad and uncle along too."

He arched his brows, sliding one arm around my waist. "Why?"

"Because if some vigilante reaper is after teenage girls, I figure he'll find an auditorium full of us pretty hard to resist. And the more *bean sidhes* that are present, the greater the chance one of us will get a look at him, right?"

"In theory." Nash frowned down at me, and I could feel a "but" coming. "But, Kaylee—" I grinned, mildly amused at having predicted something other than death "—it'not going to happen again. Not this soon. Not in the same place."

"It's happened for the past three days in a row, Nash, and it's always happened where there are large groups of teenagers. The memorial will have the highest concentration of us in one room since graduation last year. There's just as much chance he'll pick someone there as anywhere else."

"So what if he does? What are you going to do?" Nash demanded in a harsh whisper. He glanced over my shoulder to make sure no one had appeared on the porch, then met my eyes again, and I realized that behind his sudden anger lay true fear.

I knew I should have been scared too, and in truth, I was. The very concept of reapers running around harvesting their metaphysical crop from empty human husks made my stomach pitch and my chest tighten. And the

"What risks?" Wasn't the exchange rate bad enough? A new thread of unease wound its way up my spine, and I leaned against the car beside him, watching light from the porch illuminate one half of his face while rendering the other side a shadowy compilation of vague, strong features. I was pretty sure that if whatever he was about to say was as weird as finding out I was a *bean sidhe,* I'd need Carter's car at my back to hold me up.

Nash's gaze captured mine, his eyes churning in what could only be fear. "*Bean sidhes* and reapers aren't the only ones out there, Kaylee. There are other things. Things I don't have names for. Things that you don't ever want to see, much less be seen by."

My skin crawled at his phrasing. *Well,* that's *more than a little scary.* Yet incredibly vague. "Okay, so where are these phantom creepies?"

"Most of them are in the Netherworld."

"And where is that?" I crossed my arms over my chest, and my elbow bumped Carter's side-view mirror. "Because it sounds like a Peter Pan ride." Yet my sarcasm was a thin veil for the icy fingers of unease now crawling inside my flesh. It might have been easy to dismiss claims of this other world as horror movie fodder—if I hadn't just discovered I wasn't human.

"This isn't funny, Kaylee. The Netherworld is here with us, but not really *here.* It's anchored to our world, but deeper than humans can see. If that makes sense."

"Not much," I said, but with the skepticism gone, my

idea of actually looking for one of those reapers… Well, that was crazy.

But not as crazy as letting another innocent girl die. Not if we could stop it.

I watched Nash, letting my intent show on my face. Letting determination churn slowly in my eyes.

"No!" He looked toward the house again, then back at me, his irises roiling. "You heard what Tod said," he whispered fiercely. "Any reaper willing to steal unauthorized souls won't hesitate to take one of ours instead."

"We can't just let him kill someone else," I hissed, just as urgently. I resisted the urge to step back, half-afraid that any physical space I put between us during an argument would translate into an emotional distance.

"We don't have any choice," he said. I started to argue, but he cut me off, running one hand through his chunky brown hair. "Okay, look, I didn't want to have to go into this right now I figured finding out you're not human was enough to deal with in one day. But there's a lot you still don't understand, and your uncle's probably going to explain all this soon, anyway." He sighed and leaned back against the car, his eyes closed as if he were gathering his thoughts. And when he met my gaze again, I saw that his determination now matched my own.

"What we can do together?" He gestured back and forth between us with one hand. "Restoring a soul? It's more complicated than it sounds, and there are risks beyond the exchange rate."

voice sounded thin and felt empty. "How do we know this Netherworld and its…Nether-people are there, if we can't see them?"

Nash frowned. "We *can* see them—we're not human." Like I needed another reminder of that. "But only when you're singing for someone's soul. And that's the only time they can see you."

And suddenly I remembered. The dark thing scuttling in the alley when I was keening for Heidi Anderson. The movement on the edge of my vision when Meredith's soul song threatened to leak out. I had seen something, even without actually giving in to the wail.

That's why Uncle Brendon had told me to hold it in. He was afraid I would see too much.

And maybe that too much would see me.

13

NASH MUST HAVE SEEN understanding on my face—and near panic—because he wrapped one arm around my waist and pulled me closer across the waxed surface of Carter's car. "It's not as bad as it sounds. An experienced *bean sidhe* knows how to stay safe. But we're not experienced, Kaylee." It was nice of him to include himself in that statement, but we both knew I was the newbie. "Besides, we don't even know for sure that those girls weren't on the list. This is all still theory. A very unlikely, dangerous theory."

"We'll know once Tod calls," I insisted, the new information spinning around in my head, complicating what I'd thought I was prepared to do, should intervention prove necessary.

"That might not be tonight."

"It will be." He'd find out for us. Soon. Whether we'd

actually gotten through to him, or he just really wanted my last name, I'd known in the instant before he'd disappeared that he would get us the information. "Call me as soon as you hear from him. Please."

He hesitated, then nodded. "But you have to promise you won't do anything dangerous, no matter what he says. No soul singing by yourself."

Like I'd admit it if I were planning something risky. Besides… "I have no desire to see this Netherworld on my own. And my little talent's no good without yours anyway, right?"

"Good point." He relaxed a little then, and kissed me good-night. I held him tight when he started to pull away, clinging to the taste and the feel of all things good and safe. Nash had become a shining tower of sanity in this new world of unprecedented chaos and unseen peril. And I didn't want to let him go.

Unfortunately, in the world of curfews and alarm clocks, he couldn't stay.

I closed and locked the door behind him, and watched through the front window until he backed out of the driveway and drove out of sight. I was pulling the curtains closed when something creaked behind me. "Kaylee?" I jumped and whirled to find my uncle standing in the hallway threshold, watching me.

"Jeez, Uncle Brendon, you scared the crap out of me!"

His smile was more of a grimace. "You're not the only one around here with big ears."

"Yeah, well it's not the big ears that worry me so much as the big *mouths,*" I said, grateful that I could hear Sophie snoring again, now that the rest of the house was quiet. I padded across the carpet toward my uncle, then stepped around him and into the hall, desperately hoping he was bluffing. That he hadn't actually heard my little argument with Nash.

He followed me to my room, and when I tried to swing the door shut behind me, his palm smacked into the hollow wood panel, holding it firmly open. "What's going on, Kaylee?"

"Nothing." Going for nonchalance, I kicked first one sneaker then the other onto the floor of my closet.

"I heard you two talking." He leaned against the door frame, thick arms crossed over a broad chest, still well defined after who-knows-how-many years of life. "What are you planning at the memorial, and who's Tod?"

Well, crap. I shoved aside a pile of clean, unfolded clothes Aunt Val had dumped on my bed at some point and sank onto the comforter, my mind whirling in search of an answer that was at least as much truth as it was fabrication. But I came up empty. Nothing I made up would ring true to him, especially considering he knew more about *bean sidhes* than I knew about…anything.

So maybe I should just tell him the truth…. That way, if the rogue reaper *did* show up at the memorial and Nash refused to help me out of some misguided attempt to protect me, surely Uncle Brendon would step in. He might act tough, but inside he was a big teddy bear, and he could no more watch an innocent girl die before her time than I could.

"You sure you want to hear this?" I pulled my legs beneath me on the bed, fiddling with the frayed hem of my jeans.

Uncle Brendon shook his head. "I'm pretty sure I *don't* want to. But go ahead."

"You might want to sit," I warned him, reaching to pluck my iPod from my pillow. The earbuds had gotten tangled again; I guess that's what I get for falling asleep wearing them.

My uncle shrugged, then settled into my desk chair, waiting with his arms still crossed over his chest.

"Okay, here's the deal. And I'm only telling you this because I know you'll do the right thing. So technically, I think my voluntary disclosure exempts me from any penalty for what I'm about to admit."

His lips quirked, as if a smile had been vetoed at the last minute. "Go on..."

I inhaled and held the next breath for a moment, wondering where best to begin. But there *was* no good place to start, so I dove in, hoping my good intentions would bail me out during the less altruistic parts of the story. "Meredith Cole wasn't the first one."

"She wasn't your first premonition?" He didn't look surprised. Of course, he *couldn't* have forgotten the other times—including the incident preceding my trip to the hospital.

"That too. But, I mean, she wasn't the first girl to die *this week.* There was one Saturday night and one yesterday afternoon. It happened the same way with all three girls."

"And you predicted them all?" *Now* he looked surprised, his forehead crinkled, brows furrowed.

"No, I never even saw the second one." I glanced at my lap, avoiding his eyes while my fingers worked nervously at the earbuds, trying to produce two separate wires from a knot any sailor would have been proud of. "But I saw the girl who died on Saturday, and knew it was going to happen. Same thing with Meredith this afternoon." Which I assumed Aunt Val had told him.

"Wait, Saturday night?" The ladder-backed chair creaked and I looked up as he leaned forward to eye me in growing suspicion. "I thought you stayed home."

I shrugged and raised one brow at him. "I thought I was human."

My uncle frowned but nodded, as if to say he'd earned that one. Still, I couldn't believe Aunt Val hadn't ratted on me. As cool as that was of her, I couldn't help wondering *why.* Had all the "coffee" made her forget my indiscretion?

"So where did this first girl die?" He leaned back again, crossing thick arms over his chest. "Where did you go?"

Suddenly the wires now tangled around my fingers

seemed fascinating… "Taboo, this dance club in the West End. But—"

He scowled, and even with thick brown brows casting shadows across his eyes, I thought I saw some movement of the green in his irises. *I know that never happened before. I would have noticed.* "How did you even get into a nightclub?" he demanded. "Do you have a fake ID?"

I rolled my eyes. "No, I just snuck in through the back." Sort of… "But that's not really the point," I rushed on, hoping he'd be distracted by the next part. "One of the girls in the club was…*dark.* Like she was wearing shadows no one else could see. And when I looked at her, I knew she was going to die, and that panic—or premonition, or whatever it is—came on hard and fast, just like last time. It was horrible. But I didn't know I'd been right—that she'd actually died—until I saw the story on the news yesterday morning." Speaking of which… "Are the others dead too? The ones I saw last year?" My fingers stilled in my lap as I stared at my uncle, begging him, *daring* him to tell me the truth.

He looked sad, like he didn't want to have to say it, but there was no doubt in his eyes. Nor any hesitation. "Yes."

"How do you know?"

He smiled almost bitterly. "Because you girls are never wrong."

Great. Morbid *and* accurate. *Sounds like the sales pitch for a county-fair fortune-teller…*

"Anyway, after I saw the news yesterday morning, I kind of freaked. And then it happened again that afternoon, and things got *really* weird."

"But you didn't predict that one, right?"

I nodded and dropped my hopelessly knotted earbuds in my lap. "I heard about that one secondhand, but had to look up the story online. This girl in Arlington died exactly like the girl at Taboo. And like Meredith. They all three just fell over dead, with no warning. Does that sound normal to you?"

"No." To his credit, my uncle didn't even hesitate. "But that doesn't rule out coincidence. How much did Nash tell you about what we can do?"

"Everything important, I hope." And even if he'd left some gaps, that was much better than the *canyons* my own family had created in my self-awareness. Not to mention my psyche.

Uncle Brendon's eyes narrowed in doubt, and he crossed one ankle over the opposite knee. "Did he mention what happens to a person's soul when he dies?"

"Yeah. That's where Tod comes in."

"Who's Tod?"

"The reaper who works at the hospital. He's stuck there because he let this little girl live once when she was supposed to die, and his boss killed the girl's grandmother instead. But anyway—"

Uncle Brendon shot out of the chair, his face flushed so

red I thought he might be having an aneurism. Did *bean sidhes* have aneurisms?

"Nash took you to see a *reaper?*" He stomped across my rug, gesturing angrily with both arms. "Do you have any *idea* how dangerous that is?" I tried to answer, but he barreled forward, stopping at the end of my bed to stare down at me as he ranted. "Reapers don't like *bean sidhes*. Our abilities are at odds with theirs, and most of them feel very threatened by us. Going to see a reaper is like walking into a police station waving a loaded *shotgun*."

"I know." I shrugged, trying to placate him. "But Nash knew this guy before he was a reaper. They're friends—sort of."

"That may be what *he* thinks, but somehow I doubt Tod agrees." And he was pacing again, as if the faster he walked, the faster he could think. Though my doubts about that technique stemmed from personal experience.

"Well, he must, 'cause he's going to help us." No need to mention that his help stemmed more from my involvement in the matter than from Nash's.

"Help you with *what?*" Uncle Brendon froze halfway across the room, facing me, and this time his eyes were *definitely* swirling.

"Help us figure out what's going on. He's getting some information for us."

My uncle's expression darkened, and my breath hitched in my throat as the green in his irises churned so fast it made me dizzy. "What kind of information? Kaylee, what are you doing? I want the truth, and I want it right now or I swear you won't leave this house again until you turn twenty-one."

I had to smile at the irony of Uncle Brendon asking *me* for the truth. I sighed and sat straighter on the bed. "Okay, I'll tell you, but don't freak out. It's not as dangerous as it sounds—" *I hope* "—because there's this loophole in the exchange rate, and—"

"The exchange rate?" Uncle Brendon's face went from tomato-red to nuclear countdown in less than a second. And then there was more pacing. *"This* is why we wanted your father to be the one to explain everything. Or at least me. That way we'd know how much you understand and what you're still clueless about."

"I'm not clueless." My temper spiked, and I stretched to drop my iPod on my nightstand before I accidentally crimped the cord.

"You are if you think you have any business even *contemplating* the exchange rate. You have no idea how dangerous messing in reaper business can be!"

"Ignorance is dangerous, Uncle Brendon. Don't you get it?" Standing, I grabbed a clean pair of jeans and shook them out harshly, pleased when the material snapped against itself, sharply accenting my anger. "Eventually, if the premonitions kept up, I would have been unable to hold back my song. I'd have wound up delaying some random reaper's schedule and really pissing him off—not to mention

whatever *other* invisible creepies are out there—with no idea what I was doing. See? The longer you all keep me bumbling around in the dark, the greater the chance that I'll stumble into something I don't understand. Nash knows that. He explained the possibilities *and* the consequences. He's arming me with knowledge because he understands that the best offense is knowing how to avoid trouble."

"From what I heard, it sounds more like you're out *looking* for trouble."

"Not trouble. The truth." I dropped the folded jeans on the end of the bed. "There's been precious little of that around here, and even now that I know what I am, you and Aunt Val are still keeping secrets."

He exhaled heavily and sat on the edge of my dresser, scruffing one hand through unkempt hair. "We're not keeping secrets from you. We're giving your dad a chance to act like a real father."

"Ha!" I stomped around the bed to put it between us, then snatched a long-sleeved tee from the pile. "He's had sixteen years. What makes you think he'll start now?"

"Give him a chance, Kaylee. He might surprise you."

"Not likely." I folded the shirt in several short, sharp motions, then tossed it on top of the jeans, where one arm flopped free to dangle over the side. "If Nash knew what my dad had to say, he'd tell me."

Uncle Brendon leaned forward and flipped the sleeve back on top of my shirt. "Nash should *never* have taken you to see a reaper, Kaylee. *Bean sidhes* have no natural defenses against most of the other things out there. That's why we live here, with the humans. The key to longevity lies in staying out of sight. In only meeting a reaper once in your life—at the very end."

"That's ridiculous!" I tossed another folded shirt onto the stack and tugged a pair of pajama pants from the pile. "A reaper can't touch you unless your name shows up on his list, and when that happens, there's nothing you can do to stop it. Avoiding reapers is pointless. Especially when they can *help* you." In theory. But wasn't my theory about the dead girls based on the suspicion that at least one reaper *had* strayed from his purpose?

"What truth is this reaper helping you look for?" Uncle Brendon sank back into the desk chair with a defeated-sounding sigh. He rubbed his temple as if his head ached, but I was *not* taking the blame for that. If every adult in my life hadn't been lying to me for thirteen years, none of this would have happened.

"He's sneaking a peek at the master list for the past three days, to find out if the dead girls were on it."

"He's *what?*" Uncle Brendon went totally, frighteningly still, and the only movement in the room was the tic developing on the outer edge of his left eyelid.

"Don't worry. He's not taking it. He's just going to look at it."

"Kaylee, that's not the point. What he's doing is dangerous, for all three of you. Reapers take their lists very seriously. People aren't supposed to know when they're going to die. That's why you can't warn them. Once you get a premonition, you can't speak, right?"

"Yeah." I plucked at some fuzz on the flannel pants, distinctly uncomfortable with the direction the discussion was now headed, and the guilt it brought on. "I tried to warn Meredith, but I knew if I opened my mouth, I'd only be able to scream."

Uncle Brendon nodded somberly. "There's a good reason for that. Grief consumes people. Imminent death *obsesses* people. It's bad enough for a person to know he's dying of terminal cancer, or something like that. But to know the exact moment? To have the date and time stamped on your brain, looming closer to you as life slips away? That would drive people crazy."

I gaped at him, pants clenched tightly in both hands. "You think I don't know that?"

"Of course you do." He ran one hand through thick brown hair, exhaling through his mouth in frustration. "You know it much better than I ever could, and it got you hospitalized."

"No, *you* and *Aunt Val* got me hospitalized." I couldn't let that one slide.

"Ultimately, yes." Uncle Brendon conceded the point with a single crisp nod. "But only because we couldn't help you on our own. We couldn't even calm you down. You screamed for more than an hour, long after the premonition passed, though I was probably the only one who could tell when that happened."

I turned and pulled open the top drawer of my dresser, then dropped the pj's inside. "How could you tell?"

"Male *bean sidhes* hear a female's wail as it truly sounds. After a while, yours changed from the soul song to regular screaming. You were terrified—hysterical—and we were afraid you'd hurt yourself. We didn't know what else to do."

"It didn't occur to you to talk to me? Tell me the truth?" I plucked several pairs of underwear from the pile and stuffed them into another drawer, then slammed it shut.

"I wanted to. I even *tried* to at one point, but you wouldn't listen. I doubt you could even hear me over your own screaming. I couldn't calm you down, even when I tried to Influence you."

"Nash could. He's done it twice now." I sank onto my bed at the memory, absently pulling another bundle of cloth onto my lap, placated by just thinking about Nash.

"He has?" A strange look passed over my uncle's face— some odd combination of surprise, wistfulness, and concern. "He's *Influenced* you?"

"Only to calm me during those two premonitions. Why?" And suddenly I understood what he was really asking. "No! He would never try to Influence me into doing something. He's not like that."

He seemed to consider my point for a moment, then finally nodded. "Good. I'm glad he can help you control your wail, even if he has to use his Influence. That's certainly better than the alternative." He smiled as if to set me at ease, but instead, the tense line of his mouth set me on edge. "But we've strayed from the point. Kaylee, you can't get involved in reaper business. And you certainly shouldn't have asked a reaper to spy on a coworker like that. If he gets caught, it won't be pretty. They'll probably fire him."

"So what?" What was one lost job compared to an innocent girl's *life?* Besides, losing a job wasn't the end of the world; Emma was proof of that. She'd lost one every couple of months for nearly a year until I'd gotten her hired at the Ciné. "Soul-snatching seems like a pretty specialized skill, and Nash says there are reapers all over the world. Surely he can find another job somewhere else. He doesn't like the hospital much, anyway."

Uncle Brendon closed his eyes and took a deep breath before meeting my gaze again. "Kaylee, you don't understand. There's no coming back once a reaper loses his position."

"Coming back? What does that mean? Coming back from what?"

"From the dead. Reapers are dead, Kaylee. The only thing keeping their bodies functioning and their souls inside is the job. Once a reaper loses that, it's all over."

"Nooo." The socks I'd been pairing dropped into my lap as I tried to wrap my mind around what he was saying.

So when Tod said he'd almost lost his job for letting the little girl live, what he meant was that he'd almost lost his *life*. And if he got caught spying for me, that's exactly what would happen.

Not cool. Not cool at all.

Why on earth had he said he'd do it? Surely not just for my name? I wasn't *that* interesting, and my name couldn't be too hard to find on his own. He already knew where I went to school.

"But we had to do it." I met Uncle Brendon's eyes, speaking the truth as soon as I recognized it. "We *had* to know if those girls were on the list. I don't think they were supposed to die, and we won't know for sure without a peek at the list."

However, my resolve wavered even as I spoke. It was the same old moral dilemma. Did I have the right to decide whether one life was worth risking another? A girl I might not even know, for a guy I'd only met once? An *already dead* guy, who'd surely known the risk when he agreed to it.

Suddenly nothing made sense. I knew in my heart that these girls weren't supposed to be dying, but trying to save the next one would expose me to creatures I couldn't even begin to imagine in a world I couldn't see, and put several other lives in danger. Including my own.

My shoulders fell and I stared at my uncle in almost paralyzing confusion. "So what am I supposed to do?" I hated how young and clueless I sounded, but he was right. I really had no idea what was going on, and all the good intentions in the world wouldn't mean a thing if I didn't know what to do with them.

"I don't think there's anything you can do, Kaylee." Uncle Brendon looked just as frustrated as I felt. "But we don't know there's anything actually wrong yet, and until we know for sure, you're just borrowing trouble."

I tried really hard to keep an open mind. Not to jump to conclusions. After all, I wasn't exactly rolling in evidence. All I had was a bad feeling and some soul-searing guilt. And even if I turned out to be right, my options were few and far between. Not to mention far-*fetched*. I'd just found out I was a *bean sidhe* and had yet to try out a single one of my purported skills. There was no guarantee I could do anything to save the next girl's life, even if it *was* wrongly endangered.

Maybe I should just stay out of reaper business. After all, it didn't really involve me.

Yet.

But what if it did soon? One girl from my school had already died, and there was no guarantee that wouldn't happen again. And it could happen to anyone. It could be me, or any one of my friends.

"But what if I am right? If these girls are dying before their time, I can't just stand by and let it happen again if I can possibly stop it. But I can't save anyone on my own, and pulling someone else into it will just put more people in danger." Like I'd risked Tod. And Nash.

"Well then, I think you have your answer. Even if you're

willing to risk yourself—and for the record, I will not let you do that so long as you're in my care—you have no right to risk anyone else."

I abandoned the laundry for my pillow, plucking anxiously at a feather sticking out through the pillowcase. "So I should just let an innocent girl die before her time?"

Uncle Brendon exhaled heavily. "No." He leaned forward with his elbows on his knees and took a long, deep breath. "I'll tell you what. When you hear back from this reaper, if it turns out that these girls weren't on the list, I'll look into it. With your father. On one condition. You swear to *stay out of it*."

"But—"

"No buts. Do we have a deal?" I opened my mouth to answer, but he interrupted. "And before you answer, think about Nash, and Tod, and whoever else you might be putting in danger if you try to handle this yourself."

I sighed. He knew he had me with that last bit. "Fine. I'll let you know what Tod finds out as soon as I know something."

"Thank you. I know none of this is easy for you." He stood and shoved his hands into his pockets as I dropped my socks into the open drawer behind me.

"Yeah, well, what's a little mental illness and pathological screaming among family?"

My uncle laughed, leaning against the door frame. "It could be worse. You could be an oracle."

"There are oracles?"

"Not many anymore, and most of those are truly certi-fiable. If you think predicting one death at a time is hard on your sanity, try knowing what's going to happen to everyone you meet, and being unable to turn the visions off."

I could only shudder at the thought. How could there be so much out there that I'd never known about? How could I not realize that half of my own family wasn't even human? Shouldn't the swirly eyes have clued me in?

"How come I never saw your eyes swirl before tonight?"

Uncle Brendon gave me a wistful smile. "Because I'm very old and have learned how to control my emotions, for the most part. Though that gets harder to do around you every day. I think that's part of why your dad stays away. When he looks at you, he sees your mother, and he can't hide his reaction. And if you saw his eyes, you'd have questions he wasn't ready to answer."

Well, not-answering was no longer an option…. "So how old are you? For real."

Uncle Brendon chuckled and glanced at the ground, and for a moment I thought he wouldn't answer—that I'd broken some kind of *bean sidhe* code of conduct by asking. But then he met my eyes, still smiling faintly. "I wondered how long that one would take you. I turned one hundred twenty-four last spring."

"Holy crap!" I felt my eyes go wide as his smile deepened. "You could have retired sixty years ago. Does Aunt Val know?"

"Of course. And she teases me mercilessly. The children from my first marriage are older than she is."

"You were married before?" I couldn't keep shock from my voice.

That longing smile was back. "In Ireland, half a century ago. We had to move every couple of decades to keep people from noticing that we didn't seem to age. My first wife died in Illinois twenty-four years ago, and our children—both *bean sidhes*—now have grandchildren of their own. Remind me and I'll show you pictures sometime."

I nodded, numb with surprise. "Wow. So are those kids any nicer than Sophie?" I couldn't help but ask.

Uncle Brendon gave me a halfhearted frown, which smoothed into a sympathetic smile. "Frankly, yes. But Sophie's still young. She'll grow into her attitude."

Somehow, I had my doubts.

But then something else occurred to me. "Ironic, isn't it?" I took another step back, assessing him from a better vantage point—and an all-new perspective. "You're three times Aunt Val's age, but you look so much younger."

He winked, one hand on the doorknob as he turned to leave. "Well, Kaylee, I can tell you right now that 'ironic' isn't quite how she describes it."

14

MUSIC RANG OUT from the dark, the heavy, crunchy beat throbbing near my ear. I blinked and pulled the blanket over my shoulder, irritated by the interruption in my sleep, even as I was relieved by the end of my dream. Which was really more of a nightmare.

In my sleep, I'd been navigating a dark landscape dotted with peculiar, hazy landmarks. Misshapen, shadowy figures scurried and slithered all around me, always just out of sight when I whirled to face them. Farther out, larger shapes lumbered, and though they never came close enough to focus on, I knew they were following me. In the dream, I was looking for something. Or maybe looking for my way out of something. But I couldn't find it.

In my room, the music played on, and I groaned when I realized it was coming from my phone. Still groggy, I flopped over, tangling my leg in the comforter, and reached toward my nightstand. My right hand grazed the phone, still bouncing around on the varnished surface, and the vibrations tickled my fingertips.

Blinking slowly, I held the phone up and glanced at the display, surprised to realize it cast a soft green glow over half the room. The number was unfamiliar, and no name was available. Probably a wrong number, but I flipped the phone open anyway, because of the time of day displayed on the screen. It was 1:33 a.m. No one calls in the middle of the night unless something's wrong.

"Hello?" I croaked, sounding as alert as a bear in January. And almost as friendly.

"Kaylee?"

So much for a wrong number. "Mmm, yeah?"

"It's Tod."

I sat up so quickly my head spun, and I had to rub my eyes to make the lights on the back of my eyelids stop flashing. "Nash gave you my number?" That sounded suspicious even with sleep shrouding my brain like mist over a cold lake.

"No, I haven't called him yet. I wanted to tell you first."

"Okaaay…" Yet even with important information practically hanging from his lips, I couldn't dismiss the hows and whys. "Where did you get my number?"

"It's programmed into Nash's phone."

"And how did you get his phone?"

"He left it on his dresser." Tod's voice was smooth and

nonchalant, and I could almost picture him shrugging as he spoke.

"You went into his room? How did you get in?" But then I remembered him disappearing from plain sight in the hospital dining room. "Never mind."

"Don't worry, he has no idea."

"That's not the point!" I groaned and leaned over to tap the base of my touch lamp once. It flared to life on the dimmest setting. "You can't just sneak into people's houses without permission. That's trespassing. It's an invasion of privacy. It's…creepy."

Tod huffed over the line. "I work twelve hours a day. I don't have to eat or sleep. What else am I supposed to do with the other half of my afterlife?"

I leaned against the headboard and shoved tangled hair back from my face. "I don't know. Go see a movie. Sign up for some classes. But stay out of—" I sat straighter, glancing at my own surroundings in suspicion as something occurred to me. "Have you been in my room?"

A soft, genuine laugh rang over the line. "If I knew where your room is, we'd be talking in person. Unfortunately, Nash doesn't have your address in his phone. Or written down anywhere I could find without waking him up."

"Small miracle," I mumbled.

"He does have your last name, though. Ms. Cavanaugh."

Crap. With my last name, and his convenient pooflike

travel method, it wouldn't take him long to find out where I lived. Maybe Uncle Brendon was right about reapers.

"Don't you want to know why I called, Kaylee Cavanaugh?" he taunted.

"Um…yeah." But I was no longer sure the information was worth dealing with Tod-the-reaper, who seemed more and more "grim" with each word he spoke.

"Good. But I should probably tell you that the terms of our agreement have changed."

I bit my lower lip, cutting off a groan of frustration. "What does that mean?"

Springs creaked over the line as he settled deeper into whatever he was sitting on, and I could almost taste his satisfaction seeping through the earpiece. "I agreed to look at the list in exchange for your last name. I've done my part but no longer need the agreed-upon reimbursement. Fortunately for you, I'm willing to renegotiate."

"What do you want?" I asked, pleased to hear that suspicion was just as thick in my voice as delight was in his.

"Your address."

"No." I didn't even have to think about it. "I don't want you sneaking around here spying on me." Or revealing himself to Sophie, whose parents didn't want her exposed to this brave new Netherworld.

"Oh, come on, Kaylee. I wouldn't do that."

I rolled my eyes, though he couldn't see me. "How do I know that? You were in Nash's house tonight."

"That's different."

"How is that different?" I tugged my covers up to my waist and let my head fall back against my headboard.

"It...doesn't matter."

"Tell me."

He hesitated, and hinges squealed softly again on his end of the connection. "I knew Nash a long time ago. And sometimes I just...don't want to be alone." The vulnerability in his voice resonated in my heart, only further confusing me. But then his actual words sank in.

"You've done this before? What, do you hang out there?"

"No. It's not like that. Kaylee...you can't tell him!" In spite of the earnestness of his plea, I knew Tod wasn't afraid of Nash. He was afraid of embarrassment. I guess some things don't change in the afterlife.

"I can't *not* tell him. Tod, he's supposed to be your friend." At least he used to be. "He has a right to know you've been spying on him."

"I'm not spying on him. I don't care what he's doing, and I've never—" He stopped, and his voice grew hard. "Look, swear you won't tell him, and I'll tell you what I found out about the list."

Surprise lifted my eyebrows halfway up my forehead. He was willing to pay me to keep his little secret? Terrific. But... "Why would you trust me not to tell?"

"Because Nash said you don't lie."

Great. A grim reaper was holding me to my honor. "Fine. I swear I won't tell him in exchange for what you found out about the list. But you have to swear to stay out of his house."

For a moment, there was only silence over the line—Tod obviously wrestling with his decision. What could be so important about hanging out at Nash's house? Why on earth would he need to go back?

"Deal," he said finally, and I exhaled silently in relief. For some reason, I was sure he would keep his word too.

"Good." I tossed back my covers. I was awake, so I might as well be up. "So did you get a look at the lists?"

"I caught a bit of a break there. My boss was out of the office for nearly an hour dealing with some kind of complication in the northern end of the district. And since I happen to know his password—"

"How do you 'happen' to know his password?" I sank into my desk chair and plucked a blue metallic pen from a clay jar I'd made in Girl Scouts a decade earlier, then began doodling on a purple sticky pad.

"Last month he accidentally locked himself out of the system, and as the only reaper in the office who actually lived during the digital age, I'm kind of the de facto tech guy."

Oh. Weird, but I'd take it. "So what about the lists?"

"They weren't there."

"What?" I dropped the pen, anger blazing a white-hot trail up my spine, splintering to burn down to the tips of my fingers. I'd just bargained for nothing? Sworn to keep a secret from Nash only to find out that Tod couldn't get a look at the lists?

"The names. They weren't there," he clarified, and relief drenched most of my irritation. Followed quickly by renewed fear on behalf of every girl I knew. "You were right," Tod continued. "Not one of those girls was supposed to die."

AFTER TALKING TO TOD, I couldn't sleep. I needed to tell my uncle that my suspicion had been confirmed: one of Tod's fellow reapers was working overtime on some unauthorized soul-snatching. But I saw no reason to wake him after two hours of sleep, even for news of this magnitude. None of the other girls had died before noon, so if the pattern persisted, we had a while before the next one would die.

I would tell my uncle and father at the same time, so I wouldn't have to say it twice. And in the morning, so that hopefully I could avoid having to explain how a grim reaper got my phone number and why he'd called me in the middle of the night.

But telling Nash couldn't wait.

My pulse thudded as I scrolled through my contacts list for his name, my heart heavy with what I had to tell him and with what I'd sworn not to tell him. I firmly believed that keeping secrets wasn't good for any relationship; my family was living proof of that. But Tod had sworn not to go back to Nash's house, so his secret was now harmless, and thus more than worth the lives that might be saved by me keeping it to myself.

Right?

The phone rang three times in my ear, with agonizing slowness. Yet part of me hoped he wouldn't answer. That I could put off telling Nash for a few more hours too.

He answered in the middle of the fourth ring.

"Hello?" Nash sounded as tired as I felt.

"Hey, it's me." Too nervous to sit now, I stood to pace the length of my bed.

"Kaylee?" He was instantly alert, an ability I truly envied. "What's wrong?"

I plucked a round glass paperweight from my dresser and rolled it between my palms as I talked, my head crooked at a painful angle with the slim phone pinched between my shoulder and my ear. "The girls weren't on the list."

"They weren't? How do you know—" His breath hissed in angrily, and I closed my eyes, waiting for the explosion. "That bastard! He found you?"

"Just my phone number."

"How?"

"I…you'll have to ask him." I'd sworn not to tell Nash, but I wasn't going to lie.

"No problem." Something scratched against the mouth-piece as he covered it, but I still heard him shout. "Come on out, Tod!"

"You knew he was there?" I couldn't quite squelch a smile, even knowing how angry he was.

"He's not half as stealthy as he thinks he is," Nash growled.

I set the glass ball on my dresser and took my phone back in my hand, turning to avoid a glimpse of my bed-head in the mirror. "Neither are you. Your mom's going to wake up if you don't quit yelling."

"She's working eleven to seven at the hospital tonight."

"Well, I'm sure Tod's gone now." Surely he hadn't called me from Nash's house….

A door squealed open over the line, and floorboards creaked beneath Nash's feet. "He's still here."

"How do you know?"

"I just do." Another pause, and this time he didn't bother to cover the phone, because he was done shouting. "I'm not playing, Tod. If you don't show yourself in five seconds, I'm calling your boss."

"You don't have the number." Tod's voice was unmistakable, even at a whisper. He *had* called me from Nash's house!

Why? Just to rub my boyfriend's face in it?

"I told you to stay away from her." Nash's voice was so deep with anger it was almost unrecognizable.

By contrast, Tod sounded as calm as ever, which probably pissed Nash off even further. "And I haven't been anywhere near her, but that's not because of anything you said. She just hasn't invited me over." *Yet…* We all three heard the unspoken qualifier, and even through the phone I could feel Nash's rage.

Then I heard it.

"What the hell do you think you're doing?" he demanded, and his voice had gone soft and dangerous.

"I don't answer to you, Nash."

"Get out of my room, get out of this house, and stay away from Kaylee. Or I swear we'll show up at the hospital tomorrow and make your entire shift a living hell."

I froze in the middle of my fuzzy purple rug, horrified by the very thought of standing between a reaper and his intended harvest. "Nash, he was doing us a favor." But they both ignored me.

"You come to my work again, and I'll haunt your ass like the ghost of Christmas past!" Tod snapped.

"That was a one-night haunting," Nash mumbled, but the reaper made no reply, and finally Nash sighed. Then springs squeaked as he dropped onto what I assumed was his couch. "He's gone."

"Why didn't you tell me he was dead?"

"Because I was already throwing information at you left and right, and I was afraid one more supernatural fact of life might really freak you out."

"No more secrets, Nash." Irritated now, I sank onto the rug and plucked at the twisty purple threads in the dim glow of my lamp. "I'm not fragile. From now on, tell me everything."

"Okay. I'm sorry. You want to know about Tod?" His

voice went distant, as if he regretted offering before he'd even finished speaking the words.

I crawled onto my bed and turned off the touch lamp, then lay with one cheek on the cool surface of my pillow. "Not everything. But at least what's relevant to me."

Nash exhaled deeply, and I could almost feel his reluctance. Part of me wanted to take it back, to tell him he didn't owe me any answers. But I didn't, because the other half of me insisted I needed those answers. Tod's behavior scared me, and if Nash had information that could help me understand what I was getting into, I wanted it.

"I've known him forever," Nash began, and I went still to make sure I didn't miss anything. It was weird in the best possible way, talking to him in the middle of the night, in the dark, in my bed. His voice was intimate, almost like he was whispering in my ear. And that very thought made my pulse whoosh harder and warmed me all over.

"We used to be close. Then he died a few years ago, and the reapers recruited him. He took the job because that's the only way to stay here. With the living. But he had a hard time adjusting to the work." Nash paused, then his voice became almost wistful. "That's why I thought he'd be able to help you understand death—that it's a necessary part of life. Because he went through the same thing, wanting to save everyone. But he got over it, Kaylee, and his adjustment came with serious consequences. He doesn't think about things the way we do anymore. Doesn't have the same values and concerns. He's truly a reaper now. Dangerous."

I frowned, thinking of what I now knew about Tod that Nash didn't. "Maybe he's not as dangerous as you think. Maybe he just needs…company."

"He broke into my house to find your phone number. If he were human, I'd have him arrested. As it is, there isn't much I can do, short of ratting on him to his boss." Which was as good as killing Tod. "I swear, if he wasn't already dead, I'd kill him myself. I'm sorry, Kaylee. I should never have taken you to him."

Alone in my room, I sighed and turned onto my left side, holding the phone at my right ear. "He got the information for us."

"Plus a little, it sounds like." Nash exhaled heavily, and seemed to be calming down.

I sat up in my bed and slid my cold feet beneath the blankets. "He was trying to help."

"That's the thing—he's not a bad guy. But since the… change…he only helps on his own terms, and won't do anything that doesn't benefit him. Putting yourself in debt to someone like that—especially to a reaper—is a very bad idea. We should have figured it out without his help."

I had no idea what to say. Yes, Tod had crossed a very important line. Several lines, in fact. But by Nash's own admission, the reaper wasn't a bad person. And he'd come through for us—in a manner of speaking.

Springs groaned as Nash shifted in his seat. "So what's

the plan? We still don't know who the next girl will be, or if there will even be one."

I squeezed my eyes shut, unsure how he'd react to my news. "I called in the cavalry."

"The what?"

"My uncle. And my dad." Feeling mostly awake now, I touched my lamp again, and the room got brighter. "Uncle Brendon said they'd find out what was going on if I promised to stay out of it."

Nash gave a gravelly chuckle that sent a bolt of heat blazing through me. "I knew I liked your uncle."

I smiled. "He's not bad. All the lying aside. I'll tell them about the list in the morning."

"Fill me in at the memorial?"

"On the drive, assuming you still want a ride." A warm feeling trickled through me at the thought of seeing him again.

"I would love a ride."

15

IN THE MORNING, I woke to find daylight streaming into my room between the slats of the blinds, and my bedroom door shaking and thumping beneath someone's fist. "Kaylee, get your lazy butt out of bed!" Sophie shouted. "Your dad's on the phone."

I rolled over, pulling the covers askew, and glanced at the alarm clock on my nightstand. 8:45 a.m. Why would my father call when he'd see me in less than an hour? To tell me he'd landed? Or that he *hadn't* landed.

He wasn't coming. I should have known.

For a moment, I ignored my cousin and stared at the thick crown molding along the edge of the tiered ceiling, letting my temper simmer just beneath the surface. I hadn't seen my father in more than eighteen months, and now he wasn't even going to come explain why he'd never told me I wasn't *human*.

Not that I needed him. Thanks to his cowardice, I had a perfectly good set of guardians at my disposal. But he owed me an explanation, and if I wasn't going to get it in person, I could at least demand it over the phone.

I tossed the covers back and stepped into the pajama pants pooled on the floor, and when I opened my door, there stood Sophie, completely dressed and in full makeup, looking as fresh and well-put-together as I'd ever seen her. The only sign that her night's slumber had been chemically induced was the slight puffiness around her eyes, which would probably be gone within the hour.

The last time *I'd* taken one of the zombie pills, I'd woken up looking like roadkill.

"Thanks." I took the home phone from Sophie, and she only nodded, then turned and plodded down the hall with none of her usual watch-me-prance energy.

I kicked my door shut and held the cordless phone to my ear. It felt huge and cumbersome after my cell, and I couldn't remember the last time I'd actually held the home phone.

"You could have called my cell," I said into the receiver.

"I know."

My father's voice was just like I remembered—deep, and smooth, and distant. He probably looked exactly the same too, which meant my appearance would likely come as a bit of a shock to him, despite his understanding of the passage of time. I was almost fifteen the last time he'd seen me. Things had changed. *I* had changed.

"I have this number memorized, so it was just easier," he continued. That was absentee-father-speak for *I'm too embarrassed to admit I don't remember your cell-phone number. Even though I pay the bill.*

"So let me guess." I pulled out my desk chair and plopped into it, punching the power button on my computer just to keep my hands busy. "You're not coming."

"Of course I'm coming." I could practically hear him frowning over the line, and that's when I realized I could also hear actual background noise. An official-sounding voice over a loudspeaker. Random snatches of conversation. Echoing footsteps.

He was at the airport.

"My flight's been delayed by engine trouble in Chicago. But with any luck, I'll be in this evening. I just wanted to let you know I'd be late."

"Oh. Okay." *Soooo glad I didn't start by demanding he tell me everything over the phone.* "I guess I'll see you tonight."

"Yeah." Silence settled over the line then, because he didn't know what to say, and I was *not* going to make it easier on him by speaking first. Finally, he cleared his throat. "Are you okay?" His voice felt…heavy, as if he wanted to say more, but left the unspoken words hanging.

"Fine." *Not that you could fix it if I weren't,* I thought, jiggling my mouse to find the cursor on-screen. "It's all taken some getting used to, but I'm ready to have all the secrets out in the open."

"I'm so sorry about all this, Kaylee. I know I owe you the truth—about everything—but some of this won't be easy for me to say, so I need you to bear with me. Please."

"Like I have a choice." But as furious as I was over the massive lie that was my life, I was desperate to know why they'd all lied in the first place. Surely they had a good reason for letting me think I was crazy, rather than telling me the truth.

My father sighed. "Can I take you out for dinner when I get in?"

"Well, I'll have to eat *something*." I double-clicked on my Internet browser and typed the name of a local news station into the search bar, hoping for an update.

He hesitated for another long moment, as if waiting for more, and as badly as part of me wanted to speak, wanted to spare him the awful silence I'd suffered, I resisted. Birthday visits and Christmas cards weren't enough to hold his place in my life. Especially since they'd stopped coming... "I'll see you tonight, then."

"Okay." I hung up and set the phone on the desktop, staring at it blankly for several seconds. Then I released the breath I hadn't realized I was holding and scrolled through the day's headlines online, hoping to purge my father from my thoughts. At least until he showed up on the porch.

There was nothing new about Alyson Baker or Meredith Cole, but the coroner had officially declared a cause of death for Heidi Anderson. Heart failure. But wasn't that ultimately what everyone died of? However, in Heidi's case, there was no cause listed for her heart failure. As I'd known all along, she'd simply died. Period.

Frustrated all over again, I turned off the computer and dropped the home phone into its cradle on my way to the bathroom. Twenty minutes later, showered, blow-dried, and dressed, I sat at the bar in the kitchen with a glass of juice and a granola bar. I'd just ripped open the wrapper when Aunt Val wandered in, wrapped in my uncle's terry-cloth robe, rather than her usual silky one. Her hair was one big blond tangle, yesterday's styling gel spiking random strands in odd places, like a leftover punk rocker's. Eyeliner was smeared below her eyes, and her skin was pale beneath lingering blotches of blush and foundation.

She shuffled straight to the coffeepot, which was already full and steaming. For several minutes, I chewed in silence as she sipped, but by the time she brought her second mug to the counter, the caffeine had kicked in.

"I'm sorry about last night, hon." She combed one hand over her hair, trying to smooth it. "I didn't mean to embarrass you in front of your boyfriend."

"It's fine." I wadded my wrapper and tossed it into the trash can on the other side of the room. "There was too much else going wrong to worry about one drunk aunt."

She grimaced, then nodded. "I guess I deserved that."

But watching her wince over every movement—as if

contact with the very air hurt—made me feel guilty. "No, you don't. I'm sorry."

"So am I." Aunt Val forced a smile. "I can't *begin* to explain how sorry I am. None of this is your fault...." She stared down into her coffee, as if she had more to say, but the words had fallen into the mug and were now too soggy to use.

"Don't worry about it." I finished my orange juice and set my glass in the sink, then headed back to my room, where I texted Emma to make sure she was still coming to the memorial.

Her mom said she'd meet me there fifteen minutes early—at a quarter to one.

The rest of the morning passed in one endless stretch of mindless television and Internet surfing. I tried twice to get my uncle alone so I could pass along Tod's information, but every time I found him, he was with a very somber, clingy Sophie, who seemed to be dreading the memorial as badly as I was.

After an early lunch I could only pick at, I changed out of my T-shirt, hoping my long-sleeved black blouse was appropriate attire for the memorial service for someone I'd failed to save. On my way out the door, I saw Sophie sitting on the bench in the hall, her hands folded on the skirt of a slim black dress, her head hanging so that her long blond hair fell nearly to her chest. She looked so pitiful, so lost, that as badly as I hated to spoil the drive alone with Nash, I offered her a ride to school.

"Mom's taking me," she said, briefly meeting my gaze with her own huge, sad eyes.

"Okay." *Just as well.*

I pulled into Nash's driveway five minutes later and waited nervously for him to get into the car. I was afraid talking to him would be weird after his middle-of-the-night fight with Tod, and his reluctant discussion of it with me. But he leaned over to kiss me as soon as his door was closed, and from the depth of that kiss—and the fact that neither of us seemed willing to end it—I was guessing he was over the awkwardness.

The school parking lot was packed. Overflowing. Lots of parents had come, as well as some city officials, and according to the morning paper, the school had called in extra counselors to help the students learn to deal with their grief. We had to park on the side of the road nearest the gym and walk nearly a quarter of a mile. Nash took my hand on the way, and we met Emma at the front door, where one of her sisters had dropped her off. I'd promised to give her a ride home.

Emma looked like crap. She wore her hair pulled into a tight, no-frills ponytail, along with the bare minimum of makeup. And if her reddened eyes were any indication, she'd been crying. But she didn't know Meredith any better than I did.

"You okay?" I slipped my free arm around her waist as we made our way through a set of double doors, pushed along with the crowd.

"Yeah. This whole thing's just so weird. First that girl at the club, then the one at the movies. Now one from our own school. Everyone's talking about it. And they don't even know about *you*," she said, whispering the last word.

"Well, it gets even weirder than that." Nash and I guided her toward an empty alcove near the restrooms. I hadn't had a chance to tell her any of the latest developments, and for once I was glad she was grounded from her phone. If she hadn't been, I might have blurted out the whole story—*bean sidhes,* grim reapers, and death lists—before I'd thought any of it through. Which probably would have scared her even more.

"How could it get any weirder than this?" Emma spread her arms to take in the somber crowd milling around the lobby.

"Something's wrong. They weren't supposed to die," I whispered, standing on my toes to get closer to her ear, as Nash pressed in close on my other side.

Emma's eyes went wide. "What does that mean? Who's ever supposed to die?"

I glanced at Nash, and he gave me a tiny shake of his head. *We* really *should have discussed how much to tell Emma.* "Um. Some people *have* to die, or the world would be overpopulated. Like…old people. They've lived full lives. Some of them are ready to go, even. But teenagers are too young. Meredith should have still had most of her life in front of her."

Emma frowned at mc like I'd lost my mind. Or at least

several IQ points. No, I'm not a very good liar. Though technically, I wasn't lying to her.

With Emma still trying to puzzle out my odd editorial on death, Nash guided us through the crowd toward the gym, where we found seats on the bleachers near the middle of the visitors' side and smooshed in with several hundred other people. A temporary stage had been set up beneath one of the baskets, and several school officials were seated there with Meredith's family, beneath the school's banner and the state and national flag.

For the next hour and a half, we listened to Meredith's friends and family come forward to tell us all how nice she was, and how pretty, and smart, and kind. Not all of their praise would really have applied to Meredith, had she been there with us, but the dead have a way of becoming saints in the eyes of their survivors, and Ms. Cole was no exception.

And to be fair, other than being beautiful and popular, she was no different from most of the rest of us. Which was precisely why everyone was so upset. If Meredith could die, so could any one of us. Emma's eyes watered several times, and my own vision blurred with tears when Mrs. Cole came up to the podium, already crying freely.

Sophie sat in the bottom row, surrounded by sobbing dancers blotting streaks of mascara with tissues pulled from small, tasteful handbags. Several of them spoke, mostly Meredith's fellow seniors, reciting stale platitudes with fresh earnestness. Meredith would have wanted us to move on. She loved life, and dancing, and would want neither to stop in her absence. She wouldn't want to see us cry.

After the last of her classmates spoke, an automated white screen was rolled down from the ceiling, and someone played a video of still photographs of Meredith from birth to death, set to some of her favorite songs.

During the film, several students stood and made their way to the lobby, where counselors waited to counsel them. Sniffles and quiet sobs echoed all around us, a community in mourning, and all I could think about was that if we couldn't find the reaper responsible for the unauthorized reaping of Meredith's soul, it would happen all over again.

After the memorial, Nash, Emma, and I made our way slowly down the bleachers, caught up in the gradual current of people more interested in comforting one another than in actually vacating the building.

Eventually we made it to the gym floor, where more groups had clustered, gravitating en masse toward one of the four exits. Since we'd parked in front of the school, we headed for the main doors, shuffling forward inches at a time.

Nash had just taken my hand, his arm brushing the entire length of mine, when a sudden, devastating wave of sorrow crashed over me, settling heavily into my chest and stomach. My lungs tightened, and an unbearable itch began at the base of my throat. But this time, rather than silently bemoaning the onset of my dark forecast and the imminent death of another classmate, I welcomed it.

The reaper was here; we would have our chance to stop him.

16

My hand grasped Nash's. He glanced my way, and his eyes went wide. "Again?" he whispered, leaning down so that his lips brushed my ear, but I could only nod. "Who is it?"

I shook my head, each breath coming quickly now. I hadn't pinpointed the source yet. There were too many people, in too many tightly formed groups. All the bodies in dark colors were blending together in a virtual camouflage of funeral attire, and in some cases I couldn't distinguish one form from another.

A bolt of uncertainty shot through my heart, piercing my determination like a spear through flesh. *What if I can't do this? What if I can't find the victim, much less save her…?*

"Okay, Kaylee, relax." His whispered words flowed over me with an almost physical sliding sensation, trying to calm me even as his eyes churned in slow, steady fear. "Look around slowly. We can save the next one. But you have to find her first."

I tried to follow his directions, but the panic was too loud, a private, frenzied buzzing as the scream built inside my head. It interrupted thought. Rendered logic an abstract concept.

Nash seemed to understand. He stepped in front of me so that we were facing, his nose inches from my forehead. He stared into my eyes and took both my hands in his. The crowd shuffled by, parting to flow around us like water around a river outcropping. Several people glanced our way, but no one stopped—I wasn't the only young woman having a public breakdown in the gym, and most of the others were much louder than mine. For the moment, anyway.

I clenched my jaw shut, holding back the strongest soul song I'd ever felt as I let my gaze rove the crowd, passing over the boys and adults and lingering on the girls. She was here somewhere, and she was going to die. There was nothing I could do to stop that. But if I found her in time, and if I was truly capable of doing what Nash had explained to me, I could bring her back. *We* could bring her back.

Then all we'd have to worry about was avoiding the rogue reaper fury.

It may have been coincidence, or maybe my very real need, despite our strained relationship, to see that my cousin was safe, but my gaze settled first on Sophie. She stood

beneath the basket at the far end of the gym with a group
of teary-eyed friends, arms linked in a huddle of sorrow.
But none of those red, damp faces intensified my panic,
and not one of them was dimmed by a veil of shadows that
only I could see. The girls were fine, but for their grief.
Fortunately, I would not have to add to it.

Next my focus found another cluster of young women—
freshmen, if I had to guess. Everywhere I turned there
were more girls, some in dresses, some in dark pants,
others in jeans, the official uniform of adolescence. It was
like the boys and adults no longer existed. My eyes were
drawn only to the girls.

But of all the faces—freckled, tear-streaked, thin, round,
pale, dark, and tanned—none held my gaze. Not one cried
out to my soul.

Finally, after what seemed like forever, but couldn't have
been more than a minute, my gaze found Nash again. My
jaws ached from being clenched, my throat was raw from
holding back the scream, and my fingernails had left im-
pressions in his hands. I shook my head and blinked away
the tears forming in my eyes. She was still there somewhere—based on the unprecedented strength of the cry
building inside me—but I couldn't find her.

"Try again." Nash squeezed my hands. "One more
time." I nodded and made myself swallow the rising
sound—an agony like gulping broken glass—but this time
the consequences of repressing it were very real. Pressure
built in my chest and throat, and I was increasingly certain

that if I couldn't release it soon or remove myself from the source, my body would rupture into one gaping wound of grief.

Desperate now, I looked over his shoulder, where people still pressed slowly toward the exit. Everyone in that direction faced away from me, identities obscured by the anonymous backs of their heads. A thin redhead, with long, loose curls. Two heavyset girls with identical black waves. A brunette with thin, fine hair as straight as a ruler. She turned, and I saw her profile, but the panic didn't escalate.

Then one head caught my attention—another blonde, about fifteen feet away, her entire form dark with a thick, ominous shadow that somehow fell on no one else. The moment my gaze found her, my throat convulsed, fighting to release the wail my jaws held back. My chest ached for fresh air, but I was scared to take it in, afraid that would fuel the scream I wasn't yet ready to release. The blonde was tall and curvy, her hair cut straight across the middle of her back. If she'd had a ponytail, I'd have sworn it was Emma.

But whoever she was, she was about to die.

I couldn't speak to warn Nash, so I squeezed his hand, harder than I'd meant to. He started to pull away, but then comprehension widened his eyes and made a firm line of his mouth.

"Where?" he whispered urgently. "Who is it?"

Now weak from resisting the song, I could only nod in

the blonde's direction, but that was little help. My gesture took in at least fifty people, more than half of them young women.

"Show me." He let go of my left hand but still clung to my right. "Can you walk?"

I nodded but wasn't sure that I actually could. My head rang with the echo of screams unvoiced, my legs wobbled, and my free hand grasped the air. A soft, high-pitched mewling leaked from me now, the song seeping through my imperfectly sealed lips. And with it came a familiar darkness, that odd gray filter overlaying my vision. The world felt like it was closing in on me, while something else—anomalous forms and a world no one else could see—seemed to unfold before my eyes.

Nash pulled me forward. I staggered and gasped, and my jaw fell open. But he righted me quickly, and I clamped my mouth shut, biting my tongue in a hasty effort to keep from screaming. Blood flowed into my mouth, but the next step I took was under my own volition. Pain had cleared my head. My vision was back to normal.

I stumbled on, Nash guiding me, adjusting our slow course when I shook my head. It only took twelve steps— I counted to help myself focus—then the blonde was within reach, temporarily stalled in her progress toward the door by the crowd. I stopped behind her and nodded to Nash.

He looked sick. His face went suddenly pale, and his throat worked too hard to swallow back something he obviously didn't want to say. "You sure?" he whispered, and I nodded again, my jaw creaking now with the effort to hold back my wail. I was sure. This was the one.

Nash reached out, his fingers trembling as they passed into the eerie shadow shroud, and glanced at me one last time. Then he laid his hand on the girl's right shoulder.

She turned, and my heart stopped.

Emma.

She'd pulled her ponytail loose at some point and had shuffled ahead of us when I'd lagged behind, fighting the panic.

I had to make myself breathe, force my lungs to expand with my teeth still clenched together. And again my vision darkened. Went fuzzy. That eerie, dusky haze slipped over everything, so that I saw the world through a thin, colorless fog.

Emma stared at me through the gloom, wide eyes dimmed by their own private shadow. Her expression was full of understanding, yet missing that vital piece of the puzzle. "It's happening again, isn't it?" she whispered, taking my free hand in hers. "Who is it? Can you tell yet?"

I nodded, and when I blinked, two tears slid down my face, scalding me with thin, hot trails. As I watched, a boy from my biology class brushed Emma's arm, passing into and out of her personal shade without the slightest flicker of awareness in his eyes. All around us students and parents moved with slow, aimless steps, edging gradually toward the doors. Oblivious to the Netherworld murk they walked through. To what the next few moments would bring.

On the periphery of my vision, something rushed through the grayness. Something large, and dark, and *fast*. My heart thumped painfully. A spike of adrenaline tightened my chest. My gaze darted to follow the odd form, but it was gone before I could focus on it, moving easily through the crowd without bumping a single body. But it walked like nothing I'd ever seen, with a peculiar, lopsided grace, as if it had too many limbs. Or maybe too few.

And no one else saw it.

My eyes slammed shut in horror. My mind rebelled against what I'd seen, dismissing it as impossible. I knew there were other things out there. I'd been warned. I'd even caught glimpses before. But this was too much; only a thin stream of sound leaked from my tightly locked throat!

"We have to wait," Nash whispered, and my eyes opened, my attention snapping back to Emma and the terrible matter at hand. Yet the misshapen form lingered in my mind, its odd bulk imprinted indistinctly on the backs of my eyelids. "She has to die before we can bring her back, and singing too soon would be wasting your energy."

No. My hair slapped my face as I shook my head, fervently denying what I already knew to be true. I couldn't let Emma die. I *wouldn't*. But there was nothing I could do to stop it, and we all knew that. Except for Emma.

"What?" She glanced from me to Nash, confusion lining her forehead. "What's he talking about?"

Sweat gathered on my palms, and for once I was glad I couldn't talk. Couldn't answer her. Instead, I swallowed thickly, my throat tightening around the cry scalding me from the inside. The gray haze was darker now, though no thicker. I could see through it easily, yet it tainted everything my terrified gaze landed on, as if the entire gym had been draped in a translucent cloud of smog. And still things moved on the edge of my vision, drawing my eyes in first one direction, then another.

I would have given anything to be able to speak in that moment, not just to warn Emma—because that was evidently a moot point—but to ask Nash what the hell was going on. Could he see what I saw? More important, could they already see us?

My head swiveled quickly, my eyes following an eerie burst of motion, but I was too late. I spun in the opposite direction, squinting into the ghostly gloom as I tracked another movement. My jaws ached, my head pounded, and the keening deep in my throat rose in volume. Those closest to us stared at me now, only looking away when Nash drew me into an embrace, pulling my head down onto his shoulder as if to comfort me. Which was, in part, what he was doing.

"Kaylee, no," he whispered into my hair, but this time

his Influence was little help. The urge to wail was too strong, the death coming too fast—distantly I saw Emma watching us, still wrapped in an almost solid sheet of shadow. "Don't look at them."

He sees them too? That answered one of my questions....

"Focus on holding it back," he said. "Your keening breaches the gap, but I don't think they can see us yet. They will when you sing, but they're not here with us, no matter what it looks like."

Gap? Gap between what and what? Our world and the Netherworld? *Not good. Not good at all...*

I stepped out of his arms to see his face, looking for answers in his expression, but there were none to be found. Probably because I couldn't ask the right questions.

Fine. I would ignore the weird gray reality-veil, as impossible as that seemed. But what about the reaper? If Emma was going to die—even if only temporarily—I would *not* let it be for nothing.

I glanced pointedly at Emma for effect, my heart breaking a little more at the alarm clear on her face, then exaggerated shrugging my shoulders for Nash, all the while choking back the scream that now felt immediate.

By some miracle, he understood.

"You can't see him until he wants to be seen," Nash reminded me gently, stepping close to murmur against my forehead. His very words, the almost-physical satin-soft glide of his Influenced voice against my skin, made the panic abate a bit. Not enough to offer much relief, but enough to hold back the screaming for a few more seconds. "And I'd bet my life savings he doesn't want to be seen. You have to wait. Just hold it in a little longer."

"What?" Emma repeated, squeezing my hand now to get my attention. "Can't see who? Where—"

Then, in midsentence, she simply collapsed.

Emma's legs folded beneath her with my hand still clenched in hers. Her head hit the person behind her. He stumbled and almost went down. I fell forward with her, tears flowing freely now. Nash's hand was ripped from my grip as my knees slammed into the floor and the blow reverberated throughout my body. And Emma's eyes stared up at nothing, the windows to her soul thrown wide open, though it was obvious no one was home.

"Kaylee!" Nash dropped to the ground on Emma's other side. He stared at me imploringly as people turned to look, eyes wide, mouths hanging open.

I barely heard him. I no longer noticed the dimness or the odd movement creeping back into the edges of my vision. I couldn't think about anything but Emma, and how she lay there, unmoving, staring at the ceiling as if she could see through it.

"Let it go, Kaylee. Sing for her. Call her soul so I can see it. Hold it as long as you can."

I looked down at Emma, beautiful even in death. Her fingers were still warm in mine. Her hair had fallen over her shoulder, and the soft ends of it brushed my arm. I let my head fall back and my mouth fall open.

Then I screamed.

The shriek poured from me in an agonizing torrent of discordant, abrasive notes that scraped my throat raw and seemed to empty me, from my toes all the way to the top of my head. It hurt like hell. But beyond the pain, I felt overwhelming relief to no longer be the physical vessel for such an unearthly din and agonizing grief over having lost my best friend. The cousin I should have had. My confidante and, at times, my sanity.

The entire gymnasium went still in an instant. People froze, then turned to stare, most slapping hands over their ears and grimacing in pain. Someone else screamed—I could tell because her mouth was wide open, though I couldn't hear her over the much more powerful noise coming from my own mouth.

And then, before I could even process all the gawking stares aimed my way, the whole world seemed to *shift*.

That fine gray mist settled into place all around me, *over* everything normal, though that was more a feeling than a physical fact. The strange, misshapen creatures I couldn't focus on before were suddenly everywhere, interspersed with and in some cases overlaying the human crowd, ogling me just like the students and parents, but from the far side of the grayness. They were drab, as if the haze had somehow stolen their color, and they looked distant, as if I were watching them through some kind of formless, tinted glass.

Was that what Nash meant, when he said they wouldn't actually be with us? Because if so, I didn't quite understand the distinction. They were entirely too close for comfort, and drawing nearer every second.

On my left, a strange, headless creature stood between two boys in wrinkled khakis, blinking at me with eyes set into his bare chest, between small, colorless nipples. An odd, narrow nose protruded from the hollow below his sternum, and thin lips opened just above his navel.

No need to *mention* how I knew it was a he....

Horrified, I closed my eyes, and my scream faltered. But then I remembered Emma. Em needed me.

They're not here with us. They're not here with us. Nash's voice seemed to chant from inside my head. I let the song loose again, marveling at the capacity of my lungs, and opened my eyes. I was determined to look only at Nash. He could get me through this; he'd done it before.

But my gaze snagged instead on a beautiful man and woman slinking their way toward me through the crowd. They looked almost normal, except for their hazy gray coloring and the odd, elongated proportion of their limbs—and the tail curled around the female's slim ankle. As I watched, spellbound, the man walked *through* my science teacher, who didn't so much as flinch.

That's it. Enough. I couldn't handle any more weird

gray monsters. This time I would look at Nash, or at nothing.

My throat burned. My ears rang. My head pounded. But finally Nash's face came into focus directly across from me. But to my complete dismay, his gaze did not meet mine. He stared, rapt, at the space over Emma's body, eyes narrowed in concentration, face damp with sweat.

I looked up, and suddenly I understood. There was Emma. Not the body cooling slowly on the floor in front of me. The real Emma. Her soul hung in the air between us, the most amazing thing I'd ever seen. If a soul can be called a thing.

She wasn't beautiful, like I'd expected. No glowing ball of heatless light. No Emma-shaped ghost fluttering in an ethereal breeze. She was dark and formless, yet translucent, like a clear, slowly undulating shadow of…nothing. But what her soul lacked in form, it made up for in feel. It felt important. Vital.

Cold fingers touched my arm and I jumped, sure one of the Nether-creatures had come for me. But it was only the principal, kneeling next to me, saying something I couldn't hear. She was asking me what had happened, but I couldn't talk. She tried to pull me away from Emma, but I wouldn't be budged. Nor would I be silenced.

A short, round woman in a sacklike dress burst into the circle that had formed around us, shoving people out of her way. The gray creatures took no note of her, and

I realized they probably couldn't see her. Or any of the other humans.

The woman squatted by Nash and said something, but he didn't answer. His eyes had glazed over; his hands lay limp on his lap. When she couldn't get through to Nash, she tossed an odd glance my way and shot to her feet. She wobbled for a moment, then dashed around him and knelt at Emma's head to check her pulse.

More people knelt on the ground, hands covering their ears, their mouths moving frantically, uselessly. They were oblivious to the creatures peppered throughout their midst, a condition which was apparently mutual. A tall, thin man made frantic motions with both arms, and the humans behind him backed up. The gray creatures seemed to press even closer, but I saw it all distantly, as the scream still tore from my throat, burning like razors biting into my flesh.

Then my eyes were drawn back to Emma's soul, which had begun to twist and writhe frenetically. One smoky end of it trailed toward the corner of the gym, as if struggling in that direction, while the rest wrapped around itself, sinking toward Emma's body like the heavy end of a raindrop.

Transfixed, I glanced at Nash to see sweat dripping down his face. His eyes were open but unfocused, his hands now clenching handfuls of his pressed khaki pants. And as I watched, the soul descended a little more, as if the gravity over Emma's body had been somehow boosted.

People rushed all around us, staring in my direction, shouting to be heard over me. Human hands touched my arms, tugged at my clothing, some trying to comfort me and silence my cry, others trying to pull me away. Odd colorless forms gathered in groups of two or three, watching boldly, murmuring words I couldn't hear and probably wouldn't have understood. And Emma's soul moved slowly toward her body, that one smoky tendril still winding off toward the corner.

Nash almost had her. But if he couldn't do it quickly, it would be too late. My voice was already losing volume, my throat throbbing in agony now, my lungs burning with the need for fresh oxygen.

Then, at last, the lucent shadow settled over Emma's body and seemed to melt into it. In less than a second, it was completely absorbed.

Nash exhaled forcefully, and blinked, wiping sweat from his forehead with one sleeve. My voice finally gave out, and my mouth closed with a sharp snap, loud in the sudden silence. And every single gray being, every last wisp of fog, simply winked out of existence.

For a moment, no one moved. The hands on me went still. The human onlookers were frozen in place as if they could feel the difference, though they clearly had no idea what had happened, other than that I'd stopped screaming.

My gaze settled on Emma, searching out some sign of life. Rising chest, jiggling pulse. I would even have taken a wet, snotty sneeze. But for several torturous seconds, we got nothing, and I was convinced we'd failed. Something had gone wrong. The unseen reaper was too strong. I was too weak. Nash was out of practice.

Then Emma breathed. I almost missed it, because there was no Oscar-worthy gasp for air. No panting, no wheezing, and no choking cough to clear sluggish lungs. She simply inhaled.

My head fell into my hands, tears of relief overflowing. I laughed, but no sound came out. I had truly lost my voice.

Emma opened her eyes, and the spell was broken. Someone in the crowd gasped, and suddenly everyone was in motion, leaning closer, whispering to companions, covering gaping mouths with shaking hands.

Emma blinked up at me, and her forehead furrowed in confusion. "Why am I...on the floor?"

I opened my mouth to answer, but the residual pain in my throat reminded me I'd lost my voice. Nash shot me a grin of total, exhilarating triumph and answered for me. "You're fine. I think you passed out."

"She had no pulse." The round woman sat back from Emma, her face flushed in bewilderment. "She was... I checked. She should be..."

"She passed out," Nash repeated firmly. "She probably hit her head when she fell, but she's fine now." To demonstrate, he held out his hand for one of hers, then pulled her upright, her legs stretched out on the floor in front of her.

"You shouldn't move her!" the principal scolded from my side. "She could have broken something."

"I'm fine." Emma's voice was thick with confusion. "Nothing hurts."

A quiet murmur rose around us, as the news spread to those too far back to have seen the show. Whispered words, like "died" and "no pulse" set me on edge, but when Nash reached across Emma's lap to take my hand, the anxiety receded.

Until a second scream shattered the growing calm.

Heads turned and people gasped. Emma and Nash stared in horror over my shoulder, and I twisted to follow their gaze.

The crowd still surrounded us, but through gaps between the bodies, I saw enough to piece together what had happened.

Someone else was down.

I couldn't see who it was, because someone was already bent over her, performing CPR. But I knew by the straight black skirt and slim, smooth calves that it was a girl, and I knew from the pattern that she would be young and beautiful.

Nash's hand tightened around mine, and I glanced up to find his face as tense with regret as mine surely was. We'd done the unthinkable. We'd saved Emma at the expense of someone else's life. Not one of ours—an innocent, un-involved girl's.

I arched both eyebrows at him, asking silently if he was willing to try it again. He nodded gravely but looked less than confident that we could carry it off. And in the back of my mind, tragic certainty lingered: if we saved another one, the reaper would simply strike again. And again. Or he'd take one of us. Either way, we couldn't afford to play his game.

But I couldn't let someone else die for no reason.

I opened my mouth to scream—and nothing came out. I'd forgotten my voice was gone, and this time so was the urge to wail. There was no panic. No fresh pain clawing up the inside of my throat.

Horrified, I looked to Nash for advice, but he only frowned back at me. "If you can't sing, she's already gone," he whispered. "The urge ends once the reaper has her soul."

Which was why my song for Meredith had ended as soon as she'd died—we'd made no bid for her soul.

Devastated, I could only watch as people scurried around the dead girl, trying to help, trying to see, trying to understand. And in the middle of the confusion, one of the onlookers caught my eye. Because she wasn't look-ing on. While everyone else was focused on the girl lying on the gym floor, one slim arm thrown across the green three-point line, one woman stood against the back corner, staring at...me.

She didn't move, and in fact seemed eerily frozen against all the commotion surrounding us. As I watched, she smiled at me slowly, intimately, as if we'd shared some kind of secret.

And we had. She was the reaper.

"Nash…" I croaked, and groped for his hand, hesitant to take my eyes from the oddly motionless woman.

"I see her." But he'd barely spoken the last word before she was gone. She blinked out of existence, as silently and suddenly as Tod had, and in the bedlam, no one else seemed to notice.

Frustration and fury blazed through me, singeing me from the inside out. The reaper was taunting us.

We'd known the possible consequence and had taken the risk anyway, and now someone had died to pay for our decision. And the reaper had probably known all along that we couldn't stop her.

And the worst part was that when I looked at Emma, who had no idea what her life had cost, I didn't regret my choice. Not even a little bit.

17

OVER THE NEXT FEW minutes, details filtered back to us through the crowd, now thankfully focused on the other side of the room. The girl was a junior. A cheerleader named Julie Duke. I knew the name and could call up a vague image of her face. She was pretty and well liked, and if memory served, more friendly and accepting than most of the other pom-pom-wavers.

When Julie still had no pulse several minutes after she collapsed, adults began herding the students toward the doors, almost as one. Nash and I were allowed to stay because we were Emma's ride, but the teachers wouldn't let her leave until the EMTs had checked her out. However, Julie was the top priority, so when the medics arrived, the principal led them directly to the cluster of people around her.

But it was too late. Even if I hadn't already known that,

it would have been obvious by their posture alone, and the unhurried way they went about their business, and eventually wheeled her out on a sheet-draped gurney. Then a single EMT in black pants and a pressed uniform shirt walked across the gym toward us, first-aid kit in hand. He examined Emma thoroughly, but found nothing that could have caused her collapse. Her pulse, blood pressure, and breathing were all fine. Her skin was flushed and healthy, her eyes were dilating, and her reflexes were... reflexing.

The medic concluded that she'd simply fainted, but said she should come to the hospital for a more thorough exam, just in case. Emma tried to decline, but the principal trumped her decision with a call to Ms. Marshall, who said she'd meet her daughter there.

When I was sure Sophie had a ride home, Nash and I followed the ambulance to the hospital, where the triage nurse put Emma in a small, bright room to await examination. And her mother. As soon as the nurse left, closing the door on his way out, Emma turned to face us both, her expression a mixture of fear and confusion.

"What happened?" she demanded, ignoring the pillows to sit straight on the hospital bed, legs crossed yoga-style. "The truth."

I glanced at Nash, who'd pulled a rubber glove from a box mounted on the wall, but he only shrugged and nodded in her direction, giving me the clear go-ahead. "Um..." I croaked, unsure how much to tell her. Or how to phrase it. Or whether my still-froggy voice would hold out. "You died."

"I *died?*" Emma's eyes went huge and round. Whatever she'd expected to hear, I hadn't said it.

I nodded hesitantly. "You died, and we brought you back."

She swallowed thickly, glancing from me to Nash—who was now blowing up the disposable glove—and back. "You guys saved me? Like, you did CPR?" Her arms relaxed, and her shoulders fell in relief—she'd obviously been expecting something...weirder. I considered simply nodding, but no one else would corroborate our story. We had to tell her the truth—or at least one version of it.

"Not exactly." I faltered, raising one brow at Nash, asking him silently for help.

He sighed and let the air out of the glove, then sank onto the edge of Emma's bed. I sat in front of him and leaned back against his chest. I'd barely broken physical contact with him since singing to Emma's soul, and I wasn't looking to do it anytime soon. "Okay, we're going to tell you what's going on—" However, I knew when he squeezed my hand that he wasn't going to tell her *every*-thing, and he didn't want me to either. "But first I need you to swear you won't tell anyone else. No one. Ever. Even if you're still living ninety years from now and itch-ing to make a deathbed confession."

Emma grinned and rolled her eyes. "Yeah, like I'll be

thinking about the two of you when I'm a hundred and six and breathing my last."

Nash chuckled and wrapped his arms around my waist. I leaned into his chest, and his heart beat against my back. When he spoke, his breath stirred the hair over my ear, softly soothing me, though I knew that part was meant for Emma. Just in case.

"So you swear?" he asked, and she nodded. "You know how Kaylee can tell when someone's going to die?" Emma nodded again, her eyes narrowed now, fresh curiosity shining in them, edged with fear she probably didn't want us to see. "Well, sometimes, under certain circumstances… she can bring them back."

"With his help," I added hoarsely, then immediately wondered if his own involvement was one of the parts Nash wanted to keep to himself. But he kissed the back of my head to tell me it was okay.

"Yes, with my help." His fingers curled around mine, where my hand lay in my lap. "Together, we…woke you up. Sort of. You'll be fine now. There's absolutely nothing wrong with you, and the doctor will probably decide you passed out from stress, or grief, or something. Just like the EMT did."

For nearly a minute, Emma was silent, taking it all in. I was afraid that even under Nash's careful Influence, she might freak out, or start laughing at us. But she only blinked and shook her head. "I died?" she asked again. "And you guys brought me back. I *knew* I should have had that little digital health meter installed over my head, so I know when I'm about to drop."

I smiled, relieved that she could see the humor in the situation, and Nash laughed out loud, his whole body quaking against my back. "Well, with any luck, we've unlocked infinite health for you," he said.

Emma smiled back briefly, then her face grew serious. "Was it like the others? I just collapsed?"

"Yeah." I hated having to tell her about her own death. "In midsentence."

"Why?"

"We don't know," Nash said before I could answer. I let his response stand, because technically it was the truth, even if it wasn't the whole truth. And because I didn't want Emma mixed up in anything that involved a psychotic, extra-grim, female reaper.

She thought for a moment, her fingers skimming the white hospital blanket. When her hand bumped the bed's controller, she picked it up, glancing at the buttons briefly before meeting my gaze again. "How did you do it?"

"That's...complicated." I searched for the right words, but they wouldn't come. "I don't know how to explain it, and it's not really important." At least as far as Emma was concerned. "What matters is that you're okay."

She pressed a button on the controller, and the head of the bed rose several inches beneath her. "So what happened with Julie?"

That was the question I'd been dreading. I glanced at

my lap, where my fingers were twisting one another into knots. Then I shifted to look at Nash, hoping he had a better, less traumatizing way to explain it than simply "She died for you."

But evidently he did not. "We saved your life, and we'd do it again if we had to. But death is just like life in some ways, Em. Everything has a price."

"A price?" Emma flinched, and her hand clenched the controller. The bed lowered beneath her, but she didn't even notice. "You killed Julie to save me?"

"No!" I reached out for Emma, but she scooted backward into the pillow, horrified. "We had nothing to do with Julie dying! But when we brought you back, we created a sort of vacuum, and something had to fill it." Which wasn't exactly true. But I couldn't explain that there shouldn't have been a price for her life without telling her about *bean sidhes,* and reapers, and other, darker things I didn't even understand yet myself.

Emma relaxed a little but didn't move any closer to us. "Did you know that when you saved me?" she asked, and again I was surprised by how insightful her questions were. *She'd probably make a much better* bean sidhe *than I* will.

Nash cleared his throat behind me, ready to field the question. "We knew it was a possibility. But your case was an exception, of sorts, so we hoped it wouldn't happen. And we had no idea who would go instead."

Emma frowned. "So you didn't get a premonition about her death?"

"No, I…" *Didn't*. I hadn't even thought about it until she asked. "Why didn't I know about her?" I asked, twisting to look at Nash.

"Because the reason for her death—" meaning the reaper's decision to take her "—didn't exist until we brought Emma back. Which proves Julie wasn't supposed to die either."

"She wasn't supposed to die?" Emma hugged a hospital pillow to her chest.

"No." I leaned into Nash's embrace and immediately felt guilty because she'd just died, yet had no one to lean on. So I sat up again, but couldn't bring myself to let go of his hand. "Something's wrong. We're trying to figure it out, but we're not really sure where to start."

"Was *I* supposed to die?" Her gaze burned into me. I'd never seen my best friend look so vulnerable and scared.

Nash shook his head firmly on the edge of my vision. "That's why we brought you back. I wish we could have helped Julie."

Emma frowned. "Why couldn't you?"

"We…weren't fast enough." I grimaced as frustration and anger over my own failure twisted at my gut. "And I sort of used it all up on you."

"What does that mean—" But before she could finish the question, the door opened, and a middle-aged woman in scrubs and a lab coat entered. She carried a clipboard and led a very flustered Ms. Marshall.

"Emma, I believe this woman belongs to you?" The

doctor tucked her clipboard under one arm, and Ms. Marshall brushed past her and rushed to the bed, where she nearly crushed her youngest daughter in a hug.

Suddenly the bed lurched beneath us, and Nash and I jumped off the mattress, startled. "Sorry." Emma dug the controller from beneath her leg, where it had fallen.

"Um, we're gonna go," I said, backing toward the door. "My dad's supposed to get in tonight, and I really need to talk to him."

"Your dad's coming home?" Still tight within the embrace, Emma pushed a poof of her mother's hair aside so she could see me, and I nodded.

"I'll call you tomorrow. 'Kay?"

Emma frowned as her mother settled onto the bed, but nodded when the doctor held the door open for us. She would be fine. For better or worse, we'd saved her life, at least for now. And with any luck, she wouldn't catch another reaper's eye for a very, very long time.

Ms. Marshall waved to me as the door closed in front of us, and the last thing I heard was Emma insisting that she *would* have called, if she still had her phone.

Our footsteps clomped on the dingy vinyl tile as we passed the nurses' station, heading for the heavy double doors leading into the ER waiting room. It was only four o'clock in the afternoon, and I was exhausted. And the tickle in my throat reminded me that I still sounded like a bullfrog.

I'd barely finished that thought when a familiar voice

called my name from the broad, white corridor behind us. I froze in midstep, but Nash only stopped when he noticed I had.

"I thought you might want something warm for your throat. Sounds like you really wore it out today."

I turned to find Tod holding a steaming paper cup, his other hand wrapped around an empty IV stand.

Nash tensed at my side. "What's wrong?" he asked. But he was looking at me rather than at Tod.

I glanced at the reaper with my brows raised. Tod shrugged and grinned. "He can't see me. Or hear me unless I want him to." Then he turned to Nash, and I understood that whatever he said next, Nash would hear. "And until he apologizes, you and I will carry on all of our conversations without him."

Nash went stiff, following my gaze to what he apparently saw as an empty hallway. "Damn it, Tod," he whispered angrily. "Leave her alone."

Tod grinned, like we'd shared a private joke. "I'm not even touching her."

Nash ground his teeth together, but I rolled my eyes and spoke up before he could say something we'd all regret. "This is ridiculous. Nash, be nice. Tod, show yourself. Or I'm leaving you both here."

Nash remained silent but did manage to unclench his jaws. And I knew the moment Tod appeared to him, because his focus narrowed on the reaper's face. "What are you doing here?"

"I work here." Tod let go of the IV stand and ambled forward, holding the steaming cup out for me. I took it without thinking—my throat did hurt, and something hot would feel good going down. I sipped from a tiny slit in the lid and was surprised to taste sweet, rich hot chocolate, with just a bit of cinnamon.

I gave him a grateful smile. "I love cocoa."

Tod shrugged and slid his hands into the pockets of his baggy jeans, but a momentary flash in his eyes gave away his satisfaction. "I wasn't sure you'd like coffee, but I figured chocolate was a sure thing."

A soft gnashing sound met my ears as Nash tried to grind his teeth into stubs, and his hand tightened around mine. "Let's go, Kaylee."

I nodded, then shrugged apologetically at Tod. "Yeah, I should get home."

"To see your dad?" The reaper grinned slyly, and whatever points he'd gained with the hot chocolate he lost instantly for invading my privacy.

"You were spying on me?"

A door opened on the right side of the hallway and an orderly emerged, pushing an elderly man in a wheelchair. They both glanced our way briefly before continuing down the hall in the opposite direction. But just in case, Tod lowered his voice and stepped closer. "Not spying. Listening. I'm stuck here twelve hours a day, and it's ridiculous for me to pretend I don't hear stuff."

"What did you hear?" I demanded.

Tod looked from me to Nash, then glanced at the nurses' station at the end of the hall, at the juncture of two other corridors. Then he nodded toward a closed, unnumbered door on the left and motioned for me and Nash to join him.

I went, and Nash followed me reluctantly. Tod made an "after you" gesture at the door, but when I tried to open it, the knob wouldn't turn. "It's locked."

"Oops." Tod disappeared, and a moment later the door opened from the inside. The reaper stood in a small, dark storage closet lined with shelves stacked with medication, syringes, and assorted medical supplies.

I hesitated, afraid someone might walk in and catch us. A reaper could blink himself out of trouble, but *bean sidhes* could not. But then light footsteps squeaked toward us from one of the other hallways, and Nash suddenly shoved me inside and closed the door behind us.

There was a second of darkness, then something clicked and light bathed us from a bare bulb overhead. Nash had found the switch. "Okay, spit it out," he snapped. "I do not want to explain to Kaylee's father why we were caught in a locked hospital storage room full of controlled substances."

"Fair enough." Tod leaned with one shoulder against a shelf along the back wall, giving me and Nash as much room as possible—which was about a square foot apiece. "I was waiting on a guy with a knife wound to the chest. Should have been short and simple, but I stepped out to take a call from my boss, and by the time I got back inside, the doc had brought him back three times. You know, with those shock paddle things?"

"So you let him live?" Nash sounded nearly as surprised as I was.

"Um...no." Tod frowned, blond curls gleaming in the unfiltered light. "He was on my list. Anyway, when I finished with the stab victim, I came out to the lobby for a cup of coffee and heard you talking." He was looking at me now, and completely ignoring Nash. "So I followed you into your friend's room. She's hot."

"Stay away from...her," I finished lamely, remembering at the last minute that it wasn't wise to give out my friends' names to the agents of death. Not that the reaper couldn't find it on his own anyway. And not that Death didn't already have Emma's name on file, after that afternoon.

Tod rolled his eyes. "What kind of reaper do you think I am? And anyway, what fun would killing her be?"

"Leave her alone," Nash snapped. "Let's go." He turned and grabbed the handle, then threw the door open fast enough that if anyone from the nurses' station had been looking, we'd have been caught for sure. Surprised, I hurried after him and barely heard the storage closet close behind me. We were nearly to the double doors when Tod spoke again.

"Don't you want to know about the phone call?" He

only whispered, but somehow his voice carried as if he'd spoken from an inch away.

I stopped, pulling Nash to a sudden halt. He glanced at me in confusion, then in mounting irritation, and I realized with a jolt of shock that once again he hadn't heard Tod—and that I shouldn't have either. The reaper was at least twenty feet away, still in front of the closet.

"The call from your boss?" I whispered experimentally, to see if Tod could hear me.

The reaper nodded, smiling smugly.

"What did he say?" Nash growled softly, angrily.

"Come on." After a quick look to make sure none of the nurses were watching, I nearly dragged him down the hall and back into the closet behind Tod. "Why should we care about your communication issues with your boss?" I asked aloud, to catch Nash up on the discussion.

"Because he has a theory about the off-list reaping." Tod's grin grew as he leaned against the left-hand shelf, and a small dimple appeared in his right cheek, highlighted by the stark light from overhead. How could I not have noticed that before?

"What theory?" Nash asked. Apparently he could hear Tod again.

"Everything costs something. You should know that by now."

"Fine." I huffed in frustration and ignored Nash when his hand tightened around mine. "Tell us what you know, and we'll tell you what we know."

Tod laughed and pulled a plastic bedpan from the shelf, peering into it as if he expected a magician's rabbit to hop out. "You're bluffing. You don't know anything about this."

"We saw the reaper when Emma died," I said, and his smile faded instantly. He dropped the bedpan back onto the shelf and I knew I had his attention. "Start talking."

"You better be telling the truth." Tod's gaze shifted between me and Nash repeatedly.

"I told you, Kaylee doesn't lie," Nash said, and I couldn't help noticing he didn't include himself in that statement.

Tod hesitated for a moment, as if considering. Then he nodded. "My boss is this really old reaper named Levi. He's been around for a while. Like, a hundred fifty years." He crossed his arms over his chest, getting comfortable against the back wall of shelves. "Levi said something like this happened when he first became a reaper. Everything was a lot less organized back then, and by the time they figured out someone was taking people not on the list— they wrote the whole thing by hand back then, can you imagine?—they'd already lost six souls from his region."

"You're serious?" Nash wrapped one arm around my waist, and I let him pull me close. "Or are you just making all this up to impress Kaylee?"

Tod shot him a dark scowl, but I thought it was a totally valid question. "Every word of this came straight from Levi. If you don't believe me, you can ask him yourself."

Nash stiffened, and muttered something about that not being necessary.

"So why were they dying?" I asked, drawing us back on subject.

The reaper's eyes settled on me again, and he lowered his voice conspiratorially, blue eyes gleaming. "Their souls were being poached."

"Poached?" I twisted to glance at Nash with one brow raised, but he only shrugged, his mouth set in a hard line. "Why would anyone steal souls?"

"Good question." Tod fingered a box of disposable thermometer covers. His grin widened, and I was reminded of the way movie-goers sometimes cheer during murder scenes, secure in the knowledge that they're seeing fake blood and movie magic. "There's not much use for detached souls in *this* world…." The reaper left his last word hanging, and a sick feeling twisted deep in my stomach.

"But there is in the Netherworld?" I finished for him, and Tod nodded, evidently impressed that my newbie roots were no longer showing.

"Souls are a rarity on the deeper plane. Something between a delicacy and a luxury. They're in very high demand, and every now and then a shipment goes missing in transit."

"A shipment of souls?" A bolt of dread shot through me at the very thought. "In transit from where? To where?"

Nash answered, looking simultaneously pleased to know

the answer and annoyed at having to provide it. "From here to where they're...recycled."

"Reincarnated?"

"Yeah." Tod stood straighter and bumped his head on an upper shelf, then rubbed it as he spoke. "But sometimes a shipment doesn't make it, so those souls aren't passed on. They're replaced with new ones, which is one of the reasons you'll run into a brand-new soul sometimes."

I made a mental note to ask later how one might identify a new soul. "So these poached souls are going to the Netherworld?" I asked, trying to simply stay afloat in the current of new information. "You mean Meredith, and Julie, and the others were killed so some monster in another realm could make a midnight snack out of their souls?" I gripped a shoulder-height shelf for balance as my head spun. I couldn't quite wrap my mind around what I'd just said.

"That's Levi's theory." Tod picked up a roll of sterile gauze and tossed it into the air, then caught it. "He said the last time this happened, they were being collected as payment to a hellion."

My hand clutched the shelf and a protruding screw cut my finger, but I barely noticed because of the dark dread swirling in me like a dense fog. "A hellion?"

Nash exhaled heavily. "Humans would call them demons, but that's not exactly right, because they have no association with any religion. They feed on pain and chaos. But they can't leave the Netherworld."

"Okay…" My pulse raced, and I flashed back to the gray creatures I'd seen during Emma's soul song. Were those hellions? "Payment for what?"

The reaper shrugged. "Could be anything. Sometimes deals are struck. Under the table, of course. Levi'll take care of it, as soon as he finds the reaper responsible." He caught the gauze one more time and shrugged, having evidently given us everything he knew. Which was much more than I'd expected. "So…what about this reaper you saw?"

"Tell Levi he's looking for a woman." I shifted closer to Nash and accidentally bumped a shelf. Several boxes of medical tubing fell over, spilling their contents like clear plastic worms.

"A woman?" Tod's eyes widened, and I nodded.

"Tall and thin, with wavy brown hair," Nash said. "Sound like someone you know?"

Tod shook his head. "But Levi knows every reaper in the state. He'll take care of it." He hesitated, as if unsure whether or not to say the next part. "But he thinks you're going to get your own souls poached before he can get everything back under control."

"Is that what *you* think?" I wasn't sure why his opinion mattered to me, but it did.

Tod shrugged, fingering his makeshift ball. "I'd say that's a very real possibility. Especially if you keep wiggling your fingers in front of the tiger's mouth."

"We had no choice." I bent to restack the boxes I'd spilled. "The tiger was about to eat my best friend."

"You're something else, Kaylee Cavanaugh," Tod whispered, and I knew from Nash's blank, angry expression that he hadn't heard that part either, though he'd clearly seen the reaper's lips move. "It could have been you, instead of that cheerleader. It might be, next time. Or it might be him." His gaze flicked to Nash and back, and his irreverent expression darkened.

"Let Levi handle it," he said. "If you won't do it for me, or even for yourself, do it for Nash. Please."

Tod looked truly scared, and I didn't know what to make of fear coming from a grim reaper. So I nodded. "We're out of it. I already promised my uncle." I reached back for Nash's hand as Tod nodded. Then he disappeared, still holding the gauze, and I was alone with Nash in the cramped closet.

18

"WHAT DID HE SAY?" Nash shifted in his seat, staring out the passenger's side window at the passing streetlights. We were almost to my house, and those were the first words he'd spoken since we'd pulled out of the hospital parking garage.

"Is there anything else I should know about reapers?" I couldn't keep annoyance out of my voice; I was tired of being left in the dark. "Can they read my thoughts or see through my clothes?" *Which would actually explain a lot...* "Or make me stand on my head and squawk like a chicken?"

Nash sighed and finally turned to face me. "Reapers are like a supernatural jack-of-all-trades. They can appear wherever they want and can choose who sees and hears them. If they want to be seen or heard at all. They have other minor abilities, but nothing else as infuriating as the whole selective-hearing thing." He wrapped one hand around the armrest, his knuckles white with tension. "So what did he say?"

I hesitated to answer; if Tod had wanted Nash to hear, he'd have broadcast on all frequencies. *Then again, he didn't make me promise....* "He asked me not to get you killed. He's trying to protect you."

I glanced away from the road in time to see Nash roll his eyes. "No, he's trying to protect *you,* and he knows you'll be more cautious for my sake than for your own."

"How do you know that's what he's doing?"

"Because that's what I would have done."

An adrenaline-soaked warmth spread through my chest, even though I knew Nash was wrong. Tod was looking out for him, at least in part.

Squinting into the late-afternoon sun, I turned into my neighborhood. Two lefts later, my aunt's car came into sight, parked in the driveway next to the empty spot mine usually occupied. My uncle had taken the day off, expecting my father to arrive around midmorning. And surely Sophie had already made it back from the memorial. *The gang's all here....*

Nash followed me into the living room, where my uncle sat in the floral-print armchair, angled so that he could see both the television—tuned to the local news—and the front window. He stood when we came in, stuffing his hands into his pockets, his anxious gaze searching my expression immediately for any sign of trouble.

"Sophie told us what happened. Are you okay?"

"Fine." I collapsed onto one end of the couch and pulled Nash down with me.

Uncle Brendon's gaze captured mine and held it. "Val... isn't feeling well today. I just put her back in bed."

Now? I glanced out the front window to see the last rays of afternoon light just then sinking below the rooftops across the street. It wasn't even five-thirty.

"This may not be the best time for company," he continued, glancing briefly at Nash.

"I want him to meet Dad," I insisted, and my uncle looked like he wanted to argue. But then he nodded in resignation and sank into his chair. "What did Sophie tell you?" I asked. I was surprised he hadn't called me, but I'd checked my phone in the car, and there were no messages or missed calls.

But then again, he was probably pretty busy dealing with my aunt.

Uncle Brendon leaned back in his chair and lifted a sweating can of Coke from the end table. "She said Emma fainted, and while everyone was fussing over her, one of the cheerleaders fell over dead. The whole school's in complete shock. It's already been on the news."

I swallowed thickly and glanced at Nash. And naturally, Uncle Brendon caught the look.

"Emma died, didn't she?" His expression was pained, as if he wasn't sure he really wanted to hear the truth. "She died, and you two brought her back."

At his words, horror and a stunned incredulity washed over me in a devastating wave—the culmination of every terrifying thing I'd seen and done over the past few days, and I could only nod, holding back tears through sheer will.

Anger rolled across my uncle's face like fog before a storm, and he stood, his hand fisted around the can. If it had been full, he'd have been wearing most of his soda. "I told you to stay out of it. I said your father and I would look into it. You could have *died,* and as it stands now, you got someone *else* killed."

I shot to my feet, anger eclipsing my weaker emotions. "That's not fair. None of this was our fault!"

"There's nothing fair about this," Uncle Brendon roared, and I knew from his volume alone that Sophie wasn't at home. "If you don't believe me, go ask that poor cheerleader's parents."

Nash stood at my side, his stance steady and strong, his gaze unyielding. "Mr. Cavanaugh, we had nothing to do with Julie's death. In fact, we tried to save her too, but—"

We all seemed to realize simultaneously that he'd said the wrong thing. I squeezed Nash's hand to silence him, but it was too late.

"You tried to do it again?" Uncle Brendon's fury was surpassed only by his fear.

"We had to!" I was shouting now, and the entire living room swam with the tears filling my eyes. "I couldn't let the reaper steal another soul without at least trying to stop it."

A glimpse of sympathy flashed through his anger, but then it was gone, stamped out by fear born of caution. "You have to. You can't go sticking your nose into reaper business every time someone you know dies, unless you want to die with them!" He turned to Nash then, anger still spinning in his eyes. "If you're going to tell her what she can do, you have a responsibility to also tell her what she can't do."

"He did," I said before Nash could answer. "But Emma wasn't supposed to die."

My uncle's eyes narrowed in suspicion. "How do you know that?"

Nash spoke before I could, probably to keep me from digging my hole any deeper. "Tod got a look at the list. The reaper is a rogue, and none of those girls were supposed to die."

"See?" I demanded, when Nash went silent without revealing the rest of Tod's information. "We had to save her. She wasn't meant to die yet." *Plus, she's my best friend.* "Tell me you wouldn't have done the same thing."

"He wouldn't have." The new voice came from the entry, carried on a soft September breeze, and we all whirled toward it in unison. My dad stood in the doorway, a suitcase in each hand. "But I would."

I should have said something. I should have had some kind of greeting for the father I hadn't seen in a year and a half. But my mouth wouldn't open, and the longer I stood there in silence, the better I came to understand the problem. It wasn't that I had nothing to say to him. It was that I had too much to say.

Why did you lie? Where have you been? What makes you think coming back now will make any difference? But I couldn't decide what to say first.

Nash didn't have that problem. "I'm guessing this is your dad?" he whispered, leaning closer so that our shoulders touched.

My father nodded, thick brown waves bobbing with the movement. His hair was longer than I remembered it, and nearly brushed his shoulders. I couldn't help wondering how different I looked to him.

"You must be Harmony's boy," my father said, his deep voice rumbling. "Brendon said you'd probably be here."

"Yes, sir," Nash said. Then, to me, he said, "He doesn't sound like he's from Ireland."

My father dropped his bags in the entryway. "I'm not. I just live there." He reached back to pull the front door closed, then scuffed his boots on the mat before stepping into the living room. My dad took a long look at me, from head to toe, and his jaw hardened when his eyes lingered on my right hand, still clasped in Nash's. Then his gaze landed on my face, and a series of emotions passed over his.

Grief, first of all. I'd expected that one. The older I got, the more I looked like my mother. She was only twenty-three when she died—at least that's what they'd told me—and sometimes even I was freaked out by the resemblance in old pictures. He also looked sad and a little worried, as if he dreaded our upcoming conversation.

But the last expression—the part that kept me from storming out of the house and taking off in the car he'd paid for—was pride. My father's eyes gleamed with it, even as old pain etched lines into his otherwise youthful face.

"Hey, kiddo." He took a deep breath, and his entire chest fell as he exhaled. "Think I could get a hug?"

I'd had no intention of hugging my father. I was still so mad at him I could hardly think about anything else, even with everything else going on. Yet I disentangled my hand from Nash's and stepped forward on autopilot. My father crossed the rest of the floor toward me. He wrapped his huge arms around me and my head found his chest, just like it had when I was little.

He might have looked different, but he smelled exactly the same. Like coffee, and the wool in his coat, and whatever cologne he'd been wearing as long as I could remember. Hugging my father brought back the ghosts of memories so old I couldn't quite bring them into focus.

"I missed you," he said into my hair, as if I were still a child.

I stepped back and crossed my arms over my chest. Hugs wouldn't fix everything. "You could have visited."

"I should have." It wasn't quite an apology, but at least we agreed on something.

"Well, you're here now." Uncle Brendon turned toward the kitchen. "Sit, Aiden. What can I get you to drink?"

"Coffee, thanks." My dad shrugged out of his black wool coat and draped it over the back of an armchair. "So..." He sank into the chair, and I sat opposite him, beside Nash on the couch. "I hear you've discovered your heritage. And tried it out, evidently. You restored a friend?"

I met his eyes boldly, daring him to criticize my decision when he'd already admitted he'd have done the same. "Emma wasn't supposed to die. None of them were."

"None of *them?*" My father frowned toward the kitchen; obviously Uncle Brendon hadn't yet given him the details of my discovery. "Who else are we talking about?"

"There were three others. One a day, three days in a row." Nash's thumb stroked the back of mine until my father scowled at him, and he dropped my hand and leaned back on the couch. "Then the reaper took someone else today when we saved Emma."

Irritated—yet amused—I reclaimed his hand and let them both rest on my lap. Absentee fathers had no right to disapprove of boyfriends. "All four of them—five if you count Emma—just fell over dead with no warning. It wasn't their time to go."

"How do you know?"

I leaned into Nash, smiling innocently as my father's jaw tightened. "Nash's friend Tod is a reaper."

My father's brows rose in surprise, and for a moment he forgot to scowl. "Your friend's a reaper?"

Nash shrugged. "I knew him before he…died."

Dad leaned forward, elbows propped on his knees, eyes narrowed. "And this reaper told you the girls weren't on his list?"

"They weren't on *any* list," I said, drawing his scrutiny from Nash. "Tod's boss thinks there's a reaper out there poaching souls to be sold in the Netherworld. Or something like that."

Uncle Brendon froze in the doorway, holding two steaming, fragrant mugs. "Someone's selling souls in the Netherworld?" He and my father exchanged twin looks of horror and dread before turning back to us. "What do you know about the Netherworld?"

"Just that there *is* one, and that some of the locals are hot for human souls." I shrugged, trying to set them both at ease. "But that doesn't really matter to us, right? Tod's boss said he would take care of it."

The relief on my uncle's face was as thick as the tension in Nash's posture. "Good. The reapers should take care of their own problems. It really isn't *bean sidhe* business."

Frowning, I scuffed the toe of my shoe into the carpet. "Except that this psycho reaper tried to take a *bean sidhe*'s best friend. That kind of makes it my business."

Uncle Brendon scowled and looked ready to argue, but

my father spoke before he could. "Did people see you bring Emma back?" he asked, cradling his steaming mug as if for warmth.

Nash sat straighter, eager to defend me. "No one knew what was happening. Em had just collapsed, and everyone thought Kaylee was freaked out over that. And once Emma sat up, they all thought she'd just fainted."

That was mostly true, though rumors were already circulating that Emma's heart had actually stopped for a minute. The lady who took her pulse had probably started them. Not that I could blame her. The poor woman would probably need therapy.

But then, so might I. And maybe Emma.

My father shrugged, eyeing his brother sternly. "Sounds like no harm was done."

"Except for Julie," I muttered, and immediately wished I'd kept my mouth shut.

My father paused with his mug halfway to his mouth. "She's the exchange?"

"Yeah." And though I knew in my heart that Julie's death wasn't our fault, I couldn't escape the guilt that tightened my chest and made my whole body feel heavy.

Uncle Brendon sank into the other armchair and shook his head in regret. "This is why you have to stay out of reaper business. That poor girl would be alive right now if you two had just left things alone."

"Yeah, but Emma wouldn't." My free hand gripped the arm of the couch. "And we had no way of knowing for sure she'd take another one. Tod said there shouldn't be any penalty for saving a life that shouldn't have been taken in the first place."

"She?" My father slowly lowered his mug onto its coaster. "Do I even want to know how you know the reaper is a woman?"

I shifted uncomfortably on the couch and glanced at Nash, but he shrugged, leaving it up to me. So I made myself meet my father's gaze. "We…kind of saw her."

Uncle Brendon sat straight in his chair, every muscle in his body tense. "How?"

"She just showed up." I shrugged. "When they were doing CPR on Julie. She was at the back of the gym, behind most of the crowd, and she smiled at us."

"She smiled at you?" My father frowned. "Why would she show herself on purpose?"

"It doesn't matter," my uncle said. "The reapers will take care of their own. We should stay out of it."

For a moment, I thought my father would argue. He looked almost as angry as I was. But then he nodded decisively. "I agree."

"But what if they can't find her?" I demanded, Nash's hand still clasped in mine.

My father shook his head and leaned back in his chair, crossing both arms over the front of his sweater. "If you two can find her, the reapers can find her."

"But—"

"They're right, Kaylee," Nash said only inches from my

ear. "We don't even know who the reaper will go after next. If she does it again at all."

She *would*. The moment she'd smiled at me, I'd known she wasn't finished. She would take another girl soon, unless someone stopped her. But no one else seemed willing to try.

My father turned to his brother, his thoughts hidden by a calm facade. "How are your girls?" he asked, and just like that, the subject was closed.

"They aren't taking this very well." My uncle heaved a heavy sigh. "Sophie's out with her friends. The girl who died yesterday was on her dance team, and the rest of the squad is spending every waking moment together, like some sort of perpetual wake. And Val… She got a quarter of the way through a bottle of brandy this afternoon, before I even knew she'd opened it. I put her to bed about an hour ago to let her sleep it off."

Wow. Maybe Aunt Val needed to go see Dr. Nelson.

"I'm sorry, Bren."

Uncle Brendon shrugged, as if it didn't matter, but the tense line of his shoulders said otherwise. "She was always pretty high-strung. Sophie's the same way. They'll be fine once this all blows over."

But it wasn't going to blow over, and I couldn't be the only one who knew that.

Uncle Brendon stood and picked up his mug. His every movement spoke of exhaustion and dread. "I'm going to check on my wife. Val got the guest room ready for you this morning. If you need anything else, just ask Kaylee."

"Thanks." When Uncle Brendon's bedroom door closed, my father stood and faced Nash, obviously expecting him to stand too. "Nash, I can't tell you how grateful I am for how you've helped my daughter."

Still stubbornly seated, Nash shook his head. "I couldn't have done anything without her there to hold the soul."

"I mean what you did for Kaylee. Brendon says your dose of truth probably saved her from a serious breakdown." He held his hand out, and Nash floundered for one awkward moment, then stood and accepted it.

"Dad..." I started, but he shook his head.

"I messed up, and Nash picked up the slack. He deserves to be thanked." He shook Nash's hand firmly, then let go and stepped back, clearing an obvious path to the front door.

I rolled my eyes at his less-than-subtle hint. "I agree. But Nash is staying. He knows more about this than I do anyway." I slipped my hand into his and stood as close to him as I could get.

To my surprise, though he looked irritated, my father didn't argue. His gaze shifted from me to Nash, then back to me, and he simply nodded, evidently resigned. "Fine. If you trust him, so do I." He backed slowly toward his chair and sat facing us. Then he inhaled deeply and met my steady gaze. I was ready to hear whatever he had to say.

But the real question was whether or not he was ready to say it.

"I know this all should have come out years ago," he began. "But the truth is that every time I decided it was time to tell you about your mother—about yourself—I couldn't do it. You look so much like her...."

His voice cracked, and he glanced down, and when he looked at me again, his eyes were shiny with unshed tears.

"You look so much like her that every time I see you, my heart jumps for joy, then breaks all over again. Maybe it would have been easier if I'd kept you with me. If I'd seen you every day and watched you develop into your own person. But as it is, I look at you and I see her, and it's so damn *hard*..."

Nash squirmed, and I stared at my hands as my father looked around the living room, avoiding our eyes until he had himself under control. Then he sighed and swiped one arm across his eyes, blotting tears on a sweater too thick to be truly necessary in September.

Crap. He was actually crying. I didn't know how to deal with a crying father. I barely knew how to deal with a normal one.

"Um, anyone else hungry? I didn't get any supper."

"I could eat," Nash said, and I was sure he'd picked up on my need to break the tension.

Or maybe he was just hungry.

"Is macaroni and cheese okay?" I asked, already halfway

out of the room by the time he nodded. Nash and my dad followed me through the dining room and into the kitchen, where I knelt to dig a bag of elbow pasta from the back of a bottom cabinet.

I'd thought I was ready. That I could deal with whatever he had to say. But the truth was that I couldn't just sit there and watch my father cry. I needed something to keep my hands busy while my heart broke.

"You can cook?" My father eyed me in surprise as I pulled a pot from another cabinet, and a block of Velveeta from my uncle's shelf in the fridge.

"It's just pasta. Uncle Brendon taught me." He'd also taught me to hide the occasional bag of chocolate behind his stash of pork rinds, which Aunt Val would never touch, even to throw away in a frenzied junk food purge.

My father sat on one of the bar stools, still watching as I turned the burner on and sprinkled salt into the water. Nash settled on a stool two down from him and crossed his arms on the countertop.

"So what do you want to know first?" My dad met my gaze over the cheese I was unwrapping on a cutting board.

I shrugged and pulled a knife from a drawer on my left. "I think I have a pretty good handle on the whole *bean sidhe* thing, thanks to Nash." My father cringed, and I might have felt guilty if he'd ever made any attempt to explain things himself. "But why did Aunt Val say I was living on borrowed time? What does that mean?"

This time he flinched like I'd slapped him. He'd obviously been expecting something else—probably a technical question from the *How to Be a* Bean Sidhe handbook, my copy of which had probably gotten lost in the mail.

My father sighed and suddenly looked very tired. "That's a long story, Kaylee, and one I'd rather tell in private."

"No." I shook my head firmly and ripped open the bag of pasta. "You flew halfway around the world because you owe me an explanation." *Not to mention an apology.* "I want to hear it now."

My father's brow rose in surprise, and more than a hint of irritation. Then he frowned. "You sound just like your mother."

Yeah, well, I had to inherit a backbone from someone. "Wouldn't she want you to tell me whatever it is you have to say?"

He couldn't have looked more shocked if I'd punched him. "I honestly don't know. But you're right. You're entitled to all the facts." He closed his eyes briefly, as if gathering his thoughts.

"It all started the night you died."

19

"WHAT?" MY HAND fisted around a cube of cheese, and it squished between my fingers. My pulse pounded so hard in my throat I thought it would explode. "You mean the night Mom died."

My father nodded. "She died that night too. But you went first."

"Whoa..." Nash leaned forward on his stool, glancing back and forth between me and my father. "Kaylee died?"

My dad sighed, settling in for a long story. "It was February, the year you were three. The roads were icy. We don't get much winter weather in Texas, so when it does come, no one quite knows how to handle it. Including me."

"Wait, I've heard all this before." I dumped the pasta into the now-boiling water, and a puff of steam wafted

into my face, coating my skin in a layer of instant damp-
ness and warmth. "You were driving, and we were broad-
sided by another car on an icy road. I broke my right arm
and leg, and Mom died."

My father nodded miserably, then swallowed thickly
and continued. "We were on our way here, for Sophie's
birthday party. Your mother thought the weather was too
bad, but I said we'd be fine. It was a short trip, and your
cousin adored you. The whole thing was my fault."

"What happened?" I asked, my cheesy hand forgotten.

My father blinked slowly, as if warding off tears. "There
was a deer in the road. I wasn't going that fast, but the
road was icy, and the deer was huge. I swerved to avoid
it, and the car slid on the ice. We wound up sideways in
the road. An oncoming car smashed into us. Near the rear
on the passenger's side. Your car seat was crushed."

I closed my eyes and gripped the countertop as a wave
of vertigo threatened to knock me over. *No.* My mother
had died in that accident, not me. I'd been pretty banged
up, but I'd lived.

I was living proof of that!

My eyes opened, focusing on my father instantly. "Dad,
I remember parts of that. I was in the hospital for weeks. I
had two casts. We still have pictures. But I'm alive. See?"
I spread my arms across the countertop to demonstrate
my point. "So what happened? The paramedics brought
me back?"

The truth was looming, a great, dark cloud on my mind's horizon. I could almost see it, but I refused to bring it into focus. Refused to acknowledge the coming storm until it broke over my head, drenching me with a cold, cruel wash of the answers I'd thought I wanted.

I no longer wanted them.

But my father only shook his head. "They didn't get there in time. The man driving the other car was a doctor, but his wife hit her head on something, and he was trying to wake her up. By the time he came to help us, it was all over."

"No." I stirred the pasta so hard boiling water slopped onto the stovetop, hissing on the flat burner.

Nash's hand landed softly on mine, though I hadn't heard him move, and I looked up to meet his sympathetic gaze. "You died, Kaylee. You know it's true."

My father nodded again, and when his eyes squeezed shut, two silent tears trailed down his stubbly cheeks. "I had to go in through the driver's side and pull the whole car seat out. When I picked you up, you didn't make a sound, even though your right arm and leg were bent all out of shape." His eyes opened, and the pain swirling there held me captive. "I held you like a baby, and you just looked at me. Then your mom crawled out of the car and took your good hand. She was crying, and she couldn't talk, and I could see the truth on her face. I knew we were going to lose you."

He sniffled and I stood still, afraid that if I moved, he'd

stop talking. And even more frightened because part of me really wanted him to stop. "You died, right there on the side of the road, with snow melting in your hair."

"Then why am I still here?" I whispered, but I already knew the answer. "It was my time, wasn't it?" I flicked on the faucet and held my hands under the warm water, scrubbing cheese from between my fingers as I eyed my father. "I was supposed to die, and you brought me back."

"Yes." His voice cracked on that one syllable, and his face was starting to flush with the effort to hold back more tears. "We couldn't stand it. She sang for you, and it was the most beautiful thing I've ever heard. I could barely see, I was crying so hard. But then I saw you. Your soul. So small and white in the dark. It was too soon. I couldn't let you go."

I turned off the water and grabbed a towel from a drawer near my hip, dripping on the floor as I dried my hands, then leaned over the bar and stared at him. "Tell me how it happened."

He didn't hesitate this time. "I made your mother look at me, to make sure she understood. I told her to take care of you. That I was going to bring you back. She was crying, but she nodded, still singing. So I guided your soul back into your tiny little body. You blinked at me. Then, with your first breath, you sang."

"I...*sang?*" The towel slipped from my fingers and landed silently on the tiles, but I barely noticed.

"The soul song." My father pressed the heels of his hands to his eyes, as if to physically hold back tears, but his face was still wet when he looked at me again. "I thought it was for me. You needed your mother more than you needed me, and I was ready to go. But as I stood there holding you, the reaper showed himself."

"He let you see him?" Nash interrupted from my side. I'd almost forgotten he was there.

My father nodded. "He stood in the grass, on the shoulder of the road. He smiled at me, with this creepy little grin, like he knew what I was thinking. I told him I was ready to go. I gave you to your mother, and you were still singing this beautiful, high-pitched song, like a bird. I felt so peaceful, thinking that the last thing I would hear was you singing my soul song." He paused, and this time the tears actually fell. "But I should have known better, because your mother wasn't singing with you."

I stared across the countertop at my dad, mesmerized, my supper forgotten.

"The bastard took her instead." My father's fist hit the tile hard enough to shake the whole bar, and his jaw bulged with fresh fury. "He just looked at Darby, and she collapsed. I had to lunge for you, to keep you from hitting the ground when she fell."

"Kaylee, breathe," Nash said, rubbing my back. At some point during the story, I'd stopped inhaling, and didn't even realize it until Nash spoke.

"She died because of me?" My hands fisted, and my fingernails bit into my palms.

"No. Baby, no." My dad leaned forward then, to look directly into my eyes. "She died because of *me*." He took my hands and wouldn't let them go, even when I tugged halfheartedly. "Because I insisted on going out. Because I swerved to avoid the deer. Because I wasn't strong enough to make him take me instead. None of it was your fault."

But nothing he said could make me feel better. I was supposed to die, and because I hadn't, my mother had. And even if *she* hadn't, my father would have. Or maybe one of the people in the other car. The bottom line was that I was alive when I should have been dead, and my mother had paid the price.

"So…borrowed time?" I twisted the knob on the stove to turn it off, and moved the pot onto a cold burner, acting out of habit, because I was numb with shock. "I'm living my mother's life now? Is that what Aunt Val meant?"

"Yes." My father sat back on his stool, giving me plenty of space. "You'll live until she was supposed to die. But don't worry about that. I'm sure she would have had a very long life."

And that's when I burst into tears.

I'd held back until then, my sorrow eclipsed by overwhelming guilt over being the cause of my mother's death. But thinking about how long her life should have been… *That* I couldn't handle.

Nash cleared his throat, drawing our attention. "She knew the risk, right, Mr. Cavanaugh?" He stared at my father with a blatantly expectant look on his face. "Kaylee's mom knew what she was doing, right?"

"Of course." My dad nodded firmly. "She probably didn't even realize I'd planned to make the exchange myself. She was willing to pay the price, or she would never have sung for you. I just...wanted to save her too. It was supposed to be me, but I lost you both that night. And I never really got you back, did I?"

I forced back my next sob, rubbing spent tears from my cheeks with my palms. I was getting really good at not-crying. "I'm right here, Dad." I set the strainer in the sink and dumped the pasta into it, then slammed the empty pot down on the countertop. "You left."

"I had to." He sighed and shook his head. "At least, I *thought* I did. He came after you again, Kaylee. The reaper was furious that we saved you. He took your mother, but then he came back for you, two nights later. In the hospital. I would never have known it was coming if your grandmother hadn't come in from Ireland after the wreck. She practically lived in your room with me, and she got a premonition of your death."

"Wait, I was supposed to die again?" My hand hesitated over the strainer.

"No." My father shook his head vehemently. "No. Your mother and I angered the reaper when we saved you. He came back for you out of spite. Your mother wasn't hurt in the accident, and you were living on her time. There's *no way* she should have died two days after you would have. So when he came for you the second time, I called him on it."

"Did he show himself?" Nash asked, and I glanced to my right to see him staring at my father, as fascinated as I was.

My dad nodded. "He was an arrogant little demon."

"So what happened?" I asked.

"I punched him."

For a moment, we stared at him in silence. "You punched the reaper?" I asked, and my hand fell from the strainer onto the edge of the sink.

"Yeah." He chuckled at the memory, and his grin brought out one of my own. I couldn't remember the last time I'd seen my father smile. "Broke his nose."

"How is that possible?" I asked Nash, thinking of his sort-of-friendship with Tod.

"They have to take on physical form to interact with any physical object," he said, fiddling with the long cardboard box the cheese had come in. "They can't be killed, but they can definitely feel pain."

"And you know this how...?" I asked, pretty sure I knew the answer to that one too.

Nash grinned. "Tod and I don't always get along." But then he turned back to my dad, serious again. "Why did the reaper come after Kaylee a second time?"

"I don't know, but I was afraid he'd do it again." My

father paused, and his half grin faded into a somber look of regret. "I sent you to Brendon to keep you safe. I was worried that if I stayed with you, he'd end up taking you too. So I sent you away. I'm sorry, Kaylee."

"I know." I wasn't quite up to accepting his apology yet, though the fact that he clearly meant it helped quite a bit. I dumped the pasta back into the empty pot and followed it with two fistfuls of cheese cubes. Then I turned the burner on medium heat and added salt, a little milk, and a spoonful of Aunt Val's low-calorie margarine.

I stared into the pot as I stirred. "How long are you staying?"

"As long as you want me here," he said, and something in his voice made me look up. Did that mean what I thought it meant?

"What about your job?"

He shrugged. "There are jobs here. Or, if you want, you could come back to Ireland with me. I'm sure your grandparents would love to see you."

I hadn't seen them since the last time I'd seen my father, and I'd never been out of the country. But...

My gaze was drawn to Nash. When he saw me looking, he nodded, but I wasn't fooled. He didn't want me to go, and that was enough for me.

"I'd love to visit Ireland, but I live here, Dad." I sprinkled some pepper into the pot and kept stirring. "I don't want to leave." The disappointment on his face nearly killed me. "But you're welcome to stay here. If you want."

"I—"

I'd like to think he would have said yes. That he was considering a house for the two of us, hopefully not too far from Nash's, but plenty far from Sophie and her fluffy pink melodrama. But I'd never know for sure. He didn't get to finish because the front door opened, and something thumped to the floor, then Sophie groaned.

"Who left these stupid bags right in front of the door?" she demanded.

Amused by her ungainly entrance, I craned my neck to see over Nash's shoulder. My cousin knelt on the floor, one hand propping her up over an old, worn suitcase. I started to laugh, but when my gaze settled on hers, all amusement drained from me instantly, leaving me cold and empty. Her face was shadowed, her features so dark I could barely make them out, even with light drenching her from overhead.

The reaper had come for its next victim.

Sophie was about to die.

20

"Sophie?" My father stood and turned toward her without a single glance my way. "Wow, you look just like your mother, except for your eyes. Those are Brendon's eyes—I'd lay my life on it." If he'd looked at me, he'd have seen her fate. I was sure of it. But he didn't look.

Even Nash was watching my cousin.

Fear and adrenaline sent a painful jolt through my chest, and I gripped the edge of the countertop. "Sophie…" I whispered with as much volume as I could muster, desperate to warn her before the panic kicked in for real. But no one heard me.

Sophie picked herself up with more grace than I'd ever wielded in my life, brushing off the front of the dark, slim dress she'd worn to the memorial. "Uncle Aiden." She pasted on a weary smile, to match red-rimmed eyes, polite even in the grip of grief. "And Nash. Two of my favorite men in the same room."

For once, I barely registered the flames of jealousy her claim should have lit within me, because the inside of my throat had begun to burn viciously. Yes, I often wanted to shut her up, but not *permanently.*

"Dad!" I rasped, still clinging to the countertop for support, but again, no one noticed me.

Except Sophie.

"What's wrong with her?" My cousin clacked into the dining room in her dress shoes, hands propped on narrow, pointy hips. "Kaylee, you look like you're gonna throw up in your... What is that?" She eyed the half-used brick of Velveeta. "Mac and cheese?"

Nash turned to me so fast he nearly lost his balance. "Kaylee?" But I could only watch him, my jaws already clenched against the wail for my cousin's soul. "Again?" I nodded, and he pulled me close, already whispering words I couldn't concentrate on, his rough cheek scratchy against mine.

"Kay?" My father whirled toward me a second behind Nash, and a look of horror slid over his features when he recognized the look on mine. He followed my gaze to my cousin slowly, as if afraid of what he'd see. "Sophie?" he asked, and I nodded, gritting my teeth so hard pain shot through my temples. "How long?"

I shook my head. I'd had no idea my ability came with a built in time gauge, much less how to use it.

"Brendon!" my father shouted, his focus locked on me.

Sophie flinched, then stepped forward to see me better, leaning over the back of a dining-room chair, her eerily shadowed forehead wrinkled in confusion.

Nash was still whispering to me, holding me tight with his back to the stove. His lips brushed my ear, his words gliding over me with a soothing breath of Influence, helping me hold the panic in check. I breathed deeply, trying to hold back the looming wail as I stared over his shoulder, my focus glued to my oddly darkened cousin.

"What's going on?" Sophie gripped the high back of the chair in both hands, and her gaze met mine. "She's freaking out again, isn't she? Mom keeps that shrink's number around here somewhere." She started toward the kitchen, but my father put out one arm to stop her.

"No, Sophie." He glanced toward the hall and shouted, "Brendon! Get out here!" Then he turned back to his niece. "Kaylee will be fine."

"No, she won't." Sophie shook her head and tugged her arm from his grasp, green eyes wide. Her concern felt genuine. I think she was actually afraid for me. Or maybe afraid *of* me. "I know you're worried about her, but she needs serious help, Uncle Aiden. Something's wrong with her. I told them this would happen again, but no one ever listens to me. They should have let that doctor give her shock therapy."

"Sophie…" My dad's shoulders tensed, his expression

caught between fear and anger. He was going to set her straight—except that Nash beat him to it.

"Damn it, Sophie, she's trying to help you, and you…" He whirled on her, eyes churning furiously. But the moment he stepped away from me, the panic descended in full force. I pulled him back by one arm, and Nash's look of surprise melted into understanding, and he resumed whispering, as if he'd never stopped.

Footsteps pounded down the hall and I opened my eyes to see Uncle Brendon stumble to a halt in the middle of the living room. He looked from me to my dad, then followed my father's gaze to Sophie. As I watched, my uncle's features crumpled in an agony so complete, so encompassing, that I could barely stand to see it.

For several seconds, no one moved, as if afraid that the slightest twitch would draw the reaper out of hiding and bring about the inevitable conclusion. Sophie glanced from one of us to the next in total confusion. Then my father sighed, and the soft sound seemed to reach every corner of the wide-open living area. "Are you okay?" he asked, and I nodded unsteadily. I wasn't the one facing death. Not yet, anyway.

"What's going on?" Sophie demanded, shattering the quiet like a gunshot at a funeral. But no one answered. She was the source of all the trouble, yet no one even looked at her. For once, everyone was looking at me.

"Is it Sophie?" Uncle Brendon asked, walking slowly toward us, as if it hurt to move. His voice was barely audible over the unvoiced scream already reverberating in my head. I nodded, and his eyes closed as he inhaled deeply, then exhaled. "Are you sure?" He had to open his eyes to see me nod again, then the line of his jaw hardened. "Will you help me?" he asked, pain twisting his features into a mask I barely recognized. "I swear I won't let her take you."

Unfortunately, after my father's story, I wasn't sure Uncle Brendon would have any control over who the reaper took instead. Any reaper who would reap a soul not on the list wouldn't think twice about taking the *bean sidhe* who got in her way. Or everyone else in the room, for that matter.

But I couldn't just let Sophie die, even if she was a royal pain in the butt most of the time.

"What are you all talking about?" My cousin glanced at each of us in turn, like we'd all lost our minds, and sanity was getting lonely. "What's going on?"

Uncle Brendon crossed the living room in four huge steps and motioned to his daughter to join him on the couch. She went reluctantly, and he pulled her down onto the center cushion. "Honey, I have to tell you something, and I don't have time for the long, gentle version." He took Sophie's hands, and my chest ached with what could only be the splintering of my heart.

"You're going to die in a few minutes," he said. Sophie frowned, but her father rushed on before she could interrupt. "But I don't want you to worry, because Kaylee and

I are going to bring you right back. You'll be fine. I'm not sure what'll happen after that, but what I need you to know is that you're going to be *just fine*."

"I don't know what you're talking about." Confusion pinched Sophie's fine features into a scowl, and I could see panic lurking on the edge of her expression. Her world had just ceased making sense, and she didn't know what to do with information she couldn't understand. I knew exactly how she felt. "Why would I die? And what on earth can Kaylee do about it?"

Uncle Brendon shook his head. "We don't have time for all that now. I don't know how long we have, so I need you to trust me. I *will* bring you back."

Sophie nodded, but she looked terrified, as much for her father as for herself. She probably thought he'd gone over the proverbial deep end and was now drowning in it. She glared at me over his shoulder, as if I'd somehow contaminated him with my mental defect, but I couldn't summon any irritation toward my cousin—not with her moments from death.

"*Noooo.*"

Every head in the room swiveled toward the hall, where Aunt Val now stood, clutching the door frame as if that were the only thing holding her up. "It wasn't supposed to be Sophie."

"What?" Uncle Brendon stood so fast the motion made *me* dizzy. He stared at his wife in dawning horror. "Valerie, what did you *do?*"

Aunt Val? What did she have to do with grim reapers and *bean sidhes?* She was human!

Before my aunt could answer, a fresh wave of grief rolled over me and I staggered on my feet. Nash caught me before I hit the dining-room table and lowered me carefully into one of the chairs. It wouldn't be long now.

Sophie started to tremble then, and the very sight of her sent tremors through my own limbs. Anguish racked me from the inside out. My heart felt too big for my chest. My throat burned like I was breathing flames.

But beyond the physical pain of holding back Sophie's soul song, I felt my cousin's loss intensely, though the reaper had yet to strike. It was like watching my own hand laid out on a chopping block, knowing the woodsman was coming for it. Knowing I'd never get it back. And it didn't matter that we'd never been close. I wasn't in love with my feet either, but I didn't want to lose them.

"Mom?" Sophie squeaked, shifting her weight from one side to the other as she hugged herself. "What's going on?"

"Don't worry, honey," Aunt Val said from the middle of the living-room carpet, her focus darting all over the place, like a junkie on a bad trip. "I won't let her take you." She paused, without ever looking at her daughter, and threw her head back as far as it would go, blond waves cascading down her back almost to her waist.

"Marg!" she shouted, and I flinched. My hands gripped

the chair arms as I tried to regain my control after she'd nearly shaken it lose. "I know you're here, Marg!"

Marg? I hadn't told Aunt Val about seeing the reaper, or that she was, in fact, female. And I hadn't even known the reaper's name. Until now.

And suddenly I understood. Aunt Val knew the reaper's name because she had hired her.

No! Denial and devastation pinged through me. I couldn't believe it. Aunt Val was the only mother I'd known for the past thirteen years. She loved me, and she certainly loved Sophie and Uncle Brendon. She would never do business with a reaper, much less bargain with the souls of the innocent.

But the drinking, and the questions… She'd known all along why the girls were dying!

"This wasn't part of the deal!" my aunt screamed, hands clenched into fists, shaking in either fear or fury. Or both. "Show yourself, you coward! You can't *do* this!"

But that's where she was so very wrong.

21

Aunt Val's shriek had yet to fade from my ears when Sophie's legs collapsed beneath her. As she fell, she smacked the back of her head on the edge of an end table. She hit the floor with a muffled thud, and blood trickled from her hair to stain the white carpet.

Neither of her parents saw. Uncle Brendon was scanning the bright room obsessively, as if the reaper might be hiding behind an armchair, or in one of the potted plants. Aunt Val still stared at the ceiling, shouting for Marg to appear and explain herself.

As if reapers hailed from above.

But the moment Sophie died, her soul song forced itself from my throat, and I nearly choked, trying to hold it back out of habit.

Aunt Val noticed me retching and whirled around to look for her daughter. "No!" she screamed, and I'd never heard a human voice come so close to my own screech until that moment.

She dropped to her knees on the floor. "Wake up, Sophie." She stroked loose blond curls back from her daughter's face, and her fingers came away smeared with blood. "Marg, *fix this!* This wasn't the deal!"

"Sophie!" Uncle Brendon joined his wife beside his daughter's lifeless body, as Nash and I looked on in horror, too shocked to move. Then my uncle looked at me over his wife's shoulder, but I couldn't understand what he wanted. I was too busy holding back the scream.

Nash dropped into a squat by my chair and took my hands, his gaze piercing mine with quiet strength and intensity. "Let it out," he whispered. "Show us her soul so we can guide it."

So I sang for Sophie.

I sang for a soul taken before its time, for a young life lost. For childless parents, and for a girl who would never get to decide who and what she wanted to be. For my cousin, my surrogate sister, whose quick tongue would never be tempered by age and experience.

As I screamed, the lights dimmed, though I could see no noticeable difference in any one bulb. The entire room began to gray, like the gym had earlier, and I glanced hesitantly around the room, suddenly terrified of finding dark, misshapen creatures skulking around my own house.

There were none to be found. I was clearly seeing the Netherworld, but it was…empty, somehow.

But even more disconcerting than that was the sound. Or rather, the *absence* of sound. While I sang, I heard nothing else around me, as if someone had pushed the mute button on some cosmic remote control. After a few seconds, I couldn't even hear myself scream, though I knew from the fire in my throat and lungs that I was, in fact, still screeching at the top of my inhuman lungs.

Nash stayed with me, his fingers linked through mine on the arm of the dining-room chair, completely unbothered by the ungodly screech clawing its way from my mouth. My father stood still, staring at my cousin's soul, a pale, pink-tinged amorphous shape hovering several feet above her body, bobbing like a kite tethered to the ground in a brisk wind.

Her soul had risen higher than Emma's had, and some part of me understood that that was my fault. Because Nash had to prompt me to release the wail for Sophie.

Uncle Brendon stood with his arms stiff at his sides, his hands fisted, exposed forearms bulging with great effort. I couldn't see his face, but I imagined it looked like Nash's, when he'd guided Emma's soul: red and tense, and damp with sweat.

Aunt Val had collapsed over her daughter, crying inconsolably now. She was the only one in the room who couldn't see Sophie's soul, and some distant part of me found that unbearably tragic.

Uncle Brendon's shoulders fell, and he turned to me in exhaustion. "Hold her," he mouthed, and I nodded, still screaming. I would do my best, but my throat was still sore from singing Emma's song that afternoon, and I wasn't sure how long I could hold on to Sophie.

My uncle gestured to my father. I didn't catch all of what he said, but the gist of it was clear: he couldn't do it alone. For some reason, he couldn't budge his daughter's soul.

My dad nodded, and they both turned back to Sophie, working together now.

Aunt Val knelt with her hand on her daughter's sternum, facing the rest of the room. But she wasn't looking at any of us. She was talking, evidently, to the room in general. Her face was splotched with tears, and flushed with both grief and guilt. I couldn't understand much of what she said, but I made out two words based on the familiar motion of her lips.

"Take me."

And then I got it. She was talking to the reaper—Marg—begging her to spare Sophie's life in exchange for her own.

And that's when everything changed. The feel of the room abruptly *shifted,* as if all the angles had changed, the proportions recalibrated. It was like watching a movie with the screen ratio all messed up.

A slim, dark figure appeared in the middle of the weird-looking living room, only feet from my father and uncle, across the room from Sophie's body.

I recognized her instantly from Meredith's memorial.

Marg. She still wore the same long black sweater, cut to accentuate her slight figure, and soft ballet-style slippers, now half-sunk into my aunt's thick pile carpet.

The reaper spared me a glance and frowned, then dismissed me and turned toward Aunt Val. I could see only a sliver of the reaper's face now, but that was plenty. "Are you sure?" she asked, her voice like molten metal, smooth and slow-flowing, but hot enough to singe at a touch.

I was so surprised to hear her that I almost stopped singing, and Sophie's soul began to drift toward Marg. Then Nash squeezed my hand and my voice strengthened. Sophie's soul steadied once more.

The reaper didn't seem to notice. She was watching my aunt, who was saying something else I couldn't hear. I could only hear Marg, which meant the reaper hadn't forgotten about me—that for some reason, she wanted me to hear what she was saying.

Aunt Val nodded firmly in response to the reaper's question, her lips moving rapidly.

The reaper studied her for a moment, then shook her head, and what little I could see of her mouth curved into a slow, malicious smile. "Your soul will not suffice," Marg said, her voice trailing over me with an almost physical presence. "You promised Belphegore young, beautiful souls, and like your body, your soul is aging and blemished. She will not accept it."

My aunt was speaking again, gesturing angrily, and her husband flinched all over at something she said, fists still clenched in effort. Again I desperately wished I could hear both sides of the argument.

"We reached no agreement on the specific souls to be harvested," the reaper said, and chills popped up on my arms. Just listening to her was going to kill me. "I have collected the first four, in spite of piddling interference from your young minions—"

Minions? She did *not* just call me a minion!

"—and I'll have the fifth when I tire of this game. I will have your money, Belphegore will have her souls, and you will have youth and beauty like you never imagined."

Youth? Aunt Val had hired a reaper to poach innocent souls in exchange for her youth? Could anyone truly be so vain?

Aunt Val was shouting now, the veins standing out in her slim neck. But Marg only laughed. "I am in possession of four young, strong souls, and while I hold them, half a dozen *bean sidhes* couldn't take this one from me." To demonstrate, she waved one hand in the air, palm up. Pain ripped through my chest, and Sophie's soul rose a foot higher in spite of my song and the efforts of my father and uncle to guide it.

Nash stood then, and added his best to the group effort, his face flushing with the strain.

Sophie's soul bobbed, then sank slightly, but would go no farther.

The reaper whirled around then, turning her back on my aunt to focus her fury on me and Nash. "You…"

I shook harder with each step she took toward me, and my voice began to warble. I was losing it, and once the wail faded, there would be no soul for the men to guide.

"Something is…" Her sweater flared out at the sides as she walked, giving her a larger, more intimidating presence than her small frame should have carried. Then her eyes narrowed as she studied me from mere feet away, while my heart tripped its way through a few more terrified beats. Her slow smile returned. "You live someone else's life. Belphegore would surely love a taste of your borrowed life force. If you want to see the next day's sun, shut your mouth and release that soul. Otherwise, your family will watch me feed you your own tongue before I take your soul in place of hers."

Her depraved smile broadened, and the sight of such normal, even white teeth in such a vicious face sent chills through me. "And you will die in perfect silence, little one. There is no one left to sing your soul song."

"I will sing for her." The voice was soft and lyrical, and as eerie in the odd silence as the reaper's was. My head swiveled toward the source.

Tod stood in front of the closed front door. His feet were spread for an even stance, hands fisted at his sides, jaw clenched in fury. He looked ready to do battle with the devil himself, but Tod's voice didn't match the one I'd heard.

Someone stepped out from behind him, and my pulse

raced in hope. Harmony Hudson. Nash's mother. And she looked *pissed*.

"Can you hear me, hon?" she asked, and I nodded, so grateful for her presence that I didn't think to question how she'd known she was needed. "Your voice is fadin', but I can sing all night." She faced Marg then, and seemed to stand taller. "You're not leaving with her soul. Or the other one's either," she said, glancing at Sophie's soul where it still bobbed sluggishly in the air over her body.

Marg hissed like an angry cat, mouth open, teeth exposed, and for a moment I thought she'd swipe at Nash's mother with a set of retractable claws. Then she seemed to collect herself. "You'll fare no better than the child," Marg purred, slinking toward the entryway slowly. "It will take more than three of your men to steal from me while I hold four strong souls in reserve."

"How 'bout four men?" Tod said through clenched teeth. He glanced at me, then at Nash, who nodded, giving him the go-ahead for something I didn't understand. Then Tod closed his eyes in concentration, and Sophie's soul bobbed a bit lower.

My eyes widened. Tod was a reaper. Yet he was very clearly helping the others guide Sophie's soul.

Marg's eyes went dark with fury, and she whirled to face Sophie, clearly intent on taking her before she lost her chance.

And that's when my voice died.

"No!" I croaked, but no sound came out.

Yet no sooner had my scream faded from the air than true sound came roaring back to me, as if my ears had popped from a change in pressure. And the first thing to greet them was the most beautiful, ethereal music I'd ever heard in my life.

Nash's mom was singing for Sophie.

All four of the men were tugging on my cousin's soul now, with Harmony's song binding it. But Marg was pulling on it too. Sophie's soul began to rise again, and this time it edged toward the reaper, her arms spread to receive it.

"Marg, please!" Aunt Val shouted. "Take me. My soul may not be young, but it's strong, and you can't have Sophie!"

"You can't save her...." Marg sang, and, glancing around, I saw that she was right. With four souls in reserve, she was too strong for even four male *bean sidhes*. Ironic, considering how small and frail she looked....

Wait. She *was* frail. My dad had said reapers had to take on physical form to interact with their surroundings. Which meant Marg had the same physical weaknesses as the reaper who'd tried to take me. The reaper my father had *punched*...

My head spinning, throat throbbing, I ran into the kitchen. I glanced at the knife rack, then shook my head. I didn't know if I could stop her with one blow.

But I could whack the crap out of her.

I pulled open the cabinet beneath the oven and dug around for the old cast-iron skillet Uncle Brendon used for corn bread, then lugged the pan out and raced through the dining room. I passed Nash, Harmony, and Tod, and had already pulled the skillet back for a blow when I came even with my father.

Marg must have heard me coming, or seen some sign of it in my aunt's face, because she turned at the last minute. The pan hit her in the shoulder, rather than the head, so instead of knocking her unconscious, I simply knocked her down.

But she went down *hard*. Her hip hit the floor with a thud, shaking the end table two feet away.

I couldn't suppress a grin of triumph, even as a vicious ache rebounded up my arm from the blow I'd landed.

For a moment, the reaper lay stunned, glossy black waves spread around her head, arms splayed at her sides. On the edge of my vision, I saw Sophie's soul sink smoothly toward her body. Then Aunt Val let loose a shriek of rage and launched herself across the floor. I'd never seen her look less graceful or poised—and I'd never admired her more.

She landed on Marg's slim hips, straddling her, hands grasping the reaper's shoulders. Her eyes were wild, her hair nearly standing on end. She looked crazy, and I had little doubt that if she wasn't there yet, she would be soon.

"You will not take my daughter!" she shouted, inches

from the reaper's face. "So you either take me now, or you're going back one soul short of the bargain!"

Marg's lips curled back in fury as I inched forward, the skillet still gripped in both hands. She glanced up at Sophie's soul, and her dark eyes blazed in fury to find that it was gone and that Sophie was now breathing, though still unconscious.

Marg stared up at my aunt then, terror fleeting across her features. Whoever this Belphegore was, Marg clearly didn't want to disappoint her. The reaper considered for less than a full second, then she nodded. "Your soul won't fulfill the deal you made, but it will pay for your arrogance and vanity." And just like that, Aunt Val slumped forward onto the reaper, her eyes already empty and glazing over.

But Aunt Val's body hit the carpet, because Marg was gone.

I blinked, staring at my aunt in shock, and carefully lowered myself to the floor, to keep from falling flat out.

"Kaylee, are you okay?" Nash's fingers curled around my left hand, reminding me that I still clutched the cast-iron skillet in my right. Startled by what I'd done with it, now that it was all over, I dropped the skillet at arm's length, and it hit the carpet with a muffled thud.

"I'm fine," I croaked. "Considering."

Uncle Brendon stomped past me to kneel at Sophie's side. He took her pulse and exhaled in relief, then felt around her head, near where she'd banged it on the end table. Then he picked her up in both arms and laid her on the couch, heedless of the blood her hair smeared across the white silk.

Aunt Val would have had a fit over the mess. But Aunt Val was dead.

With Sophie's safety assured, her father dropped to the floor beside his wife and repeated the same steps. But this time, there was no sigh of relief. Instead, my uncle scooted backward on the seat of his jeans until his back hit the side of the couch, his hair brushing Sophie's arm. Then he propped his elbows on his knees and cradled his head in his hands. His whole body shook with silent tears.

"Brendon?" my father said, laying one warm hand on my back.

"How could she do this?" his brother demanded, looking up at us with red-rimmed eyes. "What was she thinking?"

"I don't know." My dad let go of me to kneel at his brother's side.

"It's my fault. Living with us is too hard for humans. I should have known better." Uncle Brendon sobbed, swiping one sleeve across his face. "She didn't want to grow old without me."

"This is not your fault," my dad insisted, clasping his brother's shoulder. "It's not that she didn't want to get old without you, Bren. She didn't want to get old at all."

My aunt Valerie had made a deal with a hellion, and

cost four innocent girls their lives. She'd lied to us all, and had nearly gotten her own daughter killed. And she had blasted a hole the size of a nuclear crater through our family's core.

But when the time came, she'd given her own life in exchange for her daughter's without a second thought, just like my mother had. Did that make her sins forgivable?

I wanted to say yes—that a mother's selfless sacrifice was enough of a good deed to erase her past sins. But the truth wasn't so pretty.

My aunt's death wouldn't bring back Heidi, or Alyson, or Meredith, or Julie. It wouldn't repair whatever psychological damage her loss caused Sophie. It wouldn't give Uncle Brendon back his wife.

The truth was that Aunt Val's sacrifice was too little, too late, and she'd left those she loved most to deal with the aftermath.

"HERE, KAYLEE. This will help your throat." Harmony Hudson set a small cup of honey-scented tea on the table in front of me, and I leaned over it, breathing in the fragrant steam. She started to head back into the kitchen, where the scent of homemade brownies—her favorite form of therapy—had just begun to waft from the oven, but I laid one hand on her arm.

"I would have lost Sophie if you weren't here." My voice was still hoarse, and my throat felt like I'd swallowed a pinecone. And the shock was finally starting to pass, leaving my heart heavy and my head full of the terrible details.

Harmony smiled sadly and sank into the chair next to mine. "The way I hear it, you've done more than your fair share of singing today."

I nodded and sipped carefully from the cup, grateful for the soothing warmth that trickled down my throat. "But it's over now, right? Belphegore can't leave the Netherworld, and Marg won't come back, right?"

"Not if she has any sense. The reapers know who she is now, and they'll all be looking for her." Harmony glanced to her left, and my gaze followed hers to the living room, where my aunt had died, my cousin had been restored, and I'd whacked a psychotic grim reaper with a cast-iron skillet.

Weirdest. Tuesday. Ever.

The paramedics had been gone for less than half an hour, and the thick white carpet still bore tracks from the wheels of the stretcher. They'd rolled Aunt Val out draped in a white sheet, and Uncle Brendon and Sophie followed the ambulance to the hospital, where she would get stitches in the back of her head, and her mother would be officially pronounced dead.

Sophie didn't understand what had happened; I'd known that from the moment she regained consciousness. But what I hadn't anticipated was that she would blame *me* for her mother's death. My cousin was technically dead when Aunt Val made the bargain that had saved her daughter's life, and Sophie didn't remember most of what she'd seen before that. All she knew was that her mother had died, and that I'd had something to do with it. Just like with my own mother.

She and I had more in common now than we ever had—yet we'd never been further apart.

"How did you know? About all of this?" I asked Harmony, waving toward the living room to indicate the entire disaster. But she only frowned, as if confused by the necessity for my question.

"I told her."

Startled, I looked up to find Tod sitting across from me, his arms folded on the table, a single blond curl hanging over his forehead. Harmony smiled at him, letting me know she saw him too, then rose to check on the brownies.

"How did you do it?" I brought the teacup to my mouth for another sip. "How did you guide Sophie's soul? I thought you were a reaper."

"He's both," Nash said from behind me, and I turned just as he followed my father through the front door, pulling his long sleeves down one at a time. He and my dad had just loaded Aunt Val's white silk couch into the back of my uncle's truck, so he wouldn't have to deal with the bloodstains when he and Sophie got back from the hospital. "Tod is very talented."

Tod brushed the curl back from his face and scowled.

Harmony spoke up from the kitchen as the oven door squealed open. "Both my boys are talented."

"Both?" I repeated, sure I'd heard her wrong.

Nash sighed and slid onto the chair his mother had vacated, then gestured toward the reaper with one hand. "Kaylee, meet my brother, Tod."

"Brother?" My gaze traveled back and forth between them, searching for some similarity, but the only one I could find was the dimples. Though, now that I thought about it, Tod had Harmony's blond curls....

And suddenly everything made a lot more sense. The pointless bickering. Nash knowing Tod "forever." Tod hanging out at Nash's house. Nash knowing a lot about reapers.

How could I not have seen it earlier?

"A word of warning..." Harmony gave me a soft smile, but then her focus shifted to my father. "You have to watch out for *bean sidhe* brothers. They're always more than you bargain for."

My dad cleared his throat and glanced away.

An hour later, the Hudsons had gone, and my father stood across from me at the bar, chewing the last bite of a brownie I'd had no appetite for. I set his empty saucer in the sink and ran water over it.

He slid one arm around my shoulders and pulled me close. I let him. He still knew no more about me and my life than he had an hour earlier—that much hadn't changed. But everything else had. Now he could look at me, no matter how much I resembled my mother, and see me, rather than her. He could see what he still had, rather than what he'd lost.

And he was going to stay. We'd probably fight over curfews and get on each other's nerves, but at least those things felt normal. And I needed a good dose of normal after the week I'd just had.

I sighed, staring down at the running water, too exhausted and dazed in that moment to even realize I should turn it off.

"What's wrong?" Dad reached around me to turn off the faucet.

"Nothing." I shrugged, then turned with my back to the sink. "Well, everything, really. It's just that I've only met three adult *bean sidhes* so far, and all three of you are… alone." Tragically widowed, in fact. "Do *bean sidhes* ever get happy endings?"

"Of course they do," my father insisted, wrapping one arm around my shoulders. "As much as anyone else does, at least." And to my surprise, he didn't look the least bit doubtful, even after all he'd been through. "I know that doesn't seem possible right now, considering what you saw and heard tonight. But don't judge your future based on others' mistakes. Not Valerie's, and certainly not mine. You'll have as much of a happy ending as you're willing to work for. And from what I've seen so far, you're not afraid of a little work."

I nodded, unsure how to respond.

"Besides, being a *bean sidhe* isn't all bad, Kaylee."

I gave him a skeptical frown. "That's good to hear, 'cause from where I'm standing, it looks like a lot of death and screaming."

"Yeah, there's a good bit of that. But..." My father turned me by both shoulders until I stared up at him, only dimly registering the slow, steady swirls of chocolate, copper, and caramel in his eyes. "We have a gift, and if you're willing to put up with the challenges that come with that gift, then every now and then, life will toss you a miracle." His eyes churned faster, and his hands tightened just a little on my arms.

"You're my miracle, Kaylee. Your mother's too. She knew what she was doing that night on the road. She was saving our miracle. We both were. And as much as I still miss her, I've never regretted our decision. Not even for a second." He blinked, and his eyes were full of tears. "Don't you regret it either."

"I don't." I met his gaze, hoping mine looked sincere, because the truth was that I was far from sure. What made me worthy of a life beyond what fate said I should have?

My dad frowned, like he saw the truth in my eyes, which were probably telling him more than my answer had. Stupid swirls. But before he could say anything, a familiar engine growled outside, then went silent.

Nash.

I glanced at my dad expectantly, and he scowled. "Does he always come over this late?"

I rolled my eyes. "It's nine-thirty." Though admittedly, it felt more like two in the morning.

"Fine. Go talk to him, before he comes inside and I have to pretend I'm okay with that."

"You don't like him?"

My father sighed. "After everything he's done for you, how could I not like him? But I see the way he looks at you. The way you look at each other."

I smiled, as a car door closed outside. "What are you, ancient? Don't you remember being my age?"

"I'm one hundred thirty-two, and I remember all too well. That's why I'm worried." A fleeting shadow passed over his expression, then he waved me toward the door. "Half an hour."

Irritation spiked my temper. He'd been back for all of three hours, and was already making up rules? But I stifled a retort because even my father's unreasonable curfew was better than being a long-term guest in my cousin's home. Right?

Nash glanced up in surprise when I opened the front door.   He was on the bottom step, one hand on the rail. "Hey."

"Hey." I closed the door and leaned against it. "You forget something?"

He shrugged, and the slick green sleeves of his jacket shone under the porch light. "I just wanted to say good-night without my mom looking over my shoulder. Or your dad."

"Or your brother." I couldn't resist a grin, but Nash only frowned.

"I don't want to talk about Tod."

"Fair enough." I stepped down to the middle riser and found my eyes even with his, though he stood one step below me. It was an oddly intimate pose; his body was inches from mine, but we weren't touching. "What do you want to talk about?"

He raised one brow, and his voice came out hoarse. "Who says I want to talk?"

I let him kiss me—until my dad tapped on the window at my back. Nash groaned, and I tugged him down the steps and into the driveway, out of reach of the porch light.

"So you're really okay with all this?" He spread his arms into the darkness, but the gesture included everything that had gone indescribably weird in my life over the past four days. "Most girls would have totally freaked out on me."

"What can I say? Your voice works wonders." Not to mention his hands. And his lips….

And again that ache gripped me, squeezing bitter drops of doubt from my heart. Would he be done with me in a month, once the novelty of kissing a fellow *bean sidhe* wore off?

"What's wrong?" He tilted my chin up until my gaze met his, though I couldn't see him very well in the dark.

I shoved my misgivings aside and leaned with my back

against the car. "School's going to be weird after this. I mean, how am I supposed to care about trig and world history when I just brought my best friend back from the dead, and faced down a grim reaper over my cousin's poached soul?"

"You'll care, because if you get grounded for failing economics, there won't be any more of this…" He leaned into me, and his mouth teased mine until I rose onto my toes, demanding more.

"Mmm… That's pretty good motivation," I mumbled against his cheek, when I finally summoned the willpower to pull away.

"With any luck, there will be plenty of this, and no more of that." He gestured vaguely toward the house. "That was an anomaly, and it's over."

A chill shivered through me at the reminder. "What if it's not?" After all, Marg was still out there somewhere, and Belphegore was no doubt unsatisfied.

But Nash could not be shaken. "It's over. But we're just starting, Kaylee. You have no idea how special we are together. How incredible it is that we found each other." He rubbed my arms, and I knew from the earnest intensity in his voice that his eyes were probably churning. "And we have long lives ahead of us. Time to do anything we want. Be anything we want."

Time. That was the point, wasn't it? Nash's point. My father's point.

Finally, I got it. My life wasn't just my own. My mother had died to give it to me.

And no matter what happened next, I was damn well going to earn her sacrifice.

★ ★ ★ ★ ★

Netherworld Survival Guide

A collection of entries salvaged from
Alec's personal journal during his
twenty-six year captivity in the Nether...

COMMON HAZARDOUS PLANTS

Note: Flora in the Netherworld is eighty-eight per cent carnivorous, ten per cent omnivorous, and less than two per cent docile. So keep in mind that if you see a plant, it probably wants to eat you.

Razor Wheat
- **Location** – Rural areas with little foot traffic.
- **Description** – Fields full of dense vegetation similar to wheat in structure, ranging in colour from deep red stalks to olive-hued seed clusters. Over six feet tall at mature height.
- **Dangers** – Razor wheat stalks shatters upon contact, raining tiny, sharp shards of plant that can slice through clothing and shred bare flesh.
- **Best Precaution** – Complete avoidance.
- **Second Best Precaution** – Long sleeves, full-length rubber waders and fishing boots, metal trash-can lid wielded like a shield.

Crimson Creeper
- **Location** – Anywhere it can get a foothold. Creeper can take root in as little as a quarter-inch wide crack in concrete and will grow to split the pavement open. It grows quickly and spreads voraciously, climbing walls, towers, trees and anything else that can be made to hold still.
- **Description** – A deep green vine growing up to four inches in diameter, bearing alternating leaves bleeding to crimson or blood red on variegated edges. Vines also sport needle-thin thorns between the leaves.
- **Dangers** – Though anchored by strong, deep roots, which have hallucinogenic properties when consumed, creeper vines slither autonomously and will actually wind around prey, injecting pre-digestive venom through its thorns. The vine will then coil around its meal and wait while the creature is slowly dissolved into liquid fertiliser from the inside out.
- **Best Precaution** – Complete avoidance.

- **Second Best Precaution** – Crimson creeper blooms can be made into a tea which acts as one of two known antidotes to the creeper venom; however, the vine blooms only once every three years. Blooms can be dried and preserved for up to two decades.

COMMON DANGEROUS CREATURES

Note: Whether it intends to consume your mind, body or soul, fauna in the Netherworld is ninety-nine per cent carnivorous, in one form or another. So keep in mind that if you see a creature, it probably wants to eat you.

Hellions
- **Location** – Everywhere. Anywhere. Never close your eyes.
- **Description** – Hellions can look like anything they want. They can be any size, shape or colour. Their only physical limitation is that they cannot exactly duplicate any other creature, living or dead.
- **Dangers** – Hellions feed from chaos in general, and individual emotions in particular. But what they really want is your soul—a never-ending buffet. Since souls cannot be stolen from the living, a hellion will try to bargain for or con you out of it. If you refuse—and even sometimes if you don't—the hellion will either kill you for your soul or torture you, *then* kill you for your soul.
- **Best Precaution** – Complete avoidance.
- **Second Best Precaution** – Pray.

Harpies
- **Location** – Found in large numbers near thin spots in the barrier between worlds, but individual harpies can live anywhere they choose, in either the human world or the Netherworld.
- **Description** – In the human world, harpies can pass for human at a glance, as long as they brush hair over their pointed ears and hide their compact, bat-like wings beneath clothing. In the Netherworld, harpies

appear less human, with mouths full of sharp, thin teeth, claws instead of hands and bird-like, clawed talons instead of feet.

- **Dangers** – Harpies are snatchers. Collectors. They will dive out of the air with no warning to grab whatever catches their eye, which can be anything from broken pots and pans to shiny rings—often still attached to human fingers. Also, they're carnivores and they don't distinguish between human and animal flesh.
- **Best Precaution** – Complete avoidance.
- **Second Best Precaution** – Stay inside or keep one eye trained on the sky and get ready to run.

ESCAPE AND EVASION

Note: The best way to escape a Netherworld threat is to leave the Netherworld, though that won't keep certain species, such as harpies, from crossing into the human world after you. If you are incapable of leaving under your own power, eventually something *will* eat you. But to help put that moment off as long as possible, here is a list of the most effective evasion tactics:

- Find shelter in rural areas. Netherworld creatures are attracted to heavily populated areas, where the overflow of human energy they feed from is most concentrated.
- Fibres from the *dissimulatus* plant can be woven together and worn to disguise your energy signature and keep predators from identifying you as human and thus edible.

Turn the page for a sneak peek at

My Soul to Save

the addictive second book in the
Soul Screamers series.

1

EDEN'S FIRST SONG ended in a huge flash of purple light, reflected on the thousands of faces around me, then the lights went out. I stopped, unwilling to move in the dark for fear that I'd trip over someone and land in an unidentified puddle. Or a lap. Seconds later, the stage exploded with swirling, pulsing light, and Eden now swayed to the new beat in a different but equally skimpy costume. I glanced at her, then back at Tod, but caught only a fleeting glimpse of his curls disappearing through the closed side door.

Nash and I rushed after him, stepping on a series of toes and vaulting over a half-empty bottle of Coke someone had smuggled in. We were out of breath when we reached the door, so I glanced one last time at the stage, then shoved the door, grateful when it actually opened. Doors Tod walks through usually turn out to be locked. Tod stood in the hall beyond, grinning, both backstage passes looped over one arm.

"What'd you do, crawl all the way here?"

The door closed behind us, and I was surprised to realise I could barely hear the music, though it had been loud enough to drown out my thoughts in the auditorium. But I could still feel the thump of the bass, pulsing up through my feet from the floor.

Nash let go of my hand and glared at his brother. "Some of us are bound by the laws of physics."

"Not my problem." Tod waved the passes, then tossed one to each of us. "Snoozin', loozin', and all that crap." I slipped the nylon lanyard over my neck and pulled my long brown hair over it. Now that I wore the pass, it would be seen by anyone who saw me; everything Tod holds is only as visible as he is at the time.

The reaper went fully corporeal then, his sneakers squeaking on the floor as he led us down a series of wide white hallways and through several doors, until we hit one that was locked. Tod shot us a mischievous grin, then walked through the door and pushed it open from the other side.

"Thanks." I brushed past him into the new hall, and the sudden upsurge of music warned that we were getting close to the stage. In spite of the questionable source of our backstage passes, my pulse jumped with excitement when we rounded the next corner and the building opened into a long, wide hall with a cavernous ceiling.

Equipment was stacked against the walls—soundboards, speakers, instruments, and lights. People milled everywhere, carrying clothes, food, and clipboards. They spoke into two-way radios and headset microphones, and most wore badges similar to ours, though theirs read "Crew" in bold black letters.

Security guards in black tees and matching hats loitered, thick arms crossed over their chests. Background dancers raced across the open space in all stages of the next costume change, while a woman with a clipboard pointed and rushed them along.

No one noticed me and Nash, and I could tell Tod had gone non-corporeal again by the silence of his steps. We headed slowly toward the stage, where light pulsed and music thumped, much too loud for any of the backstage racket to be heard out front. I touched nothing, irrationally afraid that sneaking a cookie from the snack table would finally expose us as backstage-pass thieves.

In the wings of the stage, a small crowd had gathered to watch the show. Everyone wore badges similar to ours, and several people held equipment or props, most notably a small monkey, wearing a collar and a funny, brightly coloured hat.

I laughed out loud, wondering what on earth America's reigning pop queen would do on stage with a monkey. From our vantage point, we saw Eden in profile, now grinding in skintight white leather pants and a matching half top. The new song was gritty, with a crunchy guitar riff, and her dancing had changed to suit it; she popped each pose hard, and her hair swung out behind her. Guys in jeans and tight, dark shirts danced around and behind her, each taking her hand in turn, and lifting her on occasion.

Eden gave it her all, even several songs into the performance. The magazines and news stories hyped her hard work and dedication to her career, and the hours and hours a day she trained, rehearsed, and planned. And it showed. No one put on a show like Eden. She was the entertainment industry's golden girl, rolling in money and fame. Rumour had it she'd signed on for the lead in her first film, to begin shooting after the conclusion of her sold-out tour.

Everything Eden touched turned to gold.

We watched her, enthralled by each pose she struck, mesmerised by each note. We were under such a spell that at first no one noticed when something went wrong. During the guitar solo, Eden's arms fell to her side and she stopped dancing.

I thought it was another dramatic transition to the next song, so when her head fell forward, I assumed she was counting silently, ready to look up with those hypnotic, piercing black eyes and captivate her fans all over again.

But then the other dancers noticed, and several stopped moving. Then several more. And when the guitar solo ended, Eden still stood there, silent, a virtual vacuum sucking life from the background music.

Her chest heaved. Her shoulders shook. The microphone fell from her hand and crashed to the stage. Feedback squealed across the auditorium, and the drummer stopped drumming. The guitarists—both lead and bass—turned toward Eden and stopped playing when they saw her. Eden collapsed, legs bent, long, dark hair spilling around her on the floor.

Someone screamed from behind me in the sudden hush, and I jumped, startled. A woman raced past me and onto the stage, followed by several large men. My hair blew back in the draught created by the sudden rush, but I barely noticed. My gaze was glued to Eden who lay unmoving on the floor. People bent over her, and I recognised the woman as her mother, the most famous stage parent/manager in the country. Eden's mom was crying, trying to shake her daughter awake as a member of security tried to pull her away. "She's not breathing!" the mother shouted, and we all heard her clearly, because the crowd of thousands had gone silent with shock.

"Somebody help her, she's not breathing!"

And suddenly neither was I.

My hand clenched Nash's, and my heart raced in dreadful anticipation of the keening that would rip its way from my throat as the pop star's soul left her body. A *bean sidhe's* wail can shatter not just glass, but eardrums. The frequency resonates painfully in the human brain, so that the sound seems to rattle from both outside and within.

"Breathe, Kaylee," Nash whispered into my ear, wrapping both arms around me as his voice cocooned my heart, his Influence soothing, comforting. A male *bean sidhe's* voice is like an audio-sedative, without the side effects of the chemical version. Nash could make the screaming stop, or at least lower its volume and intensity. "Just breathe through it." So I did. I watched the stage over his shoulder and breathed, waiting for Eden to die.

Waiting for the scream to build deep inside me.

But the scream didn't come.

On stage, someone's foot hit Eden's microphone, and it rolled across the floor and into the pit. No one noticed, because Eden still wasn't breathing. But I wasn't wailing, either. Slowly, I loosened my grip on Nash and felt relief settle through me as logic prevailed over my dread. Eden wasn't wearing a death shroud—a translucent black haze surrounding the soon-to-be-dead, visible only to female *bean sidhes*.

"She's fine." I smiled in spite of the horrified expressions surrounding me. "She's gonna be fine." Because if she were going to die, I'd already be screaming. I'm a female *bean sidhe*. That's what we do.

"No, she isn't," Tod said softly, and we turned to find him still staring at the stage. The reaper pointed, and I followed his finger until my gaze found Eden again, surrounded by her mother, bodyguards, and odd members of the crew, one of whom was now giving her mouth-to-mouth. And as I watched, a foggy, ethereal substance began to rise slowly from the star's body like a snake from its charmer's basket.

Rather than floating toward the ceiling, as a soul should, Eden's seemed *heavy*, like it might sink to the ground around her instead. It was thick, yet colourless. And undulating through it were ribbons of darkness, swirling as if stirred by an unfelt breeze. My breath caught in my throat, but I let it go almost immediately, because though I had no idea what that substance was, I knew without a doubt what it *wasn't*. Eden had no soul.

2

"WHAT IS THAT?" I whispered frantically, tugging Nash's hand. "It's not a soul. And if she's dead, how come I'm not screaming?"

"What is what?" Nash hissed, and I realised he couldn't see Eden's not-soul. Male *bean sidhes* can only see elements of the Netherworld—including freed souls—when a female *bean sidhe* wails. Apparently the same held true for whatever ethereal sludge was oozing from Eden's body.

Nash glanced around to make sure no one was listening to us, but there was really no need. Eden was the centre of attention. Tod rolled his eyes and pulled one hand from the pocket of his baggy jeans. "Look over there." He pointed not toward the stage, but across it, where more people watched the spectacle from the opposite wing. "Do you see her?"

"I see lots of hers." People scrambled on the other side of the stage, most speaking into cell phones. A couple of vultures even snapped pictures of the fallen singer, and indignation burned deep in my chest. But Tod continued to point, so I squinted into the dark wing. Whatever he wanted me to see probably wasn't native to the human world so it wouldn't be immediately obvious.

And that's when I found her.

The woman's tall, slim form created a darker spot in the already-thick shadows, a mere suggestion of a shape. Her eyes were the only part of her I could focus on, glowing like green embers in the gloom. "Who is she?" I glanced at Nash and he nodded, telling me he could see her too. Which likely meant she was *letting* us see her...

"That's Libby, from Special Projects." An odd, eager light shone in blue eyes Tod usually kept shadowed by brows drawn low. "When this week's list came down, she came with it, for this one job."

He was talking about the reapers' list, which contained the names and the exact place and time of death of everyone scheduled to die in the local area within a one-week span.

"You knew this was going to happen?" Even knowing he was a reaper, I couldn't believe how different Tod's reaction to death was from mine. Unlike most people, it wasn't my own death I feared—it was everyone else's. The sight of the deceased's soul would mark my own descent into madness. At least, that's what most people thought of my screaming fits. Humans had no idea that my "hysterical shrieking" actually suspended a person's soul as it left its body.

Sometimes I wished I still lived in human ignorance, but those days were over for me, for better or for worse.

"I couldn't turn down the chance to watch Libby work. She's a legend." Tod shrugged. "And seeing Addy was a bonus."

"Well, thanks so much for dragging us along!" Nash snapped.

"What is she?" I asked, as another cluster of people rushed past us—two more bodyguards and a short, slight man whose face looked pinched with professional concern and curiosity. Probably a doctor. "And what's so special about this assignment?"

"Libby's a very special reaper." Tod's short, blond goatee glinted in the blue-tinted overhead lights as he spoke. "She was called in because that—" he pointed to the substance the female reaper now was steadily inhaling from Eden's body, over a twenty-foot span and dozens of heads "—isn't a soul. It's Demon's Breath."

Suddenly I was very glad no one else could hear Tod. I wished they couldn't hear me, either. "Demon, as in hellion?" I whispered, as low as I could speak and still be heard.

Tod nodded with his usual slow, grim smile. The very word *hellion* sent a jolt of terror through me, but Tod's eyes sparkled with excitement, as if he could actually get high on danger.

I guess that's what you get when you mix boredom with the afterlife.

"She sold her soul…." Nash whispered, revulsion echoing within the sudden understanding in his voice.

I'd never met a hellion—they couldn't leave the Netherworld, fortunately—but I was intimately familiar with their appetite for human souls. Six weeks earlier, my aunt had tried to trade five poached teenage souls in exchange for her own eternal youth and beauty, but her plan went bad in the end, and she wound up paying in part with her own soul. But not before four girls died for her vanity.

Tod shrugged. "That's what it looks like to me."

Horror filled me. "Why would anyone do that?"

Nash looked like he shared my revulsion, but Tod only shrugged again, clearly unbothered by the most horrifying concept I'd ever encountered. "They usually ask for fame, fortune, and beauty."

All of which Eden had in spades.

"OK, so she sold her soul to a hellion." That statement sound wrong in *sooo* many ways… "Do I even want to know how Demon's Breath got into Eden's body in its place?"

"Probably not," Nash whispered, as heavy black curtains began to slide across the front of the stage, cutting off the shocked, horrified chatter from the auditorium.

There are only eight breeding female werecats left. And I'm one of them.

Female werecats are disappearing and the Pride is helpless to stop the stray responsible. Then Faythe Sanders ends up in the claws of the kidnapper himself.

Now, armed with nothing but animal instinct and a serious attitude, Faythe must free herself and stop the kidnappers before they rob her Pride of its most valuable asset: its own continued existence.

www.mirabooks.co.uk

MIRA

Meghan Chase has a secret destiny...

Meghan has never quite fitted in at school...or at home. But she could never have guessed that she is the daughter of a mythical faery king and a pawn in a deadly war.

Now Meghan will learn just how far she'll go to save someone she cares about...and to find love with a prince who might rather see her dead than let her touch his icy heart.

First in the stunning *Iron Fey* series

Available 21st January 2011

www.mirabooks.co.uk

CHOOSE:
A QUICK DEATH...
OR A SLOW POISON...

About to be executed for murder, Yelena is offered
the chance to become a food taster. She'll eat the
best meals, have rooms in the palace – and risk
assassination by anyone trying to kill the
Commander of Ixia.

But disasters keep mounting as rebels plot to seize
Ixia and Yelena develops magical powers she can't
control. Her life is threatened again and choices
must be made. But this time the outcomes
aren't so clear...

www.mirabooks.co.uk

MIRA